LOVE TO SPARE

Aja Jorgensen

ISBN: 9798354176465

Cover design by: Sarah Schneider
Library of Congress Control Number: 2018675309
Printed in the United States of America

For Sarah,
This book would not exist without you.

And Josh for getting it through to the end.

1

"That's a turkey! I just got a turkey!" Maddie screams after she bowls her third strike in a row. Everyone jumps up and down, reacting as if she just won a gold medal. She spins around and points directly at me, laughing, "that means you have to ask him out!"

It's the first day of summer and I'm with a group of students celebrating our high school graduation. There's youthful freedom in the air between everyone that makes us feel elated. This exact feeling made me foolish enough to agree to a bet that would result in me having to ask out the cute guy behind the counter.

"There's no way I can do that!" I exclaim, glancing over my shoulder at him.

"I know you're waiting for a romantic meet-cute but honestly, sometimes you just have to wing it," Maddie says.

She's been my best friend since we were in 6th grade. We navigated the awkward middle school years together and have been best friends ever since. She's been there through the highs and lows and knows me better than anyone else. Sometimes it's hard when someone knows you so well.

I open my mouth to respond but realize I don't have anything to say. She's not wrong. I deflect and continue the game, focusing instead on conversations about our future. Maddie and I are going to Duke University together and will be rooming together. We talk about career aspirations, class schedules, and make a promise to meet back here every summer.

We finish the game and go to return our shoes. Maddie playfully shoves me towards the counter and winks. I roll my eyes at her as I shakily make my way towards him. The boy behind the counter looks to be about our age. We noticed how cute he was right away. I caught him watching us a few times throughout the night, which spurred the turkey bet in the first place.

"Pretty cool your friend got a turkey," he smiles as I reach the counter.

"Yeah, super cool," I reply, feeling my cheeks flush. I suddenly feel embarrassed knowing exactly how much he has been watching us.

"So, uh, are you here all summer?" I choke out, trying to be smooth.

The guy kinks an eyebrow at me, "yes, I am." He doesn't offer any more information. His eyes crinkle with his smile, and I notice how blue they are. Such a cliché to think piercing blue, but that's precisely the word I think when he looks back at me. His brown hair has a slight wave of a curl to it. I'm not sure if I'm staring, but he runs his hand through it and slightly chuckles.

"Cool," I swallow nervously. I peek over at Maddie standing in the corner watching me.

I'm about to lose my nerve so I take a deep breath and quickly blurt out, "Okay, so I promised my friend that if she bowled a turkey I would ask you out but I know that's totally crazy and weird and I don't know you so let's just pretend like I asked and you said no and we just won't make it a big deal."

The corner of the guy's mouth turns up and I freeze, my face turning red.

"This is so embarrassing," I admit. "Seriously, say no and just pretend this never happened."

He lowers his voice and says quietly, "I can't turn you down without at least an excuse."

I blink, slowly comprehending his words. "So you are turning me down?"

He chuckles softly, "I wasn't even sure if it was a real invitation." After a pause he adds, "but yes, I would have to ask for a rain check on that question. I'm finally breaking free of the dark place I've been and I'm not ready to date yet."

His words catch my breath. It's such an honest and vulnerable answer from a complete stranger. I struggle knowing exactly how to respond to something so sincere.

"Okay," I mutter, "yeah. I'm sorry. That was stupid. I uh, hope things get better for you."

"Thank you. And don't be so hard on yourself. It wasn't stupid. Asking someone out is a big deal. Don't ever let someone judge you for your feelings," he replies.

I smile back at him and take a few steps towards Maddie. She's staring at me from the corner, a look of awe splashed across her face, but my mind is still caught on his words. I've spent a lot of my life letting other people have opinions about my emotions, maybe he's onto something.

2

Four years later

I stand in the bowling alley parking lot, feeling like I was just here yesterday celebrating graduating from high school. But this time, we are celebrating college graduation. It feels good to be back. This place always felt like such a big part of home. Looking up at the building and the sky, I hear a shriek from behind me, "Jennaaaaaa!"

Before I can fully turn around, I feel Maddie wrap her arms around me.

"How was the drive?" Maddie asks as we pull apart.

"Good! I enjoyed my extra day of silence," I reply, smirking.

Maddie glares at me in response. Maddie and I were roommates at school together all four years. Fortunately, it only made our friendship stronger.

We had kept our promise about coming back once a year while we were in school. Now that we were about to become real adults with real jobs, this felt like it might be the final time. We both knew it; we both felt it. While we were scared to admit it, it hung heavy in the air over us.

The bowling alley has been getting nicer and nicer as the years pass. Towards the end of high school, it was starting to fall apart, and people were going there less. At first, I noticed subtle changes, and it was nice to see it being put back together. More people started to come the nicer it became. It's fully upgraded now with new TVs and new seats. It doesn't even smell like a bowling alley anymore.

A few hours pass and the bowling alley turns into a blacklight party. This is always our favorite time to bowl. I run over to the row of bowling balls so that I can choose my favorite ball for blacklight. I always choose a light pink one because it glows the brightest. As I reach my hand down, another hand reaches for the same ball.

"Oh, sorry!" I say, pulling back.

"No worries, gorgeous. You want to hold my ball?" a deep voice says.

I turn to see a large man standing beside me. He's flashing a way too big smile at me and opens his arms wide. "I'm Ty," he adds.

"Excuse me?"

He smiles at me again and winks. Then opens his arms wider and steps closer. I find myself staring at him, confused. Maybe it's the sheer audacity of this man, but it takes me a few moments exactly to understand what he's implying.

When I do, I take a step back and reply, "I'll go get a different one."

"Mine are better than the rest, baby!" I hear him call as I walk away.

I rush back to my Maddie and tell her what just happened, my voice dripping with disgust. She looks just as disturbed as I feel. I see Ty and his friends on the other end of the bowling alley. They are laughing and their laughter just makes me feel more annoyed.

It's 2 in the morning by the time we decide to leave. Maddie honks a goodbye as she pulls out of the parking lot. I'm looking for my keys when I hear footsteps and turn to see Ty right behind me. He reaches my car at the same time as me and puts his hand on the car behind me.

"You didn't seem to appreciate my joke earlier," he says, talking down to me.

"I didn't think it was very funny," I reply, looking at his arm next to my face.

He scoffs, "You just think you're too good for my jokes."

"In this case, yeah, I am."

He leans in closer, too close. I can smell his breath as he says, "I promise you, baby, you are not too good for me."

He lifts a finger and roughly runs it down the side of my face, stopping under my chin and pulling up hard, forcing me to look him in the face. Lust and hate are burning in his eyes and I feel like I'm going to throw up.

I try to scoot out from under his arm just as he's coming in closer. My stomach squirms and I feel my throat get tight. I anxiously glance to my side, desperate to find an escape. Then I hear a loud "Hey!" from behind Ty.

Ty stands up and away from me a little as I hear footsteps coming closer. I try to lean around and see who it is but Ty is blocking my view.

"Thanks for waiting for me, Jenna."

Ty is fully standing now and looking between the guy that was talking and me. I slide out from under his arms and shakily say, "Yeah no problem." I look at the guy now, but I don't recognize him.

He comes and stands right next to me, holding my eye contact until the last second. "Hey man, what's up?" He says, turning his attention to Ty.

"Uh, nothing," Ty grunts.

"Good. Cause if it *were* something, we would have a problem." He says it quietly but seriously. He's looking Ty right in the face. I see the irritation cross Ty's face as he looks at the guy up and down, sizing him up. While Ty isn't what I would consider small, the other guy is taller and more muscular. Ty glances at me, decides I'm not worth it and walks away with a shrug. I realize I'm fully shaking now as I turn to my car, desperate to get inside.

"Hey, are you okay?" I look up and notice the guy is still here. I try to nod.

"Let me take you home, or at least go with you. Which one would make you more comfortable?" he asks. He's standing close, but not too close.

"I'm not getting in your car," I say, glancing at him and opening my door.

He chuckles, "Smart girl. Can I at least ride with you in yours? I'm not comfortable leaving you alone."

I look him straight in the face now. He looks familiar to me. It must be his friendly face, the kind blue eyes. I nod once, and he closes my door behind me and runs around to the passenger side.

It's quiet as I'm pulling out of the parking lot; I'm still shaking. I can feel his eyes on me as I drive.

"I'm Oliver," he says after a few minutes of silence.

"Jenna," I reply.

As the car falls silent again, my mind starts to spin. My heart is still racing, and my breath feels shallow. I can feel the panic attack coming as I start to comprehend what just happened and what exactly could have happened.

"Did you know most stars travel the galaxy in companions or clusters?" Oliver suddenly says.

His voice, and this random fact, shock me from my replaying of events.

I quickly glance at him, a questioning look on my face, and then turn back to the road.

"Yup, it's true. They are created together and travel the galaxy together."

"How do you know this?" I ask.

"My sister, she's obsessed with all things space. She's only 12, but she is a genius."

We pull up to my house now. "Uh, thanks for your help tonight," I say as I open my car door.

"No problem," he says as we get out. I realize he's standing by the car, waiting for me to go inside. I walk to the front door, still aware of him watching me. When I reach the porch, I turn and lift my hand in a wave. I see him wave back and then turn and run off the other way. Only as I shut the door and lock it do I realize that he had called me Jenna in the parking lot. Before I ever told him my name.

3

I wake up early the following day and tie up my running shoes. I'm still reeling from the night before and the incident with Ty. I come downstairs to find my parents in the kitchen, both are dressed and ready for the day.

"Good morning, dear. Up and ready for work?" My father asks as he grabs his suitcase. I look at my leggings and running shoes as I reply, "I'm going for a run." He pauses and looks at me, "Oh yes, I see. Well, have a good day." He kisses my mom and then squeezes my shoulder as he leaves.

My dad and I have an interesting relationship. He doesn't share his emotions openly, although his nonverbal expressions and grunts clearly show his negative feelings. He's a great car salesman, which means he can be a great people person, but it feels like he wastes that energy on others most of the time and we get the leftovers at home. Which means everyone in town loves him. Everyone sees him as the bright, bubbly personality that he is at work. A salesman must have the right personality, and it's not the grumpy, tired one that we all get at home. He's never said he's proud of me. I guess we have different ideas of success in our lives, and my choices don't line up with his visions of a future. He wants me to work with him. He thought he could train me to be a saleswoman, and then together, we could take over the dealership. He loves that place and the importance it makes him feel. But I've always been more creative than that. I love the creativity at my job. I love collaborating with companies and bringing their visions to life. It's something I don't think he can ever understand. I just wish he would accept our differences.

My mom is a go-getter in her own way. She's an English professor with a few published novels on the side. Growing up, she was very busy and never had much time for my brother or me. My brother, Robby, is three years older than me. He lives in NYC and is a financial guru. He's made an amazing life for himself. I remember when we were younger, I would snuggle up in bed with him and ask what our futures would look like. He told me he would move to a huge city with so many people that he could blend in and not have any expectations to live up to. Of course, any expectations he placed on him, he passed with flying colors. He's excelled in his career and Mom and Dad constantly talk about how successful he is. I try not to take it personally, but it always feels a little personal. I've always felt like I'm trying to prove myself to them. Robby and I have a close relationship though, even if we don't get to see each other as often as I'd like. When I get the chance, I love going to visit him in the city.

I put my headphones in as I step outside. I huff out a sigh and try to breathe out the negative feelings with it. My mom has told me countless times that working as a freelance designer is not ambitious enough. I view it as the opposite; I'm my own boss. I find my clients and create continuous relationships with them. I don't know what could be more ambitious than creating something all on my own. It's been successful too. I have four companies that I work with on a daily and monthly basis, and I have other random projects from people who frequently contact me. It's been enough to get me through school and enough to continue to support me now. It's frustrating that they can't see it.

They have planted a seed of doubt in me that I'm constantly fighting. It's been that way since I was young. Small comments made here and there about the way I look or the choices I make, constantly second-guessing me, have led to a life full of doubt and fear. I love them. I just wish they made me feel like I am enough for them the way I am.

I turn right out of my neighborhood and head down a side trail that loops around the lake. I like coming back home. The familiarity is comforting. I remember running this same trail all through high school. Mostly trying to escape my parents and their nagging about college. It was such a relief when I was accepted at Duke, and my dad clapped me on the back and said, "There ya go!"

The trees are full and green now, providing a shady trail to run. My shoes pound the ground and take me farther away from last night. It feels like I can't stop replaying it. The sneer on his face as he cornered me. The smell of his breath as he leaned in close. I shut my eyes and come to a stop, bending over and breathing heavily. I try shaking my head to clear the memories away.

My immediate feeling is that I'm overreacting. Nothing actually happened, and therefore I should not be feeling the way I do. I'm too sensitive. I have to proactively quiet that voice in my head because I know it's wrong. Thanks to a few years in therapy, I've learned to ignore those unhealthy thoughts that stem from my childhood. My feelings are valid. I'm allowed to feel this way. No one has the right to judge my feelings. I repeat it over and over in my head. I stand up shakily and continue running, desperate to leave the memories behind. As I near the dock on the lake, I see a familiar shape out on the edge.

"Joan!" I exclaim as I reach the dock. She turns and gives me a big smile. Joan sets down her fishing gear and pulls me into a hug. Her hugs are all-encompassing and instantly feel like home.

"Jenna! How are you? Are you home for the summer?"

Joan is my first-ever client. She's 70 years old and owns her own fishing company online. She started posting videos of her fishing and they went viral fast. She has the perfect southern lady charm as she fishes and gives out life advice. She ended up creating how-to videos that people loved so much that she created a whole business out of it. She sells fishing journals to track your locations and catches with blank lines to write down any advice she gives. Now she's expanded to different fishing tackles and baits and some clothing with her quotes on it. I still do all of her graphic design work. She tries to say that I'm half of the reason she's successful, but we all know she did it on her own, people can't help but love her.

"Yeah, I just graduated and moved out a few days ago!" I reply.

"So what's the plan now?" she questions, moving over so I can sit on the bench by her.

"Well, I plan to continue building up my business. But really, I can do that from anywhere. So I'm just kind of hanging out here and seeing where I want to go next."

"How wonderful! A job you can do anywhere. That's my kind of job," she says, winking at me.

"Joan, you have a job you can do anywhere."

"Exactly!" she says, laughing. She throws her line back in the water and then adds, "I would love to be able to work with you in person. Video and phone calls are great, but sitting down and working together over some sandwiches would just be wonderful!"

I smile at her and lean on her shoulder, "That sounds wonderful to me too."

Joan has always felt like a grandmother to me. I don't remember any of my grandparents. They passed away before I was born or shortly after. She was always the first customer at my lemonade stands and quickly supported my visual design dream. She is more supportive than my parents, and I have clung desperately to that.

"So, tell me about the man in your life," she declares.

I sit up and look at her, "Joan, you know I don't have a man in my life."

"And there ain't nothing wrong with that," she remarks, "But are you at least having some fun with men in your life? You won't be young and beautiful forever." She gestures to her face and body, and I laugh. Joan is flawless. Sure, she has aged. But she looks as beautiful as ever.

"Don't let Dave hear you talk like that!" I scold her.

"Oh pah, Davey is blinded by love," she replies, waving her hands.

Dave and Joan have been married for 48 years and are the ultimate couple goals. Even after all this time, the look in his eyes is just as rich and in love as it has ever been. They have been through it all together. War, kids, sickness, and Joan's new successful business.

They've loved each other through it all. I love seeing them together. Any time they are close enough, they are touching. He's always holding her hand, putting his hand on her leg, leaning on her, it's like he still can't keep his hands off her. It's the kind of marriage I hope for.

"No, I don't have anyone right now," I respond.

"That's a shame. Get on one of those swipe apps and go have some fun!" she replies.

It's true, I don't have anyone right now in my life. I was dating Mike during my last year of school, but it never felt like it was going to go anywhere. I didn't have that eagerness with him. If we couldn't see each other for a few days, that was fine by me. I would forget to text him back and sometimes, we would go a few days without talking, which never bothered me. I never fully let him in because I just didn't care enough.

Unsurprisingly, he ended things with me after he said he felt like he cared more than I did. Surprisingly, it hurt. I was sad about the break-up. I don't know why I couldn't care more about him. I never really gave him a chance. He was a great guy, and I wish that I could have cared more but I just couldn't force it. It always seemed to feel that way for me. I've never felt that crazy head-over-heels feeling. I've never had the constant want and desire to be with someone.

Joan and I say our goodbyes promising to meet up in the next few days to sit down and work together in person. I run back to my parent's house, feeling much better than before. I'm grateful to open the door to a quiet house. My parents are already at work and won't be home until late. I run upstairs to shower and get ready. After pulling on some shorts and a shirt, I decide that I want to swing by the bowling alley to thank Oliver again for last night. As I pass a mirror, I stop and put on some pink lipstick, smile, and head out the door.

As I pull up to the bowling alley, I notice there are a few other cars here belonging to some morning bowlers. As I walk inside, I'm greeted by the smell of fresh popcorn, and I look around to see if I can find Oliver. I'm still surprised by how much this place has changed in the last four years. I guess change is inevitable. I'm just glad in this case, it's a good change. I have too many memories here to let it go. I head up to the counter and wait until a young girl comes. She's way too young to be working here.

"Hi," she says, staring at me with her big milky brown eyes.

"Hi, uh, do you by chance know if there is an Oliver here?" I ask, looking around.

Her eyebrows raise, and she says, "Ollie? Yeah, he's here somewhere. I think he's behind the lanes fixing something." She points towards the back right and then smiles at me. "Who are you?" she asks.

"Oh, I'm Jenna."

"Jenna," she replies, still staring at me.

I shift uncomfortably and say, "Well, I'm going to see if I can find him. Bye."

I head towards the back of the lanes, where she pointed. I peek over my shoulder and see that she has disappeared into the back again. When I reach the back of the lanes, I tentatively step down and look around.

"Hello?" I call out.

I don't hear anything, so I walk a little farther back.

"Hello?" I say again.

I hear a banging and some muttering, so I follow the

sounds until I see Oliver lying on the ground under one of the machines. He's wrestling with a tool under it, and I can't help but notice how his arm flexes each time he moves. He scoots a little farther back, and it pulls his shirt up, exposing just a tiny strip of skin on his lower abs. I catch myself staring and quickly look away. I clear my throat loudly and say, "Oliver?"

He jumps at the sounds of my voice and quickly slides out from under the machine. He seems genuinely surprised to see me.

"Jenna? What are you doing back here?" he asks, sitting up. He has a little bit of grease smeared on his cheek and I have the urge to reach out and clean it.

"I wanted to talk to you and the girl at the front told me you were back here."

"She talked to you?" he questions quickly, "I told her she's not supposed to talk to people when she's alone," he adds, seemingly to himself.

"Anyway, I just wanted to come by and say thanks again for last night," I say, bringing his attention back to me.

"You're welcome. Really. How are you feeling today?" he asks, standing up and wiping his hands on a rag. I notice now that he stands taller than me. He's easily at least 6 feet tall.

"I'm good," I reply.

He looks at me, his eyes questioning, but seems to let it go. Instead, he asks, "Do you want some nachos?"

"It's 10:30 in the morning," I reply with a laugh.

A small smile appears on his face, "So?" he counters, his eyes crinkling.

"Okay, sure," I reply, chuckling.

He leads me out of the back area and to the front. I see

the younger girl inside the office, nose buried in a book about planets. Suddenly, I realize that she must be his sister. He sees me glance at her, and he nods, "Yeah, that's my sister Olivia. Like I said, she loves space."

"Your name is Oliver, and her name is Olivia?" I ask.

"Yeah, my mom has a sense of humor, I guess," he replies, shaking his head and smiling.

He leads me to the concession counter and starts making our nachos. I perch on the edge of the seat, looking around at all the different lanes. There are only a handful of people here, but I'm still a little surprised that anyone is here in the morning. When I came here growing up, it didn't even open until after lunch because no one was here this early.

There's a cute family at the lane on the end and a group of middle school girls a few lanes over. They keep giggling and looking over at Oliver. I smile fondly watching them and thinking about the many times my friends and I used to come here.

It's much nicer now than it used to be. The permanent stickiness on the old tables is gone and the new chairs don't have any rips in them. I turn back to see Oliver putting triple the amount of cheese to chip ratio. He catches me watching him, and he smiles.

"I've got it down to a science," he explains, adding cheese. "You need lots of extra cheese, so you can dip the parts of your chips that don't get cheese in the first place. Then I like some pulled pork on top," he pauses and looks at me for approval.

I nod, and he continues, "A few green onions, sour cream, and..." he pauses while holding a tomato and then looks at me and sets it back down. I'm glad because I've never liked tomatoes, especially on nachos.

"Shredded cheese for the top," he adds finally.

"More cheese?" I question.

He stops, looks at me seriously, and replies, "You can never have too much cheese," then he smiles and pushes the nachos closer to me. He leans across the bar, and I scoot closer on my seat.

"After you," he says, gesturing at the nachos.

I grab a chip, cheese stringing up with it, and take a bite.

"Delicious!" I exclaim as the cheese warms my mouth. The sauce from the pulled pork mixes with the cheese perfectly, and the green onions add the perfect amount of spice.

Oliver beams at me with pride. "That's right!" then he digs in, grabbing a few chips and shoving them in his mouth.

"Thanks for the nachos," I say after I swallow another bite.

"Don't mention it. Or do actually, I'm quite proud of my nacho expertise."

He spins around and fills up a big cup of Dr. Pepper for me. He sets it down, and I look at him, surprised. "How do you know I like Dr. Pepper?"

He pauses briefly and looks at me. "Who doesn't?" he shrugs after a pause.

"So, since you work here, do you get to bowl for free?" I ask, looking around.

"I do, but don't you try to use me now," he says, smirking at me.

"I would never," I reply, smiling back. "My friends and I have been coming here ever since high school. We even made a pact to come back once a year in the summers to meet here. Usually, it ended up being a lot more than the one time."

"Hmm," he says, looking out at all the lanes, "Sounds like some good memories were made here. I have a lot of great memories here too." The conversation falls silent until a red light pops up on the screen behind him.

"Oh, got to go fix that," he says, and he quickly runs off towards the middle school group. A few of the girls are giggling and watching him. Oliver plays with the screen, showing them how to reset the lane. I watch as the girls exchange looks and giggles with each other. I chuckle as one of the girls points at Oliver's arm and the other one nods eagerly. Oliver smiles at them as he continues teaching them. I'm finishing off the last few chips when Oliver comes back.

"Oops," I say, smiling at the empty plate.

He laughs as he shrugs and replies, "My loss."

"Well, I should get going. Maybe I'll see you around." I say, standing up.

"Definitely. Come back anytime."

"Do you work here a lot?" I ask.

He chuckles a little and rubs the back of his neck. "Yeah, I'm here a lot."

"Sorry, that's nothing to be embarrassed about. It seems like a fun job," I quickly say, backpedaling a little.

"Yeah, I actually..."

"Ollie!" a voice from the office calls, interrupting him.

"Yes?"

"The phone is for you."

He looks back at me and smiles. "I should get that. Have a good rest of your day."

"You too," I reply as he turns and runs towards the office where Olivia is waiting.

A few days later I'm eagerly checking my email. I've been trying to convince this up-and-coming brownie company to work with me for a while now. We did a trial run a few weeks back, and they seemed impressed with my work but haven't officially signed anything with me yet. I pitched them a few ideas during the trial and showed them a whole new website refresh with different logo animations that would be fun. I've been refreshing my email constantly, waiting for their final decision.

This is the biggest company I have pitched myself to and I find myself losing confidence with each day that passes. In my career, it's not easy to separate myself from the business, so when I'm rejected, I feel it in all areas of my life.

My mom comes into the backyard, where I'm sitting out in the sun and sits down next to me. She doesn't have class today, so she's working on her next novel. Having her next to me adds to my anxiety as I refresh my email again and again.

"How are you, honey? Planning for your next steps?" she asks.

"Working on it right now, actually. I have a big client that I'm hoping works with me. I worked really hard on this trial run and I think they were impressed. But it's so stressful waiting to hear back."

"Ah yes, that is the struggle of working on your own. You just never know when you'll be getting that next paycheck."

"It's not just about money, though. I really enjoy what I do. I like when I can accomplish what the client wants and bring their vision to life. It's just stressful trying to convince them to take a chance on me. It's hard constantly proving myself." I swallow, realizing how completely vulnerable that was. I'm not just talking about my job, but my whole life has felt like I am constantly proving myself.

My mom makes a noncommittal sound, so I move the conversation, "I saw Joan, and we made a plan to sit together and work in person on her site. She's really excited about it."

"Hmm? Really? That must be nice. Her business seems to be doing well."

"Yeah, it's taken off fast. Can you believe she's been my client for six years now?"

She chuckles and replies, "Of course, those beginning high school years of you trying to work for her were just so cute."

It takes all my willpower to not roll my eyes. "Mom, I was 17. I wasn't just a cute little kid *trying* to work for her. I was creating her brand and designing her website, all while learning CSS. That's something most people would consider impressive."

She pats my leg, "I wasn't trying to offend you, honey, relax. It's not a big deal. I was just saying it feels so long ago."

I lean back into my chair and choose to let it go. Refreshing my email again…nothing yet. It's hard constantly living under this expectation and criticism. My parents view success very differently than I do. One day I'll show them that I can be successful on my own. My hard work will pay off. I keep telling myself that, hoping the more I say it, the more I'll believe it.

My phone pings, and I look down to see a text from Maddie.

Dinner tonight? she asks.

Yes! Please! I reply quickly.

Another ping goes off, and this time it's my email. I click on it to see a message that says, "Just signed the agreement and sent over the first payment. Very excited to be working with you, Jenna. You have such an excellent vision and I think this partnership will take us far."

4

"Jenna, this is great!" Maddie squeals. "I knew you'd get it! This is huge!"

She's not wrong. It is huge. They are my first big client, and they are paying me double what most of my other clients do. I dig into the french fries in the middle of the table, feeling giddy about the news. It felt so good to tell my mom that the company believed in me enough to hire me.

"So, it turns out I'll be sticking around all summer," Maddie says.

"You are?"

"Yes, and I think you should too! We can do all the fun stuff we used to do when we were in high school. It's like reliving the summer after our senior year. Except we are smarter and obviously more beautiful," she jokes.

Before I can answer, she's continuing. "Think about it! We can go swimming every day, go to the drive-in movies, have sleepovers, go bowling and just be kids again!"

"Okay, that does sound amazing. But I still have to work," I reply slowly, thinking about it.

"I know, I know. And I know you're planning on moving somewhere and settling down, but I would love one more summer that is carefree and fun. I have stuff I need to do to prep for school, too, and I'm still doing some internship work, so I have work things too. I promise you'll still get work done. But we both still have enough time to play this summer!"

It doesn't take me long to think about it, "Let's do it!" I exclaim, and Maddie squeals again. I can always use some distractions from my self-destructive thoughts, and Maddie has always been the perfect distraction partner.

A few days later, the perfect summer day has Maddie and I are lying on the dock, our feet dangling in the lake water. One of our favorite summer activities has always been drinking milkshakes and enjoying the sun.

"Let's take a picture!" Maddie says, squeezing us closer together.

We smile as she snaps a photo, then looks at it, "Perfect! That is so cute! I'm sending this to Ben!"

She's giggling at her phone and takes another picture of just herself in her swimsuit.

"Oh, he's going to love that one," I tease with a wink.

"Stop!" she laughs, smacking my arm, then adds, "He definitely will, though."

I chuckle as I roll my eyes. I'm so happy for her, and a little bit envious. It was pretty much love at first sight for Maddie and Ben. They met at the first dorm meeting freshman year and wouldn't stop talking the whole time. Ben was nice and tried to set me up a few times so we could double date, but they never really lasted. Mike was my longest relationship, and well, you already know how that turned out. Maybe I'm broken.

"Have you thought any more about what Joan said about trying out a dating app?" Maddie asks, as if she's reading my mind.

"I'm not just looking for a hook up though."

"They aren't just for hooking up. Ben is coming to

town soon, let's do a double date!"

I look at Maddie with her sweet, eager face and find myself smiling. I may not have a head over heels romantic love yet, but I lucked out in the friend department. So I find myself saying, "Okay, fine. One double date."

I promised Joan that I would come over for sandwiches and work later that day. Even though we both knew there probably wouldn't be much work involved. I start off by telling her about the promise I made to Maddie and she was all too excited to help me set up my profile. Soon enough, we are eating little finger sandwiches, drinking wine, and scrolling through profiles.

"Mustache? No." Joan says, swiping left for me.

"Oh, hello, blue eyes," she laughs and swipes right.

Joan has done most of the swiping, allowing me to veto a few when needed. Mostly, I let her choose and have a great time listening to her commentary.

"Oh my. This looks just like Dave when he was younger!" Joan says.

"Are you calling me old?" Dave jokes, coming into the room.

"Of course you're old, dear."

He chuckles and leans down to kiss Joan on her temple.

"Should I ask why you are looking at a shirtless man flexing on your phone?" he asks, bemused.

"Trying to find Jenna a man to date," she replies, unfazed as she continues scrolling photos.

"Technology these days," he says, shaking his head, "It really can do everything, huh?"

Joan turns back to me and shows me a cute guy. He

has blonde hair and brown eyes and a nice smile.

"He's cute," I offer.

"Very cute," she counters, scrolling through the rest of his pictures.

She stops on a shirtless one of him and raises her eyebrows at me.

"Swipe right," I sigh, rolling my eyes a little.

My phone dings and she jumps, "Oh, what does that mean? Are you a match? Did he already swipe on you?" She hands my phone back and I see that not only did we match but there is a message waiting for me.

"Hey, happy to see we matched." My mouth falls open a little, and I show the message to Joan. She claps and urges me to reply.

"Yeah, me too. My friend has been bugging me to try this app for ages, but I was sure it would be full of weirdos."

"It's definitely full of weirdos. If you look hard enough, though, there are a few good ones. We may have just lucked out today."

His name is Jensen, and he's not bad to talk to. He makes me laugh a few times and he doesn't say anything weird so we decide to meet up on a double date with Maddie. I text Maddie and ask for her and Ben to choose a time, and I'll let Jensen know when he can casually meet up with us. *Casually*, I say again to remind both Maddie and Jensen.

Maddie texts me back immediately and says *Thursday night, 7:00, let's go bowling!*

5

I look at myself in the mirror one last time before I leave. My blonde hair has loose waves, and I put on soft red lipstick. I'm going for the casually cute look, even though I tried on five outfits and my insides are a nervous wreck.

Jensen is going to meet us at the bowling alley, and Maddie and Ben are picking me up at my parent's house. I planned this strategically just to emphasize how casual this night is. My parents are at a meet and greet for potential students at the college, and I was grateful that I didn't have to answer any prying questions.

When I hop into Maddie's car I notice how radiant she looks. She seems to glow just a little brighter when she is with Ben. It has always intrigued me. The perfect way they balance each other; their natural ebb and flow. It's electric for both of them. They light up and buzz with each other, somehow both seeming even brighter and better when together.

"Hi, Jenna! How's it feel being a college grad and living at your parent's house?" Ben jokes.

Maddie laughs loudly, winks at me, and then answers, "Oh, she's about to have the best summer ever."

I see Ben squeeze her hand and whisper something that makes Maddie's cheeks flush and a little giggle escapes her lips.

A few minutes before we pull up to the bowling alley, Maddie says, "Okay, what's our code word? Y'know, in case you want to get out of here."

"How about my feet hurt?" I suggest.

"A little on the nose, don't ya think?" Maddie says.

"What about pineapple?" Ben exclaims.

Maddie shrieks and says, "Yes! Love it! Ben brought me a pineapple on our second date. He knows it's my favorite fruit and that I'm dying to go to Hawaii. So instead of flowers, he showed up with a pineapple." Maddie tells me as if I haven't already heard the story a million times.

We pull up to the bowling alley now, and I feel my nerves kick back in. I'm already picturing a middle-aged man waiting for me. I'm so prepared to be catfished; honestly, I'm expecting it, so when I see Jensen at the counter I'm surprised. He gives me a wave and starts walking to meet us.

"Oookay, not bad at all," Maddie whispers, bumping her hip into mine.

"Jenna, nice to officially meet you," he says, reaching out his hand. It seems a little too proper, but I shake it anyway. "You look beautiful," he adds, smiling.

"Thank you. I'm really glad you're not a middle-aged creeper," I blurt back.

Maddie gives a roaring laugh and she says, "Definitely not!"

Jensen chuckles and adds, "I'm also glad I'm not."

Jensen and Ben go up to the counter to pay, and Maddie pulls me closer as she says, "He's funny! I like him!"

Jensen is just about 6 feet tall. He has very light blonde hair that you know has already seen plenty of sun. His skin is a darker hue, thanks to the summer sun, I'm sure. I can't lie to myself, he's very easy to look at. As I'm staring, he turns around and catches me. His face lights up in a smile, and he waves us over for our shoes.

Maddie and Ben grab their shoes and are already heading towards the lane as Jensen politely waits for me. "Your friends seem nice," he says, looking over at Ben and Maddie.

"Yeah, they're great," I respond as I grab my shoes and we make our way towards them.

It turns out Jensen is really good at bowling and Ben isn't. Maddie and I have gotten pretty good over the years. In the first game, we get 145 and 137, Jensen gets 157, and Ben gets 105. Jensen pats Ben on the back and says, "Half was just luck, man. Don't worry about it. I'll go buy the first round and some nachos for everyone."

Maddie takes this chance to slide over to me and ask, "Sooo, what do we think?"

"He seems really nice," I offer. I don't actually have much else to say. I learned that he's an only child, he grew up here but went to a different high school from us. He got a degree in business and is working at a local shipping company running all of their excel reports. It's mostly a bunch of small talk, and that's my least favorite part of first dates. That's another reason I haven't been anxious to get out there and find someone new. I was so comfortable in my last relationship, and we were way past the small talk get to know you conversations. I hate going back to that.

"Who's ready for round two?" Jensen asks as he walks back with our drinks, nachos, and a pizza.

Ben stands up proud and replies, "Let's do this!" Maddie jumps up to cheer him on, and I see Jensen chuckle.

"Gotta give it to him, he's got a great attitude when he's so far behind all of us. I'm a lot more competitive than that," Jensen says, sitting down and handing me a drink. I reach towards the nachos and use another chip to wipe off some of the tomatoes.

"Are you?" I sip my drink and look up at him expectantly.

"Oh yeah. It's not a great trait, I know that. Runs in my family, I guess. My dad is very competitive, and he signed me up for just about every sport. I wasn't any good at them, though. It sure ticked him off. I guess I'm just better with numbers."

"You seem pretty good at bowling," I offer up.

He laughs, "Yeah, if only my dad could see me now!"

"I'll take a picture for you. You can send it to him," I tease, holding out my hand for his phone.

He looks away from my eyes as he replies, "Thanks, but, uh, he passed away."

"Oh," I breathe out, letting my hand fall back to my side. "That's awful."

"Yeah, after that, I stuck to the sidelines. I love sports, I went to all the games, but it will always remind me of him."

It's my turn to bowl so I give him a gentle smile and hop up. Jensen was opening up in ways that kind of surprised me for a first date. Especially one from an app. Maybe I judged this whole process too quickly, and I really need to give it more of a chance. I bowl a strike, and Jensen jumps up to high-five me and then takes his turn. It gives me a little time to think more about what he said and how he doesn't feel like his dad would be proud of him.

When Jensen comes back, I say, "I get what you were saying earlier about your dad being ticked off about not being good at sports. I know it's not the same thing, but my parents expect more from me than what I'm currently doing."

"Graphic design?"

"Yeah. I love it, but they don't understand. They don't believe that it will support me or lead anywhere."

"I think it's pretty impressive," Jensen says.

"Honestly, I'm not even worried if it doesn't lead me anywhere. I'm only 22. Right now, I'm trying this, and I'm enjoying it. If it doesn't work out, then I'll do something else. That's the part that really kills them, that I'm okay if it doesn't work out. They view that as a lack of ambition," I realize I'm rambling and I bite my lip. "Sorry. It's a little heavy sometimes."

"Well, I disagree with them. I think it's very ambitious to even try in the first place. To try and create a living from something you love to do, it's very cool," Jensen replies.

I find myself smiling up at Jensen as I say "thank you." I scoot in a little closer so that our knees are touching. Jensen has pretty eyes, they are a dark milky brown, and now that I'm close enough, I can see the flecks of color in them, pops of lighter brown and green.

Suddenly, Jensen breaks eye contact and looks over my shoulder. He seems surprised as he calls out, "Oliver?"

I turn slightly and see Oliver standing behind me. He's wearing a blue and white plaid button-up shirt with the sleeves rolled up. It's unbuttoned to reveal a white t-shirt underneath.

"You're Oliver Hayes, right?" Jensen says, standing up.

"Yeah, that's me," Oliver replies, looking at me and then at Jensen.

"Oh man, I went to high school with this guy! He's

a few years older than me, but man, can he throw! He was our quarterback!" Jensen explains excitedly, talking to me now. Maddie and Ben come over to see what we are talking about.

Oliver looks a little uncomfortable as he introduces himself to Maddie and Ben.

"You went to Alabama, right? I heard about what happened, tough break," Jensen says, turning back to Oliver.

"Yeah, Bama was great. They were really understanding with me," Oliver answers, glancing at me again.

Jensen notices Oliver's glance and puts his arm around me, pulling me into him, as he replies, "Life just isn't fair sometimes, am I right?"

So there's his competitive side. I can see it now with Oliver here. This is the most physical contact we've had all night. It's too much to be a coincidence and it makes me uncomfortable. I pull away slightly and feel Jensen's grip tighten. He throws a quick smile at me and then looks back at Oliver.

Oliver glances down at our nachos and I see the corner of his mouth turn up. Then he looks directly at me. "Needs more cheese," he says, throwing me a smirk before turning and walking away.

I slide out from under Jensen's arm, and Maddie looks at me, "Do you know him?"

"Oliver? I met him last time we were here," I reply.

"That's cool. He was a really awesome quarterback," Jensen cuts in. "Kind of sad to see him just working at a bowling alley. Talk about a waste."

I look over to see Oliver behind the counter. I'm glad he can't hear what Jensen is saying.

We play a few more games, and Jensen offers to give me a ride home. It was a nice date, and I had a good time with Jensen, so I accept his offer.

"This was fun," he states as we drive.

"Yeah, I had a good time. It was fun to have a little competition other than Maddie. For as long as I can remember, Maddie and I have been going to that bowling alley and trying to win. You beat us both tonight though."

"Can't always win," he says, laughing. "So, would you be interested in going out again? Maybe on our own this time? Maddie and Ben were great, but I would love to take you out to dinner, just us," he asks.

"Yeah, I think that would be fun."

"Great! I'll text you." He pulls over in front of my parent's house and gets out to walk me to the door. I see some lights inside and figure my parents are probably watching, so I keep my distance, trying to send him a hint. He seems to get it because when we reach the front step, he stops and says, "Well, it was fun. I'll see you again soon." Then he turns and heads back to his car. I give him another little wave and open the door.

My mom and dad are sitting in the front room reading their books. Without looking up, my dad says, "Did you have a good night?"

"Yup, I went bowling," I say, heading upstairs.

"With a boy?"

I pause and come back down the few stairs I had gone up. "Yes."

My mom puts down her book and smiles, "Let's hear about him!"

"His name is Jensen."

"What does he do?"

"He's an analyst for a shipping company."

"Ooh, analysts can do very well these days," my dad says to my mom.

"Exciting, maybe we should invite him over," she says to me.

"It was a first date," I reply trying to emphasize how casual it was.

"It's not a big deal, just dinner or drinks! It will be fun. I'll check our calendar," my mom says, already pulling out her phone and looking over her schedule.

I start to reply and realize it's pointless, so instead I quiet turn and walk upstairs.

6

The next day is full of work tasks. First thing I need to do is create a presentation for the brownie company that agreed to work with me. They started off small but grew so fast they couldn't keep up. Suddenly, they are selling brownies in malls and grocery stores, and at least every state has one of their bakeries. I pull my hair up, put on some shorts, and get to work.

A few hours later my stomach grumbles telling me to take a break and eat lunch. My mom is reading by the pool so I make myself a sandwich sneak back to my room. I check my phone and see that I missed a call from Maddie as I sit down at my desk. I call her back, knowing she'll want to hear all about the car ride last night.

"Jennaaaaa," Maddie sings my name when she picks up. Then she exclaims, "Tell me everything!"

"Hi, Maddie. There really isn't much to tell."

"Did he kiss you? Did you kiss him? Do you like him? Are you going out again? There's plenty to tell!"

"No, we didn't kiss. Yes, he asked me out again. And yeah, he was nice."

"Nice?" Maddie repeats it like it's a question.

"Yeah, he was nice."

"Like swoon-worthy nice or like, boring nice?"

"Uhh, is there an in-between choice? I just don't know him that well."

"When it's right, it doesn't matter how well you know him. You just feel it."

I scoff and she hears me.

"It's true, and you know it! That's what you're waiting for! Don't act like it's not."

"I'm hoping for it, sure, but realistically, I'm not sure that exists."

"It does."

I fall silent, knowing it's not worth the argument. Sweet Maddie means well, she always does. But love just fell in her lap. She's one of the lucky ones.

"Ben and I are going out for dinner tonight if you want to join," Maddie breaks the silence.

"No, thanks, you two go and have fun."

"Okay! Keep me updated. Love you long time!"

"Love you long time," I reply, hanging up.

I finish up my presentation and send it off to Jennifer, my contact for the company. I feel pretty confident about it, but I already find myself anxiously refreshing my email, waiting for a response. I check the time, 5:08, and decide I'll reward myself with some retail therapy.

As I pull into a spot at the mall, I get a text and look down to see a message from Jensen.

"Like I promised, here's a text asking you out again."

"Glad I didn't scare you away. Would love to go out."

"I don't scare easily, remember? I'm competitive. I'll fight for what I want. How does next Friday sound? There's a good seafood place we can go."

He's saying I'm what he wants? Pretty bold at this point, but also kind of sweet.

"I'll be honest, I don't love seafood. But I'm sure I can find something."

"Great! I'll pick you up at 7:00."

I spend the next hour mostly window shopping and eating one of those delicious baked pretzels that only malls and airports have somehow perfected. I find a pair of jeans I like and head to the dressing room to try them on. Just as I'm going in one door, I pass a girl coming out of the other one. I pause, "Olivia?" I ask. She stops and looks up at me, confused.

She stares at my face for a second and then points at me and says, "Bowling alley girl."

I laugh, "Yeah, I guess that's me."

"You're friends with my brother."

"Uh, not really. He just helped me out the other night."

Olivia gives me a blank stare and then shrugs. She has a pile of clothes over her arm, and I notice a NASA t-shirt.

"Cool shirt," I say, pointing to it.

"Thanks. People call me a space geek."

"And you're okay with that?"

"Yeah, it's true," she states matter of factly. I don't mention that Oliver actually did mention her love of space to me.

"I'm a design geek," I tell her.

"Like clothing design?" she asks, her eyebrows raised.

"Not quite, more like logos, stickers, websites, things like that. Although I do help design some shirts and sweaters for a fishing company."

"That's pretty cool. You'll have to design me a space shirt."

I laugh and notice that she looks serious, so I add, "Yeah, maybe I'll try that for you."

"Cool. I'll see you around," she gives me a little wave and leaves.

I decide to buy the jeans after trying them on. They

are the kind of jeans that fit just right and make you feel confident and cozy. I'm a firm believer that everyone needs a pair of jeans like that. As I'm walking out to my car, I see Olivia and Oliver walking in front of me towards their car. Olivia is animatedly talking, and Oliver is listening intently. I watch as he laughs and then wraps his arm around her shoulders.

Maddie is busy with Ben all week, so our summer plans don't happen much the next few days. We met up and went swimming at the lake on Wednesday, where she made me relive the date all over again and talk about the upcoming date on Friday. I had plenty of time to work, and I met up with Joan twice to go over some new ideas she had.

She wants to put some of her quotes on bumper stickers, so I spent some time working on different designs with her. The first one we design is a fish on a hook with words from the fish saying, "I ain't dead yet!" This is something Joan frequently says as a reminder to live every day to the fullest. People have started calling it her catchphrase.

Joan is equally interested in the Jensen situation and asked if his pictures matched his body in real life. She was disappointed when I told her that he kept his shirt on while we were bowling. As I listen to Joan talk about her hot date night plans with Dave, I find myself doodling and playing with a new sticker idea. I don't notice what I'm making until I finish it and realize it's a rocket ship. I add in a small girl's face, smiling wide, in the window of the rocket.

"I didn't think you were that serious about not liking seafood," Jensen says. It's Friday night, and we are out at the restaurant Jensen wanted to take me. Jensen looks good. He's in khakis and a tight black polo. It makes his blonde hair look even more blonde, and his skin look darker. The restaurant is definitely a seafood restaurant. Even the smell grosses me out a little.

Usually, I can find something on the menu that I like, but this place really puts fish in everything so I am only eating the free bread. The restaurant is nice, though. Other than the weird fish decor, it's quite fancy.

"I told you I don't," I reply and then add, "But the bread is great."

Jensen frowns slightly, looking down at his plate. "I feel a little silly eating all of this while you snack on bread."

"Well, I'm quite enjoying the bread."

Jensen looks up at me, "Sorry, I just want to make sure you're enjoying yourself."

"So, how are things going with work?" He asks.

"Great! I sent off my big presentation this week and am waiting to hear back. It's for Townie Brownie. I'm making some large changes to their website so hopefully they like it. The idea is that they want to start creating brownies specialized for each state. So Alaska will get a baked Alaska brownie, and Georgia will have a peach brownie, and New York will get a cheesecake brownie."

"Okay, that sounds delicious! What about North Carolina?"

"I think they said they are working on some type of donut brownie since Krispy Kreme started here."

"Yum, they all sound amazing."

"Yeah, and they also want a logo update, so I sent them some ideas that I think are pretty fun."

"You can do everything they need you to?" he asks.

I feel a little bit of anger bubble up at his comment. Of course I'm capable of doing it. I hesitate to answer, not wanting to overreact.

"I just mean, this is your first big client, right?" he continues.

"Other than Joan, yeah," I say a bit sharply.

"Joan is the one you mentioned the other night? The one you've been with from the beginning?"

"Yeah, she's great. She's the one that set me up on the app."

Jensen chuckles and says, "Guess I'll have to thank her when I meet her."

He scoops a fork full of his food up and holds it out towards me, "Here, try this, it's delicious."

"No, thanks, really I don't like any seafood."

"C'mon, you won't even try it?"

"No…I know I won't like it. It's all yours."

"But you won't even try it? That's seriously lame."

I throw him a look, and he sighs. "Fine, not a big deal. Just thought you might change your mind." He shoves it in his mouth and makes an exaggerated mmmm sound.

"Do you ever think it's ironic that you work for Joan but you hate seafood?" he asks, his mouth still full of food.

"Not really, I don't have to like fish to be good at my job."

He shrugs, "guess not."

"So, do you enjoy your work?" I ask, hoping to change the subject.

"Yeah, I'm a numbers guy. I spend most of my day

finding cool shortcuts in Excel. It's the way I get creative with it."

"I don't love numbers, but I definitely get the creative part. Would you say you're a creative person?"

"Yeah, I think I'm more left-brained than right, but I like to draw. Usually, I'm just doodling and sketching things during meetings and things. I enjoy it. Growing up, I used to draw dorky comic strips and things."

I chuckle a little and reply, "I would love to see that."

"Oh, I'm sure I have them hidden somewhere."

"How is your meal going?" the waitress asks as she refills our drinks.

"It's wonderful, thank you," I reply.

Jensen nods and then asks, "Do you have a pen I can borrow?"

I look at him, questioning, but he smiles at me and continues to eat.

A few minutes later, she brings a pen back and Jensen grabs my napkin and starts doodling. I try to peek, but he hides it and grins at me.

"Tell me about your parents," he tries to distract me.

"Oh geez, you want to have that talk?" I sigh, leaning back.

"Well, you already heard my story. Time for your sob story," he replies while still sketching.

"It's not really a sob story. They are still together and happy. We just have a...different relationship. I kind of told you about it last week."

"Yeah, the whole wasting your time thing?"

"Yeah, that. Guess they don't have much faith in me. They feel that way about most people. They have very specific expectations of what makes someone successful."

"Although, they seemed to be impressed with your job," I add.

He stops sketching and peeks up at me, "You told them about me?" he asks, a smile growing on his lips.

I blush a little, realizing how that sounds. "Uh yeah, I mentioned it after our date."

He now gives me a full smile and slowly looks back down at his drawing.

"Analyst just sounds smart, it's nothing special," he says kindly.

Jensen finishes up the drawing, looks down at it one more time, then spins the napkin around to me.

I look down to see a comic strip of a man looking at his phone with hearts in his eyes. The next few squares show him checking his phone constantly with an overly large smile. The last square shows a girl walking through a door and the man's eyes bug out of his head and his heart coming out of his chest. There are words on the bottom of the last square that says, the beginning...

"This is really good!" I exclaim, adding, "And it's really sweet."

"It's cheesy but also true. Like I said, my comics were usually pretty cheesy. It's all in good fun."

"Can I keep it?" I ask.

He lights up and looks at me, surprised. "Yeah, of course! If you want it, it's yours."

The rest of the date goes well. I notice that he's kind to our waitress, and he leaves her a big tip, although he seems a little too showy about it. I was feeling pretty unsure at the beginning of the date but Jensen seemed to get better as the date went on.

"Are you still hungry?" Jensen asks as we are on the way back to my house.

"I'm fine, thanks."

"You sure? I feel bad that you only ate bread."

"I like bread. I'm fine, really."

He looks at me again but seems to believe me, so he continues driving. He fidgets with the radio a little but ends up just turning the volume down. The car is quiet as we drive. I find myself feeling a little uncomfortable with the silence. It seems like the longer we go without speaking, the more awkward it becomes. I finally look over at him and ask, "Did you have fun tonight?"

"Are you kidding? Of course, I did!"

"Not that you could say otherwise," I joke.

"Oh, I 100 percent could say otherwise. It would be rude, though."

I laugh, feeling a little better about the quiet car ride. Still not good enough to leave it though, so I say, "Just making sure this silence isn't a bad silence."

Jensen looks over at me and smiles, "I don't mind silence. Do you?"

"Uh, I guess it depends on the moment."

"Like now?" he questions.

"Well, kind of, I guess."

He gently puts his hand on my knee and says, "It's not bad silence. I promise." He looks at me briefly and then takes his hand back.

When we get to my house, he walks me to the door this time.

"I had fun tonight," he smiles down at me.

"Me too." I'm trying to think about how to handle his next move, but he opens his arms and pulls me into a hug. I'm instantly relieved when he doesn't try to kiss me. Jensen is cute but I'm still not ready to kiss him. I feel his hands slide a little lower on my back and pull me in tighter. My body tightens and I pull away a little. He reacts and let's go, taking a step back.

"Well, hopefully, I'll see you again soon," he says as he steps back towards his car.

"Yeah. Let's do it again," I reply, turning and walking inside.

This time when I get inside, the lights are off, and my parents are in bed. I'm thankful and hungry so I sneak to the kitchen and eat a bowl of ice cream before bed. As I'm eating my favorite creamy chocolate moose tracks ice cream, I'm thinking about the end of the date with Jensen. The awkward hug. Did I make it weird? Was he uncomfortable? Why is dating so exhausting? With Mike, it felt easy. I knew how he was feeling, what he was thinking, it was all predictable. I guess in the end, that was the problem. I never felt the spark with Mike, just the comfort. Now with Jensen, I'm not sure what I feel. I'm attracted to him, but I'm not overly comfortable; maybe that's the spark I've been waiting for?

I look down at the napkin on which he drew his comic, and I find myself smiling. Thinking about the date makes me smile, and for now, I'll just have to go with that. I ignore my racing thoughts and try to focus on the good. It's enough to make me pick up my phone and text him first.

Thanks again for tonight. The bread was delicious ;)
Typing bubbles popped up almost immediately, and he replies, *I'm so glad you liked it. Next time, you pick the place. I'm hoping there will be a next time?*

Definitely.

7

The following day, I wake up and eagerly check my email. I still haven't heard from Townie Brownie, and I've been refreshing my email constantly. Sure enough, they replied!

Unfortunately, it's not good news. She said they had some thoughts for me. They are having a meeting with the team today and will get back to me today or tomorrow. My stomach and chest tighten as I read it. What do they mean by thoughts for me? Good or bad thoughts? My mind instantly starts thinking bad things. Why couldn't she just say what her thoughts were and give me some idea? I flop back into bed, knowing I'll be an anxious mess all day. I go back over my presentation a few more times, wondering what the thoughts could be. Maybe they're good, I try to tell myself. There's a chance they loved it or maybe they just want more? I sigh and roll out of bed. I don't even believe that it's good news, so of course, I can't tell my parents. It would only be extra ammunition for them. So instead, I text Maddie a screenshot of the email with a frowny face.

She replies quickly, *Hey, that doesn't mean it's bad! It could be good news!*

I feel like if it was good, there would be some kind of implication of that. There's not even an "I love it" or "great job."

If they don't love it, then they suck.

Thanks, but I think that means I suck.

NO WAY! Don't say that. Let's do one of our summer activities today to get your mind off of it.

Like what?

Snow cones in the park?

Deal.

It's a beautiful summer day. There are no clouds in the sky only a slight breeze, and the perfectly warm sun on my skin. Maddie and I are lying on a blanket at our favorite park. We've been coming here since we first met. I'm leaned up on my elbows, wearing denim cut-off shorts with a white tank top tucked in. I slide out of my black sandals and breathe deeply, trying to ignore my nerves. I attempt to keep my focus on the beautiful day and not the doubts racing through my mind.

Maddie ordered her favorite snow cone, pina colada. I'm pretty sure she just gets it because it comes with a tiny umbrella. I slurp down the last bit of my raspberry cheesecake and lay down on my back, closing my eyes behind my sunglasses. I'm making an effort to be in the moment, to feel the sun on my legs even though my mind is racing. I can't ignore my worries about the email from Townie Brownie. I fidget and take a few deep breaths.

"Stop stressing," Maddie says next to me.

"I'm not stressing."

"I can literally feel the stress coming off of you."

"Okay, well, I'm *trying* to be in the moment."

Maddie slurps the rest of her snow cone down loudly, I open my eyes at her, and she laughs. "Me too!" then she pulls her shirt over her head and lies down by me.

"What are you doing?"

"What? It's basically a bikini top." She shrugs and laughs.

Typical Maddie, I think. She's too carefree. But in the best way, in the way I wish I could be. She's always been great at living in the moment while I stress about the future. It's been like this ever since we were kids. I would stress about the test coming up on Monday, and she would be playing and enjoying her weekend. I would worry too much about what dating someone would be like, that I never actually dated anyone. On the other hand, Maddie went on tons of dates and was carefree about them all. She got her heart broken once or twice, but she still swears she wouldn't change a thing. Even when we were applying to college, I was so concerned about getting accepted and what would happen if I didn't. She always shrugged it off and told me to enjoy my senior year. I loved her for it. She always brought me back to the moment and made me believe that somehow everything would work out in the end, which is why I was glad to be spending the day with her. She kept me here in the moment and not completely spinning out about the email coming soon.

"I miss Ben," Maddie sighs.

"When will you see him again?"

"Oh, I don't know. He's supposed to come again in a few weeks. But I might go visit him first, or after that. I don't know. I hate being away from him."

"He liked Jensen, ya know," she adds, nudging me with her elbow.

Of course, I had already told her all about my date last night. She patiently let me re-read the email from Townie Brownie to her again but then she wanted to hear every little detail about the date. She thought the napkin was adorable and got mad when I said I didn't kiss him.

"He's likable," I reply, simply.

"Ugh, give me something, girl! Give *him* something!" Maddie says, leaning up onto her elbows.

"I am trying!"

"You *try* too hard, though. Just let it flow!" she replies, leaning back.

"It's not flowing on its own. I just want what you have."

"Yeah, it's pretty perfect, not gonna lie."

Now it's my turn to elbow her in the side and she just laughs, leaning into me.

Then she suddenly sits up, "Hey! You're Oliver!"

I look up as a shadow falls over us. He's wearing black sunglasses, black shorts, and a tight black t-shirt. The only thing not black are his crisp white sneakers. He looks good in all black and I feel my cheeks flush when I look at him.

"You seem to always be with people that know me," Oliver says, smirking at me.

"Yeah, I remember you from the other night!" Maddie says. "We were at the bowling alley, on a date." she explains unnecessarily because Oliver replies, "I remember."

I look at Maddie, wondering if she's uncomfortable lying there in her bra with a boy she hardly knows. She seems completely unfazed, so I peek back at Oliver, fully expecting him to be checking her out because, honestly, she's gorgeous. However, he's looking right at me, and asks, "How was the date?"

"Well, it was Jenna here's first date with him! She met him on an app," Maddie answers, raising her eyebrows and looking at me.

"Maddie, he doesn't care," I whisper, embarrassed and thankful for my sunglasses.

"Oh, I love hearing dating app horror stories." Oliver smiles.

"What makes you think it was a horror story?" I blurt out.

He raises his eyebrows, and his smile drops a little. "Wasn't it?"

"No, actually, he was nice. We went out again last night." I don't know why I'm telling him or why I feel the need to justify it.

Oliver listens to this and then plops down next to me. "Okay then, seems like not all app dates are horror stories. I just figured that was more for the hit it and quit it, crowd."

"Hit it and quit it," Maddie snorts.

"Anyway," I say, rolling my eyes behind my sunglasses, "What are you doing here?"

"Enjoying this beautiful weather. I like to walk in the park to clear my head."

"Why are you clearing your head?" I ask, genuinely curious.

He rubs the back of his neck, "I have some decisions to make."

"Jenna is trying to clear her head too! This park is perfect for it, huh?"

"Why are you clearing your head?" he asks me.

Before I can answer, Maddie replies, "She's freaking out because her big brownie client said that they had some "thoughts" to share with her about her proposal. And of course, that means Jenna started spiraling and thinking they didn't like it or her."

I feel my cheeks heat up a little and say, "Thanks,

Maddie, it's embarrassing enough without everyone knowing."

Oliver turns to look at me. He slides his sunglasses on top of his head and his blue eyes scrunch a little like he's inspecting me. Then he says, "There's nothing to be embarrassed about. At least not yet," he winks.

"Ugh!" I sigh, falling onto my back and covering my face with my hands.

"I'm kidding, I'm kidding. There's nothing to be embarrassed about. Are you proud of what you did?" he asks.

"Yes," I say from behind my hands.

"And did they say they hate it, or hate you?" he continues.

"No."

"Okay then, maybe we just wait until they do respond and then decide how to react from there."

I peek out from behind my fingers. He leans in just a tiny bit and smiles at me as I peek out from my hands.

"Okay, I know. I'll try." I reply, sitting up.

Maddie throws her hands up in the air and says, "Not like I've been telling her that literally all day, but a cute boy comes along, and she's totally fine listening to him."

Oliver barks out a loud laugh and then says, "Cute, huh?"

"Her words, not mine," I say, smiling.

"You don't agree?" he asks, turning towards me.

My cheeks flush bright red as I open my mouth to respond. Maddie is giggling next to me, and thankfully my phone rings. I struggle to pull it out of my pocket and see that it's my mom calling.

I quickly stand up and answer it, happy for an excuse to walk away from Maddie and Oliver.

"Hey, Mom, what's up?"

"Hey, hon, just calling to make sure you're still coming to the event tonight?"

I quickly check my watch. I still have 4 hours before I have to leave, but she was right. I had completely forgotten about the cocktail party. My mom had asked me a few days ago to come to keep her company at a grad student party tonight. "Yeah, of course! I'll be there."

"Great, don't be late. And dress up nice, please."

"Sure, thing Mom."

I hang up but stay looking at my phone, hoping enough time has passed from the question earlier. As I walk back over to Maddie and Oliver, Maddie laughs and says, "She sounds fun!"

"Who?" I ask, sitting down next to them.

"My sister. She told me about seeing you at the mall," he replies.

"Yeah, she seems cool," I say.

"She really is."

"Seems like there's a big age gap there, but you're still close?" I ask.

"Yeah, there are 12 years between us. But we've always been close."

"Wow, that's cool. So you're 24?"

"I just turned 25."

Suddenly, Maddie screams and covers her head as a football comes flying toward us. Oliver reaches out and easily grabs it.

"Sorry!" a voice from a group of guys yells out. He lifts his hands up, waiting for Oliver to throw the ball back. Oliver is holding it in his hands, and I notice how his hands easily wrap around it and flex, the veins in his hands strong. He looks up from the ball and then pulls back and sends it soaring perfectly back to the guy.

"Nice throw!" the guy yells and waves.

"What is it with you always saving me?" I mumble and laugh.

"Wait, what do you mean saving you?" Maddie asks, confused.

I swallow, realizing I never told her about what happened when she left. I knew she would feel responsible and angry. I decided it would just be easier to deal with it on my own. Oliver looks between her and me but doesn't speak.

"Uhhh, yeah, that's actually how I first met Oliver," I start, avoiding Maddie's face. I find myself looking at the ground, my hands, anywhere except her face. I look up at Oliver, and his face has softened as he looks back at me. He gives me a small smile and a tiny nod, encouraging me to continue.

"Remember that guy at the bowling alley that made that disgusting joke to me?" I ask.

"Yuck, yes, of course."

"Well, he kind of cornered me at my car when I was leaving."

"What!" Maddie yells. She pulls up her sunglasses and grabs my arms. "Jenna! Why didn't you tell me? What happened?"

"Nothing, really. I mean, like I said, Oliver came and told him to leave."

"You did?" she asks, turning to Oliver.

"Yeah, I just made sure she was okay. It didn't look right."

"Thank God you were there. Unlike me! I can't believe I just left you there!" Maddie says.

"That's why I didn't tell you. You couldn't have

known. And nothing happened. Really, I was fine," I respond.

"But you almost weren't," she whispers.

"Okay, I don't know what would or could have happened. But it's not a big deal."

"Don't say that!" Maddie exclaims at the same time Oliver says, "Yes, it is."

I look up and meet Oliver's eyes, and he says again, "Yes, it is. It's a big deal, Jenna. Whether or not something happened. It's a big deal. It's okay to feel your emotions."

I swallow and feel tears well up in my eyes. A lump grows in my throat, and I cough and look away. The way Oliver looked at me as he said those words. It felt familiar and safe. I was allowed to feel my feelings without any shame or belittling. I knew he wasn't judging me or thinking less of me. He was validating me and accepting me. It was something I don't feel often.

Maddie pulls me into a hug and says, "I'm so sorry that happened to you." Then she looks over my shoulder at Oliver and adds, "And I'm so glad you were there to take care of her."

"Me too," he replies, and I can hear the smile in his voice as he says it.

"I should go," he says. "Come on by the bowling alley sometime. The first game will be on me."

"Oooh, yes! We'll be there!" Maddie cheers, releasing me from the hug.

Oliver gives me another soft look and then says, "See ya later, Jenna."

The way he says my name makes my stomach flip. I like the way it sounds coming from him.

It's a few minutes before we have to leave for the cocktail party, and I'm looking in the mirror, running my hands down my dress to smooth it. It's a simple black dress with thin straps and a high slit up the side. I look in the mirror and give a little turn to the side. My hair is straightened, my make-up light and simple, and I'm wearing thin, black high heels. I look nice, and I feel great.

"You look wonderful!" My mom says, poking her head in my door.

"Thanks, Mom."

"Are you ready to go?"

"Yeah, let's go."

"Great, now remember, let's try to make a good impression."

I throw her a look and reply, "Do I ever try to make bad ones?"

"I just need you to be extra aware."

"Why are you trying to impress these people?"

"I'm not. But you never know where something like this could lead," she replies. She moves her hands around as if to shush any further comment and then turns and walks away.

"Your father is meeting us there," she calls from down the hall. "He had to finish up late at work."

I roll my eyes even though no one is there to see it. Then I put on my best smile and follow my mom downstairs.

The cocktail party is at a small bar downtown. The college rented out the place, so it's a little more quiet than usual. Everyone is dressed up, and as we walk in, I see my dad in his work suit, animatedly talking and laughing in the corner. My mom saunters up to him, kisses him on the cheek, and then goes to the bar to get a drink. I hover in the corner, testing out the place. It's a solid mix between grad students and professors. Most of them are split off into small groups with a few stragglers caught looking around uncomfortably. My mom waves me over to the bar, so I smile and make my way toward her. She slides me a mojito even though she knows it's not my favorite drink. We've had the conversation a few times, but I smile and accept it anyway.

"Find me in a minute so I can introduce you to people," she says, as she waves and calls out, "Hey, John! How are you?" She's gone before I can respond. I take a sip of the mojito and then slide it to the side and order a glass of wine.

I lean against the bar, watching the crowd. My dad is on one side of the room, still telling some hilarious story that captures the attention of even more people. My mom is on the other side of the room, talking to the dean of her department and a few other professors I recognize from other parties. I continue sipping my wine when my phone buzzes.

Still thinking about today. I'm really glad you're okay. I want to kill that guy. It's from Maddie.

Don't waste the energy.

Ugh, why are guys so awful.

You got me there. But don't let Ben hear you say that.

Ha! Ben is one of a kind.

Another message pops up as I'm reading Maddie's message. It's an email from Townie Brownie. I quickly click on it and read over it, my heart racing.

Jenna, I like a few of these thoughts, but they don't seem on-brand for us. After discussing with the team, they agree.

We would like a change, a refresh, but we still want to be on brand, and these website ideas don't match what we are looking for. The logo is okay. But we want to be blown away, and this just doesn't accomplish that for us. Can you send us a few more of your other designs? I think we will be a good team together, but we need to really nail down some specifics and figure out the best way to work together.
Thanks

I read the email three more times. My ideas are off-brand? I'm suddenly questioning everything I sent them. They wanted something new and fresh while staying on brand. I knew that, and that's what I was trying to do. But they still didn't like it. I feel the disappointment and doubt come flooding in. I only have two other designs for the logo I was playing with, and neither of them is as good as the one I sent. My fear of not being good enough seems to be coming true. I can hear my parent's voices in my head telling me they knew it all along. I drink the rest of my wine, order another glass and, respond.

Thank you for the feedback. I'm grateful for any way that I can improve. I can send over some other logo designs and chat more specifically about what you do and don't like for the website design. What exactly feels off-brand for you? Can we set up a time to chat?

My mom calls me over right as I send the email. I'm discouraged. Of course, I wanted them to be happy with my work. I expected some changes, but I also expected some good news too. It feels like they didn't like anything I sent and I can't help but take it personally. I swallow the rest of the wine left in my second glass. I don't have the energy to put on a fake smile as I wander to the group my mom is with.

"This is my daughter, Jenna! She just graduated!" my mom raves in her happiest party voice.

I smile politely as the dean says, "Congratulations! What is next for you?"

I open my mouth to tell them about my visual design company, but my mom interrupts and says, "She's taking some time to plan for her next steps! Lindsay, here is a law student! Isn't that interesting?"

"Uh, yes, how are you liking it?" I ask.

Lindsay chuckles, "It's hard! But I love it."

"And this is Tommy, he's one of my English grad students. He's going to be the next great American author," my mom says, gesturing to the guy to my left. He's in a nice button-up with a bow tie and glasses. He looks exactly like what I might expect the next great American author to look like. He smiles kindly but looks uncomfortable with the attention on him.

"I don't know about that," he chuckles.

"Oh, don't be modest! You've worked so hard!" My mom declares.

That's when it hits me. It seems so obvious now. I'm not here just to keep my mom company. She's trying to convince me to go to grad school. She's made this argument to me in the past and refused to listen when I told her it wasn't what I wanted. So instead, she's brought me here to convince me through other people. I'm so frustrated at this point. I've continually tried to give her the benefit of the doubt and she can never do the same for me. My body is getting hot as my mom continues raving about Tommy and how hard he worked on his book. She is mid-sentence talking about Tommy's success when I interrupt.

"Actually, I own a visual design company. So if you need help designing your book cover, let me know. Now, if you'll excuse me," I blurt out curtly, and I turn and walk away, leaving behind my mom frozen in shock.

I'm furious. My mom just does not give up. I run into my dad as I'm storming away, and he stops me, "Hey, hon!"

"Did you know about Mom's secret agenda?" I snap at him.

His smile disappears, and he replies, "She means well. She's trying to do what's best for you."

"She has no idea what's best for me."

"She is your mom. She has some knowledge, you know."

I give him a flat look, and he sighs. "Don't be so stubborn, Jenna."

"I'm not being stubborn. You are. Both of you are. You refuse to give me a chance. Would it be so bad to just believe in me?" I spit back.

"It would be if we stood by while you crash and burn."

I feel tears well up in my eyes, but I refuse to let him see; so I turn sharply on my heel and walk out the door. As the door slams open, I feel the warm night air surround me, and my hair blows back over my shoulders. I breathe in deeply, lean down and take off my heels. I hold them in my hand and practically run down the street. I'm not ready to go back home yet. I need a minute to process the email, my disappointment, and my parent's behavior.

I stop when I remember that I rode with my mom and decide I'm more than happy to walk. I can feel the warmth of the wine inside me and the sidewalk under my feet. Downtown always looks magical at night. It's not overly big. But we have one magical main street. It's full of restaurants and bars, antique shops, and boutiques. They are always lit up at night and there are lots of people out walking. The energy is high as I hear passing strangers laughing and talking. As I'm walking past a bar, I look through the window and see Jensen. He's standing at the counter and laughing with a friend. I turn and walk inside.

"Hey Jensen," I say, walking up to him.

He turns, and his eyes widen, "Wow, Jenna, you look great!" I give him a coy smile and a shrug, and he says, "This is Bobby, Bobby, this is Jenna, my girlfriend," he pulls me in close.

Jensen seems to puff out his chest a little with his arm around me. Bobby looks impressed, a little too impressed, so I say, "Technically, we haven't discussed labels," as I wiggle out from under his arm.

Jensen chuckles and says, "Keeps me in line, doesn't she? Won't just let me win with her."

His words make my stomach churn. It all feels gross. Between that and the proud look on his face, I can feel my anger rising again.

"What do you mean, win with me? Like I'm your prize?" I question, my eyebrows lowering.

"Looking like that, most definitely!" he declares loudly.

Jensen and Bobby bust out laughing and high-fiving each other. When Jensen finally stops laughing, he looks at me and realizes I'm not amused. I'm very obviously mad.

"I'm not a prize for you," I say sternly.

"Oh geez, Jenna. I didn't mean it like that. Don't overreact." He gives Bobby a look that only adds to my anger. "It was supposed to be a compliment," he adds.

I take a deep breath and close my eyes. This night just keeps getting better and better. "I don't take that as a compliment," I reply.

"Ooooo," Bobby says, chuckling and hitting Jensen on the shoulder, "I think your girl is mad."

I can't help but roll my eyes at his sloppy friend.

"You're overreacting. Most girls would love to be called a prize. It's flattering," Jensen replies.

I look between Jensen and Bobby and quickly decide I don't have the energy for this. "Look, I've had a long night, and I don't need this right now," I say.

Jensen holds up his hands. "Hey, I'm sorry. It really was a compliment."

"Yeah. I think I just need to go home."

"No big deal, it's fine. You really do look great," Jensen says, trying to pull me into a hug. I give him a stiff side hug and lean around him to grab his shot off the bar. It burns my throat on the way down but it feels good. He looks at me with his eyes wide and then smiles. I give him one last look and then turn and walk out the door.

8

I finish walking the main road and turn left, I don't even recognize where I'm going until I see it come into my view; the bowling alley. It's lit up and comforting. It reminds me of the easy high school nights with Maddie when it felt like midnight cosmic bowling was the biggest adventure.

I walk through the front door and my mouth waters instantly at the smell of the popcorn. I beeline straight for the counter but no one is here. The place is buzzing, and almost every lane is full. I wait around for a minute, but no one comes to the food counter. I lean over the edge and see some popcorn bags right next to the machine, so I slip behind the counter, grab a bag and start filling it up with popcorn. I pop a piece in my mouth and close my eyes, the butter is perfect. It practically melts in my mouth. I open my eyes and come out from behind the counter when I see Oliver. He's walking towards me, looking at the ground, then he glances up and freezes. I freeze too.

His mouth opens a little, and he breathes out, "Whoa, you look…stunning."

I feel my cheeks blush and say, "Thank you," finding it hard to make eye contact with him.

I unfreeze and make my way to the barstool on the right side of the counter. He continues to watch me, his eyes piercing through me. He closes his mouth, shakes his head a little, and then walks closer and goes behind the counter.

"I see you're already comfortable here," Oliver chuckles, looking at the popcorn bag in my hand.

"Sorry, couldn't help it. It smelled too good."

"So what brings you here, all dressed up like that?" he asks, leaning on his arms across the counter.

I find myself watching his forearms flex as he puts his weight on them. He's wearing a denim button-up rolled up just enough for me to see his forearms and his veins as he moves. I realize I'm staring, so I quickly look up and meet his eyes. He looks amused, he couldn't possibly know what I was thinking, right?

"I had to go to a cocktail party designed to convince me that I'm not doing enough with my life."

"What?"

"My mom. She thinks my life is a joke and that my design career will get me nowhere. So she tricked me into going to a cocktail party and introduce me to people in an effort to convince me to go to grad school."

"Ah, I see. That sounds like it went well," he jokes.

"Yeah, just a grand old night. At least the wine was good."

Oliver laughs, it's a soft laugh, and he says, "So that's why the popcorn is extra delicious. It seems to pair well with wine."

I laugh with him this time and emphasize throwing a piece of popcorn into my mouth. He opens his mouth, and I throw one to him, he dives to the left and catches it in easily.

"Impressive!" I cheer.

I see a customer walk up to the counter and Oliver says, "I'll be right back," as he runs to take care of them.

He smiles at them like they are his old friends as he takes their money and hands them their shoes. They laugh and thank him and it impresses me how friendly he is with each person he interacts with. He makes his way back to me and leans across the counter again. This time his shirt pulls up a little farther, and I see the tip of a scar across under his elbow.

"Ouch, what happened there?" I ask, pointing at it.

He looks down and rolls up his sleeve a little higher to reveal it all. It's a big, white scar stretching across his right elbow. "I got in a car accident. Broke my elbow pretty badly."

"Wow," I say, reaching forward to touch it. Just as I touch his skin, I realize what I'm doing and quickly pull my hand back. "I have a thing for scars," I blurt out, my cheeks flushing as I realize what I'm saying.

Oliver chuckles softly and replies, "Good to know." Then he adds, "It happened six years ago."

"Oh, so that's what Jensen was talking about," I mumble, comprehending.

"Jensen?"

"My date from the other night."

"Right. Yeah. I had a scholarship to Alabama to play football. I was their starting quarterback as a Freshman. It was my dream, and it was incredible. But I got in a car accident after my first season there. Messed my elbow up pretty bad. I had to have surgery to get it all put back together. I did tons of physical therapy and worked with the school a lot to try and get back, but I just couldn't get to 100%. They were really kind about it, but I knew I'd never be the same."

"That's awful, Oliver. I'm so sorry."

"Thanks. It was hard at the time, but I'm just grateful

I got that first season at all."

"You threw that football today at the park!"

"Yeah, I can still throw," he replies, laughing and shaking his head, "Just not good enough to be a professional."

"Right, of course," I reply, feeling embarrassed. But he's looking at me kindly, and I add, "Well, I'm sorry you lost your dream."

"It was just one of them. Dreams change and evolve. That was my dream then, and I lived it for a season. Now they have changed, and I hope I get to live those too."

"You need a refill?" he asks, breaking me out of my stare.

I nod, but he's already filling a bag up and handing it to me. He scoops up another bag and then looks around and cocks his head to the right, "You want to play a game?"

"I don't have socks, and I'm definitely not using community socks. That sounds disgusting."

Oliver's eyes glimmer as he laughs loudly and says, "Fair point. What if you don't have to wear bowling shoes? Even though I think they would look incredible in that outfit."

I smile back at him. "Hmm, then I suppose you should get ready to lose," I reply, hopping off the stool.

"You sure you can play while working?" I ask as we walk towards the lane.

"Yeah, it will be fine. No one has the VIP lanes tonight, so we'll play over there."

He leads me to a door and opens it. It's dark inside but he follows closely behind me and flips on a switch. The room lights up with a disco ball and black lights. There are three private lanes and no one else in the room.

"Okay, this is cool!" I exclaim, twirling around. I catch Oliver watching me with a smile, and he says, "Yeah, this is a new addition. It's pretty fun."

Oliver hands me a bright pink ball and walks over to the machine to type in our names. As I'm holding the ball in my hands, I smile, "How did you know I'd want this ball?" I ask.

"Huh?" he asks, looking up from the computer.

"This pink ball. I always use this color when these lights are on."

A look crosses his face as he says "Oh," then he pauses and says, "I just figured that's a cool color." I smile down at the ball as he finishes typing our names.

"So you're pretty confident you're going to beat me, huh?" Oliver challenges, setting his ball down next to mine.

"I mean, I'm pretty good," I tease.

"Let's make it interesting then. For each round, the one with fewer points has to answer a question. Truthfully."

"Deal!"

"Ladies first," he gestures towards the lane.

I pick up my ball and step up to the lane. I've never bowled barefoot before, it feels oddly free. In some way, it feels perfect for tonight. To break the rules and stand barefoot while bowling. I breathe and then let the ball sail down the lane, knocking down 9 pins. Oliver claps, and I turn to give him a curtsy. When my ball comes back, I throw it back down the lane. I don't even watch as it rolls. I throw my hair over my shoulder and saunter back towards Oliver as I hear the ball knock the last pin over.

"This is going to be good," Oliver says, his eyes glowing as he watches me.

Oliver knocks down 7 pins on the first roll and 2 after that, meaning I get the first question.

"Okay, whatcha got for me?" He asks, plopping down in the chair across from me.

"You acted pretty nonchalant and okay back there, talking about the accident, but honestly, how hard was it?"

A pained look flashes across his face and settles into a frown. "You're very intuitive, Jenna."

I smile and wait patiently.

"It was incredibly hard. Devastating. I haven't had any alcohol since."

I feel my body tense at this response. "You were drinking?" I ask, shocked.

"No! Of course not!" Oliver replies quickly. He sighs and shakes his head, "But the guy that hit me was."

"Oh…Oliver, that's awful."

"Yeah. He was fine, of course. Hardly even a scratch. They say that happens a lot with drunk drivers. How infuriating is that? My whole life was changed because of his decision. So yeah, it was devastating. Olivia helped me through it. She was my light."

"I'm so sorry that happened to you. What about your parents? Were you dating someone then?" I ask.

Oliver looks up and smiles at me, his blue eyes twinkling, "Those sound like more questions to me. You've got to earn those," he smirks.

I stand up and make my way to the lane, I can feel his eyes watching me and it makes my hands a little shaky. I swallow, focus, and throw the ball down the lane, knocking down five pins.

I turn and see Oliver smile big at me. I stick my tongue

out at him, grab the ball and throw it down the lane. Three pins.

Oliver stands up and walks past me, giving me a wink. He confidently grabs the ball, and it sails down the lane, knocking down all the pins, a perfect strike.

"Soooo," he says, walking back towards me. "Tell me, what do you see in Jensen?"

"You mean the tall, handsome blonde?"

Oliver lets out a short laugh as he sits in his seat and says, "Yeah, that one."

"Well, like I said, he's very handsome and he's smart. And he drew me a comic of the first time we met."

Oliver nods as he listens.

"Is that it?" I ask.

"I only get one question," he shrugs.

"But you didn't even respond."

"Oh, sorry, yes, he sounds dreamy."

I roll my eyes and take my turn, getting a strike.

"So, did you have a girlfriend when the accident happened?" I ask.

"Hang on, you have to give me a chance to tie," he smiles and sends the ball down the lane. One pin is left standing.

He shakes his head and puts his hands up, "Okay then, yes, I did."

"And?"

"And what?"

"Well, what happened? Are you still together?"

"Technically, I answered your question."

"Oh, c'mon! There was no actual information!"

"Fine, fine. No, we aren't together anymore. Like I said, it was a hard time. At first, I was in denial. I thought for sure I would still be able to play and have my old life back. Then when I realized that wasn't going to happen, I was devastated. Depressed. I don't blame her for leaving, it was a hard time for all of us."

The rest of the night continues like that, although we ease up on the questions a bit. I find out that his lucky number is 3 and that it was also his jersey number. He's dated two girls seriously but refused to tell me how many girls he kissed or slept with. Which means I also refuse when he tries to ask me, but I do tell him about Mike. We talk about my love for design, and I tell him about Joan.

"I've seen her videos!" he exclaims excitedly.

He tells me more about Olivia, how she's too smart for her own good, but that she has a good group of friends and he's so happy about that. He's protective of her, even though she can take care of herself. I tell him about my brother, Robby, and how he lives in NYC, so I don't see him as much as I'd like.

Oliver ends up winning the first game and gives a low bow as I clap for him. "Thank you, perk of this place, I guess," he says, gesturing around the room.

"So, my client got back to me tonight and told me my ideas were off-brand," I say slowly, pulling out my phone to show him the email.

His eyebrows pull together, and he walks over and takes my phone. Our fingers brush slightly as he grabs it, and then he plops down next to me. I watch as he reads it; I'm fidgeting and embarrassed. He looks up at me and then hands my phone back, his body moving with the movement, pushing his knee against mine.

"I'm sorry, Jenna. That's never what you want to hear. I'm sure you're discouraged."

"Yeah. It's just hard to get the confidence in myself to send more ideas."

"So much of this world is full of us putting ourselves out there and hoping that people like it."

I nod, putting my phone away and swallowing the lump in my throat.

"Hey, maybe you could help me. This bowling alley needs a new logo. Maybe that could be a fun distraction for you. Of course, you will be paid for your time too."

"Yeah? That could be fun! I can draw up some ideas and show you!" I reply, getting excited about the chance to design something for a place special to me.

"Great! Sounds like a deal!"

I check the time, and it's past midnight. "I should probably get going," I say, standing and putting my shoes back on.

"You sure? Do you need a ride? I have some things I need to finish up here, but I can give you a ride if you'd like."

"Uh, sure, I guess. Do you need help?"

He chuckles and says, "No, just make yourself comfortable."

I follow him out the door, he turns off the light and locks the door behind me. He twirls the keys around his fingers as he walks. Only a few people are finishing up their games, so I follow Oliver to the food counter. He slides a cookie to me, smiles and then walks over to start putting away the other bowling balls.

How was the cocktail party? My phone dings, a message from Maddie.

A nightmare. Tell you all about it tomorrow.

My phone dings again. This time it's Jensen.

Hey, hope you're doing okay. Did you get home safely?

Not yet, but I will. Thanks for checking in.

I take a bite of the cookie, and it's perfect with a soft

center and crisp edges. I finish it in a few quick bites.

Oliver makes his way back to me, "How was the cookie?" he asks.

"Delicious! Who knew bowling alley food could be so good?"

He laughs candidly, and I find myself thinking how nice his laugh is and how freely he gives it.

"I'll try not to take that personally," he chuckles.

He waves goodbye to the final people as they walk out the door, and turns to me, "Alright, let's go."

We walk towards the door, him swinging his keys around his finger again with a little pep in his step. When we reach the doors he says, "Would you like to do the honors?" pointing to the light switch.

I take a step and turn off the three light switches on the wall, and the bowling alley goes dark.

"Ah, just like the movies," he whispers and opens the door for me.

Oliver leads me over to the last car in the parking lot. I don't know enough about cars to know what it is, but it seems like a nice car, especially for someone that works in a bowling alley. As we get closer, I realize it's a Lexus. It's one of the few cars I actually know because it's Robby's dream car. He follows me to the passenger side and opens the door for me, then runs around to his side.

"This is a nice car," I say as he slides in.

"Thank you. Are you a car person?" he asks.

I laugh, "Definitely not. The only reason I know this is nice is because of my brother."

He laughs with me and then declares, "I never got my final question from the game."

"Hmmm, seems like there's probably a time limit for

that."

"I would say I'm well within the limit," he kinks up an eyebrow at me.

My insides squirm and I find myself blushing and looking away. "Okay, go ahead."

"How are you doing? You know, after the incident the other night."

My stomach drops. It's a question I wasn't expecting and one that I wasn't sure how to answer. I sit quietly as we drive. Oliver waits patiently. Then I say, "Honestly, I don't know. I feel a little silly letting it affect me. Because other people have it so much worse..."

"It's never good to compare," Oliver says, interrupting me.

"I know, I know. But I do and I'm so grateful that it wasn't as bad as it could have been. And no matter how much I tell myself that nothing happened, I still find myself thinking about what could have happened. I think it's the idea that I know I couldn't have done much to stop him, and that scares me. It's scary comprehending what kind of a world I'm living in." The words come tumbling out of me.

Oliver is quiet as he listens. I'm worried that I said too much. He steals a glance at me as we are pull up to my house now and I add, "I can't help feeling like I'm making a bigger deal out of it than it really was."

He stops the car and turns towards me. "You worry too much about that. If you're making too big of a deal out of something. In reality, it's all about how it makes you feel. That's what's important. There is no correct measurement for what is and isn't considered a big deal to someone."

"Yeah... I guess you're right," I reply quietly. I swallow

hard, his words bringing tears to my eyes. I peek up at him and he's staring right back at me. How is it possible that his eyes can be this bright and beautiful even in a dark car?

"Thanks for the ride," I express, opening my door.

"No problem."

I step out of the car just as Oliver says, "Jenna."

I lean back into the car a little, "Yeah?"

"Remember, no one has the right to judge your feelings."

I smile and close the door. A mixture of gratitude and acceptance force tears into my eyes. I hear him wait until I get inside to drive away, his words still echoing through my head.

9

After Oliver drops me off, I go upstairs and fall asleep instantly. I sleep well and wake up feeling refreshed and motivated to work. If anything, last night has just given me more incentive to work harder.

My mom is in the kitchen when I come down the stairs but as usual, she pretends like nothing happened last night. She gives me a big smile and happily says good morning. I'm not surprised, she's great at ignoring the bad or uncomfortable things in life. I can play her game too. I plop down to eat breakfast next to her. I look at my phone to see a good morning text from Jensen. I groan a little and my mom looks up.

"What's wrong?" she asks.

"Jensen. He was kind of a jerk last night," I reply.

"Hmmm, really? That doesn't seem like him. What happened?"

I'm irritated by her response. Even in something like this, she seems to doubt me. She doesn't know him, so I'm not sure why she would think it doesn't seem like him. This is one of the reasons she hasn't met him yet. I bite my tongue and reply, "He was acting like I was some prize, like his prize girlfriend."

She smiles at me, "Oh dear, that's just a compliment! He's proud you're his girlfriend."

"But I'm not his girlfriend," I retort. "And even if I was,

I'm not some prize he should just brag about," I add.

"Kids these days are so silly. He was just being sweet. There's no need to get defensive. I'm sure you just misunderstood his intentions."

I think back to last night. I'm annoyed by my mom's reaction, but it's enough to make me doubt my response. After the cocktail party, I was a bit extra defensive and a maybe a little tipsy from the wine. Had I overreacted? Is my mom right? Maybe I'm making too big of a deal out of it.

"Yeah, you might be right," I say finally. I finish my breakfast in silence and decide to spend some time alone in the pool before I start working.

The sun is warming my skin a little too much, so I roll over onto my back. After swimming for a little bit, I grabbed a notebook and got to work on new logo ideas. I've felt inspired and filled a page with new ideas for Townie Brownie.

I hear the back door slide open, and I look up to see Jensen walking toward me. He's in a white short sleeve shirt, denim cut-off shorts and black sunglasses. He's holding a bouquet of beautiful flowers and holds them out for me when he reaches me. I stand up and take them, breathing them in deeply.

"What're these for?" I ask, surprised.

He lifts his sunglasses and steps closer to me. He gently puts his hands on my waist and I'm surprised to feel the heat that comes from his fingers on my bare skin. His brown eyes look extra warm in the sun, those flecks of gold shining bright. Suddenly, I feel a little exposed in only my swimsuit.

"I'm really sorry about last night. About whatever happened with your parents, and also about how I reacted to it," Jensen says.

"Thank you." I bite my lip and look up at him, then I step onto my tiptoes and give him a small peck on the cheek. I wave him over to follow me and we go to the pool to dip our toes in.

"Do you want to talk about what happened with your parents?" he asks.

"Not really."

He nods. "For the record, I don't think you're my trophy girlfriend. But, I will be proud to show you off to anyone that will listen."

I give him a small smile, "That's sweet, Jensen." I don't know how I feel about his apology but his body relaxes a little and he seems to be happy with my response.

He smiles at me as he suddenly stands up and pulls off his shirt. I feel my mouth drop open a little. The pictures on the app did not lie. He has so many abs I can't even count them. He smiles down at me and then jumps into the pool, causing the water to splash me. He comes out of the water, right in front of me, smiles and then leans close to me.

"Don't you dare," I say, leaning back.

Jensen smiles wide, grabs me, and pulls me under with him.

When we come up, we are both laughing. He's standing close, and I teasingly splash a little bit of water at him. He pulls me closer, and I can feel the muscles in his arms as they wrap around my back. I hesitate, thinking briefly about Ty in the parking lot and how scared I was. I'm safe, I tell myself.

Jensen looks down at me, a small smile on his face, and dips his head a little. I slowly lean my head up to bring my lips to his. The kiss starts soft, then he pushes back just a little harder, separating my lips and dipping his tongue in to explore. He pulls me in tighter, his hand going a little lower and pulling me closer to him. I reach my hands up behind his head, pulling him down closer, allowing the fire in me to take over. When we separate, he has a big smile on his face, and he wraps me up in a hug. He starts spinning me around the pool and cheering. I close my eyes and laugh. As we come to a stop, I open my eyes and see my mom watching us and smiling from behind the glass door.

We playfully swim for a few hours, and when we get out, I laugh at his shorts, completely soaked. He shrugs it off and says they will dry as he lays down on a chair next to me. He leans over and looks at my sketches.

"Working on some more logo ideas?"

"Yeah, they didn't like my other one."

"What's that?" he asks, pointing in the lower corner.

"Oh, Oliver asked me to work on a logo for the bowling alley."

"Really? When did he ask that?"

"Last night," I reply, not looking at him while I continue doodling.

I hear him shift uncomfortably and his voice changes when he says, "You were with him last night?"

I look up, surprised to see his eyebrows pulled down and his jaw tense.

"Yeah, I went over to the bowling alley."

"After you saw me? You were out really late...with him," he says, but it's not really a question.

"Yeah. We played a few games and then he drove me home."

He continues to stare at me, his jaw flexing. He leans

over, grabs my notebook, flips a few pages past my logos and then rips a piece of paper out.

"What are you doing?" I exclaim.

"I'm going to draw. It helps distract my mind," he retorts sharply.

"Distract your mind?" I blurt, honestly confused.

"Yeah, I do NOT want to think about you and Oliver last night," he shoots back, his voice is low.

I feel shocked by his reaction, and my instinct is to snark back at him but I bite my tongue, take a deep breath and say, "I'll go get you a pen."

I shake my head a little as I walk inside. It feels like Jensen needs a reminder that I'm not his property and that if I want to spend time with someone else, I'm more than welcome to. I'm getting a little tired of this behavior from him.

"Jenna! Is that Jensen?" my mom sings from the kitchen as I walk in.

"Yes."

"He's handsome!" she gushes.

"Mhm."

"What are you doing?"

"Getting him a pen," I reply, wiggling the pen at her as I walk back out the door.

I throw the pen down on the chair next to him, angrily. He flinches and looks up at me, surprised, but swallows whatever he's thinking and starts doodling on his paper. I sit down and focus again on the Townie Brownie logo. We draw in silence until I hear the door open, and my mom comes out. She's carrying two glasses of water, a big smile plastered on her face.

"Hello," she says brightly. "I'm Jenna's mom. You must be Jensen!"

"I am, it's nice to meet you," Jensen replies, flashing a smile right back at her.

"I've heard so much about you!" my mom gushes, leaning down to hand him a glass.

"Have you?" he asks, shooting me a flirty look.

I glower at my mom and pointedly say, "Thanks for the water."

"Oh, it's no problem. So Jensen, tell me about yourself!"

I listen as Jensen starts telling her about his job, and she excitedly makes noises and nods while she listens. He tells her about the charity work he did right after high school in Africa and how it changed his life. He's laying on the perfect guy charade pretty thick. I start tuning him out and focusing more on the logo I'm working on. It's a simple sketch right now, I'll do it on the computer later but I like this one a lot.

"I like to draw as well," I hear Jensen say as he shows my mom his paper.

"Interesting. And you keep that as a side hobby?" my mom asks.

Jensen looks at me and I can see that he realizes her intention behind the question. He hesitates and replies, "If I could make money from it, I would love to do that."

I give him a small smile in return, my heart swelling in gratitude, but my mom only says, "Yes, well then, it was wonderful to meet you!" She stands up with a little wave and walks away.

"Thanks for that," I say, smiling at him.

He turns back towards me a little, "I'm sorry."

"For what?"

"For her, and...earlier."

I swallow, unsure how I want to reply. I settle and say,

"It's okay," even though my gut is screaming at me. "What are you drawing?" I ask, scooting a little closer.

His eyes twinkle, and his lips turn up as he grabs my chair and pulls it right next to him so our arms and legs are touching. I can feel the warmth from his body, and my heartbeat picks up a little.

"I was just doodling, messing around," he says. It's a bunch of squiggly lines making up a big circle. Honestly, it still looks a little angry to me, but it inspires me, and I grab my paper and start sketching. He leans close, and I can feel his breath against me, but I keep my focus on the paper. It's a circle with the bowling pins making up the edge lines and then the squiggly lines coming from a ball shooting towards them.

"Hey, that's pretty cool," he says, his mouth very close. "Kind of looks like what I was doing."

"Guess you inspired me."

"Gotta give me a cut of that check then," he says against my ear.

I chuckle, and then I feel him put his hand on the other side of my face and slowly turn it towards him. He's so close that I can smell the chlorine on his skin from the pool. He opens his mouth to say something, but I lean the rest of my body into him, bringing our lips together.

His lips are fast and serious this time, moving with eagerness. His hands are tangling in my hair as I drag my hand down his chest, feeling his muscles ripple beneath my fingers. His arms flex, and he pulls me onto his lap. I'm caught up in the heat of the moment, and how his body feels against mine, the way he's pulling me closer to him like I can't possibly get close enough. I like how free it feels letting my attraction to him take over. His lips release mine, and he starts moving down my jaw to my neck. I can feel my skin tingle in the spots he touches. He's going lower and lower down my neck, too low. I push back against him. He resists, and I say, "Jensen, wait." He stops and looks up at me as I push back more.

"We're at my parent's house," I say.

"So?"

"So, this is a bit much for me."

"We can go somewhere else," he says, the corners of his mouth turning up.

"Not now, okay?"

He smooths out his hair and runs his hands down his shorts. He sighs loudly in a way that makes his disappointment clear. I crawl back into my chair and feel him scoot closer, so we are touching again.

"We can stay close still, right?" he winks.

"Yeah, we can do that," I say. I force a smile back at him but there's an uneasiness spreading through me now.

That night I finish up the different logo ideas for Townie Brownie. When I send them over, I get an email back immediately.

Yes! I love these! Let me share them with the team and I'll get back to you.

I smile and let out a big sigh of relief. It feels good to get a little validation. Since the cocktail party, I've just been trying to prove myself even more. I've been swirling between extreme discouragement and intense motivation all week. It's exhausting.

Earlier this week, I listed Joan's new bumper stickers on her site, and they've been doing great. She posted all about the new launch and already has 50 new orders. Even though she handles the order and delivery process, I love seeing how many orders come in; it helps me feel like my work is valuable, even if it's just a funny bumper sticker. At least I can see success in something I'm doing.

Looks like the launch is going well! I text her.

It's going wonderfully! But of course, it is, you're a magician.

As are you!

Davey and I are going out for dinner tonight as a little celebration. Would you like to join us? You can bring that new hunk of yours!

Thanks for the offer, but I'm due for a night in.

As much as I love Joan and Dave, I'm exhausted. It feels like the last few days have been emotionally and mentally draining. I want nothing more than to curl up with some food and relax. I throw on some sweatpants and head downstairs to grab dinner. My parents are in the living room, and they are dressed up. My dad is wearing his favorite blazer, and my mom is in a low-cut red dress.

"What event are you off to tonight?" I ask.

"No event, just taking your mom out for a nice date," my dad says, grabbing his keys.

"Oh, a date night? How fun!"

"We still have to make time for each other," my mom says, pulling my dad in close. He mumbles something quietly to her, and she giggles.

"Okay, you two, go have fun," I say, averting my eyes.

"Have a good night, sweetie," my dad says, pulling my mom through the door.

I settle on some leftover pasta and bread, take it over to the couch and turn on my favorite sitcom. It's easy for me to listen to and laugh at, which is exactly what I do for the rest of the night, and I head to bed before my parents even come home.

10

Maddie is pounding down my front door a few days later.

"I'm finally free from studying," she says, pushing past me and sitting in the kitchen.

"You've been doing school stuff?"

"Don't tell me you haven't even noticed my absence?" she places her hand over her heart in pretend pain.

"Sorry, I've been in my own little world the last few days. Mostly focusing on getting new clients and wallowing in self-pity a bit."

"Self-pity?"

"I've just been in my feelings lately."

"Oh yes, feelings. It must be so hard having a big new client and a hot new boyfriend," she winks and then stands up and starts looking through the fridge. She sees a beer, shrugs, and then hops up onto the counter and starts drinking it.

"Your dad has some interesting taste in craft beer," she says, looking at the label.

"You don't have to drink it. And he's not my boyfriend. We haven't officially said that yet."

"Fine, your boy toy then."

"Ew."

"I could say something much worse," she says, then looks around the house and whispers, "But *they* could be listening."

"Haha," I reply flatly. "You know we haven't had sex."

"Let's go hang out. I'm tired of being cooped up. Let's go to the lake, or a bar, or anything, please?" she begs, hopping off the counter and sticking out her bottom lip.

"Alright, fine, you choose," I give in.

"Oooh!" she claps, "I was hoping you would say that! There's a new club I've been dying to try downtown!"

I love a good chance to dress up, and Maddie is always the perfect partner to dress up with. I put on my best sparkly mini dress and sky-high heels. Is it too much? Probably. Will my feet hurt by the end of the night? Definitely, but I know it will be fun. I put on dark makeup, curl my hair and Maddie and I are ready to go. Maddie makes us take a selfie before we leave and she texts it to Ben. Then she sends it to me and tells me to text it to Jensen. I hesitate and tuck my phone into my bag without sending it.

The rest of the night is a blur of dancing, singing and sweating. Maddie and I spend the whole night in the middle of the dance floor, shaking our hips and loudly screaming along to each song. We accept the free drinks, dance with some guys from a safe distance and tell all the creepy guys that we are a couple.

Halfway through the night, Jensen texts me asking what I'm up to. I send him the photo of Maddie and me from before we left, then I pull her over to my side and take another photo, this time our hair is a little more flat and we have a shine to our skin from dancing. I send him both photos and say, *started like this and ending like this!*

He sends back a heart and *don't have too much fun without me.*

We end the night collapsed on my bed, too exhausted

to change. We slide under the covers together and Maddie leans her head on my shoulder.

"Tonight was perfect," she says sleepily.

I nod in agreement, too tired to verbally agree. It was the perfect distraction from work and Jensen. I needed this break to ignore the doubt constantly bombarding my thoughts. It's exhausting always asking yourself if you're doing the right thing. I hear my phone vibrate and look to see a text from Jensen.

Did you make it home safe?

I drop it back on the nightstand, exhausted, and promise to reply tomorrow.

When I wake up, I see a few missed texts, all from Jensen.

Jenna?

You okay?

I'm a little worried.

Hope you got home okay. Please let me know.

"He's kind of obsessed with you," Maddie mumbles, reading over my shoulder. "It's cute."

"Is it?" I ask.

Maddie shrugs in response and grabs her phone.

Home safe, I was asleep last night. I reply and then pull up my email. The first thing I see is an email from Townie Brownie.

Jenna, the team, and I talked and we think we need to meet in person to really nail down these specifics in the beginning. When can you come to New York?

Maddie shrieks, and I turn, thinking she has been reading over my shoulder again. But she's looking at her phone. She turns to me and exclaims, "Ben bought me a ticket to see him!"

"Wow! When?"

"This weekend!"

She jumps up onto the bed and starts dancing. I giggle, and she pulls me up with her. My head is pounding as I give her one quick, half-hearted shimmy and collapse back on the bed.

"What summer thing are we crossing off today?" she asks, falling back down next to me.

"Bowling?" I ask.

"Oooh, yes! Maybe Oliver will be there!" she declares.

My stomach flips and I smile involuntarily. "Yeah, maybe." She gives me a knowing look and starts raiding my closet for clothes.

When we pull up to the bowling alley Maddie bursts through the door, yelling, "Oliver! Oliiiiiiver!"

I see Oliver lean out from the office, a smile spreading across his face when he sees us.

"There he is!" she shrieks and runs towards him.

A lopsided smile pulls on his mouth, his eyebrows raised. "A little early to be drinking, don'tcha think?" he asks.

"No alcohol needed for this one, she's just easily excitable," I reply.

"It's true," she adds with a flair of her hands, "but also, I'm going to see Ben in a few days! And we went dancing last night," she says, pulling out her phone to show him the picture of us.

"Wow," he breathes, leaning in closer "You look great," he says, looking up at me.

I feel my cheeks flush red, and I look away.

"So, about that free game you promised us?" Maddie asks, bumping into Oliver with her shoulder.

He chuckles, “Of course, let’s get you some shoes.” Maddie claps, tells her the right size and runs off to choose a lane.

“She’s full of energy, that one,” Oliver chuckles as he grabs our shoes.

“She is. It’s slightly exhausting,” I reply with a smile.

“Did you have fun last night?” he asks.

“Yeah, probably too much fun.”

He laughs, “That’s great. You deserve it. Any news from Townie Brownie?” he asks, handing me my shoes.

“Actually, yeah, they want me to come to New York to meet them in person.”

Oliver stops and gasps, “Wow! That’s awesome!”

I laugh, “I mean, I’m not sure if that’s good news or not.”

“Well, at least you can have some fun while there!”

“I guess. I’ll probably just be a nervous wreck.”

Oliver steps from behind the counter and starts walking with me towards the lane. “Why don’t we make it fun? Let’s do a road trip! I’ll come with you! I love New York!” he exclaims.

“Are you serious?”

“Yeah! Why not? It will be fun!” he says.

I hesitate, and he adds, “I’ll drive!”

“Okay…that could be fun,” I say slowly, thinking about it.

“And look, if there’s only one bed, I promise I’ll be a perfect gentleman and let you have it,” he says, the corner of his mouth turning upward.

“One bed? What are you talking about?” Maddie demands.

We’re standing at the lane now and Maddie is facing us, a questioning look on her face. I hadn’t even thought about where we would stay. Would we stay in the same room? I'll see if we can stay with Robby. His apartment is small, but I've stayed with him before while visiting.

"Jenna has to go to New York to meet Townie Brownie. I offered to drive her," Oliver explains.

"Oh yes! When? I love road trips!" she says, clapping her hands.

"We would probably leave in a few days. I think the sooner the better..." I reply. My stomach is a knot of nerves. I don't know if it's because of the meeting with Townie Brownie or the thought of an 8-hour road trip alone with Oliver.

"Aw, I'll be visiting Ben," she replies, disappointed. "But I'll be having fun in other ways," she adds, wiggling her eyebrows at us.

Oliver laughs and shakes his head. "I'm going to go do some work, but I'll swing back around later and play a game with you if you're still around."

As he leaves, Maddie shimmies next to me and says, "So a road trip with Oliver, huh? Just you two? *And* he's already thinking about the bed?" she winks at me.

"Stop! It's not like that."

"What would your parents say?" she asks, fanning herself dramatically.

"Ha! Like my parents would even care about the boy that works at the bowling alley. They wouldn't even view him as an option. My mom is 100% sold on Jensen," I snort.

"Oliver doesn't work here," a voice behind us says.

Maddie and I spin around and see Olivia behind us. She's holding a rag and cleaning spray and must have been cleaning the balls behind us.

"Oliver owns it," she states.

“He does?” I ask, wondering why he hasn’t told me.

“Yeah, he bought it a few years ago,” she responds.

“Okay, that’s super cool!” Maddie exclaims.

Olivia looks at us for a few seconds with an unreadable expression and then turns and walks away.

“Wonder what your parents would think now,” Maddie says, laughing and turning back to the game.

“So you’re riding with a guy you don’t know?” Robby asks through the phone.

“I know him,” I reply.

“But you just met him.”

“Earlier this summer, yeah.”

“Then yes, you’re definitely staying with me,” he replies seriously. “And it will be fun to see you,” he adds.

“Thank you!”

Robby is expecting us, and I already talked to my parents about it, so the next person is Jensen. Honestly, I’m nervous about his reaction. Lately, it feels a bit like walking on eggshells with him. I never know exactly how he’s going to respond. Some days he’s sweet and completely fine; other days he seems to get upset about the smallest things. It’s a bit of an emotional rollercoaster for me. We are going out for dinner tonight, and I leave with Oliver tomorrow morning.

When Jensen picks me up he’s in a nice blazer and black pants. He leans in and gives me a soft kiss. “You look lovely,” he whispers down at me.

“Thank you, you look great too,” I reply. His hand is on my lower back as he leads me to his car.

In the car, Jensen tells me all about his day. He’s been

working so hard on a certain project because he knows it will lead to a promotion if he does a good job. He's saying things that I don't fully understand, but I nod my head anyway and listen.

"Anyway, enough about my work. What's new with you?" he asks.

We pull into the restaurant and my stomach grumbles. After he tells them our reservation we follow them to a booth in the corner.

"Joan is great. The bumper stickers are selling like crazy," I say as we sit down.

"Yeah? That's awesome!" he replies.

I quickly move on, "Townie Brownie is good too. They liked the last stuff I sent over to them, but now they want me to go to New York and meet in person."

"Oh, wow."

"Yeah. I'm leaving tomorrow morning."

"Tomorrow? For how long?"

"Just a couple of days."

"Oh, Jenna, I wish you had told me. I would have offered to come with you. I don't want you to go alone, but I can't afford to leave work on such short notice," Jensen says. He reaches out and grabs my hand softly from across the table.

"I'm actually not going alone…"

"Who are you going with?"

"Well, I told Oliver about the email, and he offered to drive with me," I say cautiously.

I see his jaw tighten, and he pulls his hand back abruptly. "You're going with Oliver?"

"Yeah, we'll be staying with my brother."

He stays quiet and still. I see his jaw flex a few times as he thinks.

"I mean, I don't love that idea, Jenna. I don't want my girlfriend driving to New York with another guy," he says, his voice low.

Anger bubbles inside me, "I'm not your girlfriend. We are going out and getting to know each other, but you don't own me. Besides, Oliver and I are just friends."

"I don't care," he spits back.

I'm stunned by his sudden harsh tone.

"I'm not saying you can't go," he says, quieting down a little, "But–"

"Good. Because I don't need your permission to go," I interrupt.

"You don't care how I feel?" he practically yells. "That's pretty selfish, don't you think?" He slams his hand down on the table as if to emphasize his words.

I see people turning to look at us, and I shrink back slightly. He breathes deeply and puts his fingers against his temples, rubbing them in circles.

I fidget uncomfortably with my silverware. I don't know what to say. I swallow shakily and say, "Look, I'm pretty nervous about this meeting, and it's really nice of Oliver to offer to come with me. I could use a little more support from you."

He looks surprised by my words, and he pauses. Then his eyebrows pull together. "You don't need him."

"Well, of course, I don't *need* him. But it's nice of him to offer."

"I would have offered!" his voice raises again.

"I never said you wouldn't!" I spit back. I'm trying to whisper as more and more people look over at us.

He sighs angrily. "I don't like it," he says.

"You don't have to like it," I reply.

He studies me for a minute and I see his brown eyes

soften a little. He holds his hand back out for me, and I slowly put mine back in his, avoiding eye contact with the strangers gawking at us. He slowly traces circles on the back of my hand with his thumb.

"I really like you," he offers quietly.

I still feel the embarrassment coursing through my body, and my hand is shaking a little. But no one is looking at us anymore and Jensen seems to be remorseful.

"I like you too," I finally reply quietly.

"Maybe it's cheesy, but I'm going to miss you."

I can't fully meet his gaze but I feel him desperately looking at me, so I say, "I know, me too."

He flashes me a wide smile and starts eating his dinner.

"Dinner was delicious," I say as we pull up to my parent's house. The rest of the meal passed smoothly. Jensen was a little extra sweet, maybe to make up for not being with me the next few days, or maybe because of his reaction earlier. While at dinner, he drew another comic for me on a napkin. This time it was a remake of us swimming in the pool. It ended with us kissing and saying, "To be continued..." It was very sweet, but I still felt a little on edge from earlier. His reaction was so sudden and so public, it made me really uncomfortable. I wasn't sure how or if I should bring it up. Jensen spoke most of the car ride home, not even noticing my lack of response.

"Much better than seafood," Jensen replies with a grin, pulling me out of my thoughts.

I look at him and smile, then look back out the window, my hand on the door handle.

"Jenna, I'm sorry about earlier," he suddenly says.

I swallow and pause.

"I care about you a lot. I know it's fast, but I can see a future with you," he continues. "Can you forgive me? Please? I would hate for you to leave and be mad at me just for caring too much."

I finally look over at him. He's turned towards me, his face sad and his eyes soft. I try to remember if I've ever had someone care this strongly for me. Somehow, I actually start to feel a little bad for him. I nod slowly, "I don't want to be mad at you either," I say gently.

He chuckles, "Glad we're on the same page."

"But that made me really uncomfortable," I add quickly.

"Of course. I'm so sorry," he apologizes.

"And I don't like this possessive act of calling me your girlfriend. I'm not ready to be exclusive yet, I feel like I'm still getting to know you," I continue.

He leans close to me and puts his hand on the back of my neck, pulling our foreheads together.

"But you forgive me?" he whispers.

I swallow the lump in my throat and say, "Yeah, I forgive you."

He sighs deeply and tucks his face to give me a soft kiss on my neck. His lips wander across my collarbone and lower neck, causing chills to run through me. This part with him is so easy. I'm attractive to him and he likes me, that's all that matters right now.

I tilt my head down and feel his lips meet mine with a sense of urgency. He pulls me closer, tighter, and then leans back and pulls me with him. His hands go to my waist, his fingers gripping me tightly. At first, I hold back. Unsure how to react at this moment, remembering the look on his face earlier at dinner. I throw him a playful smile, buying myself time, but he pulls me closer, his lips exploring my chest. It feels good to be wanted. It's comforting to have this one thing in my life that I don't have to question. He cares about me so much.

I give in and reach around to his back, dipping my fingers up his shirt, just a little. He takes this as an invitation to repeat the action for me and slides his hands up my shirt. The higher he gets, the more uneven my breathing becomes, and the minutes turn into hours.

"Do you have to go?" Jensen asks, his face inches from mine. We are still curled up together in his seat.

"Yeah, I have to wake up early tomorrow," I whisper.

He sighs deeply. "This was fun," he says.

"Mhm," I say, leaning forward to give him a long, gentle kiss.

"Thank you for being patient with me," I say.

"Of course," he replies.

I feel relieved to hear him say that. In the past, other guys haven't been as patient and understanding with me which led to a lot of hard feelings. After his reaction at dinner, I feared that Jensen would be just like the others. But I told him I'm not ready. Especially after what happened tonight, I don't want to rush it. I don't want to have sex with him until my emotions can catch up to his. Even if I find it extremely flattering and comforting knowing how much he cares.

He gives me another warm look and a soft kiss. "Text me tomorrow? Let me know you're safe?"

"I will," I promise.

I give him a quick kiss and then hop out and wave goodbye as he drives away.

The next morning, Oliver picks me up right on time.

He meets me at the door as I'm yelling goodbye to my parents. As I turn to face him, he pulls a sub sandwich out from behind his back.

"Is that your breakfast?" I ask curiously.

"First of all, it's never too early for a sub," he replies playfully and then adds, "But actually, I want to start this trip off on the right foot."

"Okay," I say tentatively.

"This is a turkey sub," he says, his eyes staring at me meaningfully.

"Okay?" I ask, confused.

"I'm giving it to you. As a way to tell you that I remember you. That we've met before...when Maddie scored a turkey four years ago." He's still staring at me, and a nervous smile grows on his face.

I frown, confused. I think back to four years ago when we were celebrating at the bowling alley. I remember her scoring the turkey, still the only time I've seen three strikes in a row. I remember the cute boy behind the counter that she made me ask out. The one with brown curly hair and bright blue eyes. The one that told me people don't need opinions about my emotions. The one that allowed me, a stranger, to see his vulnerable side. I've thought about what he said so many times in the last few years. I tried looking for him the first summer I went back but he wasn't there. I fooled myself twice that summer into thinking I may have seen him but he never seemed to recognize me. I gave up and figured he didn't work there any more.

"You told me to not let people judge my emotions!" I exclaim. Then I chuckle and add, "I asked you out."

He rubs the back of his neck nervously. "Yeah. I've been meaning to tell you."

"Why didn't you?"

"If you didn't remember me, I would have felt weird. Like that moment, that memory, only mattered to me."

"That's how you knew my name," I realize as it all clicks in my head.

"What?"

"That first night you rode with me home, you called me by my name even though I never told you."

"Oh, yeah. I've also seen it on the screen every summer since then," he smiles.

"I tried looking for you that first summer," I say. "But I never saw you."

"I was around, but I may have hid behind the lanes some days," he replies sheepishly.

I laugh loudly, "that's creepy."

I snatch the turkey sandwich from his hand and walk toward the car. He rushes after me and grabs my bag, puts it in the trunk, and then runs around to my door and opens it.

"For the record, that memory matters to me too," I say as he closes my door for me. His eyes blaze in response.

11

Things I've learned about Oliver on this road trip so far:

1- He likes all genres of music. He will rap along with Eminem and then follow it up by knowing every word in a Taylor Swift song.

2- He's generous with the air conditioning and fully lets me control it. I'm kind enough to turn it off when I notice goosebumps on his arms.

3- Snacks are a must-have. It's honestly amazing that he stays in such good shape considering how much junk food I'm watching him eat.

4- He loves to stop at random roadside attractions. We have already stopped at a giant rooster and a large nutcracker.

Now we are pulling over to see a giant roller skate.

"This is great!" he shouts enthusiastically. "Look at it!"

I'm looking at him and laughing. His face is lit up in pure glee, he looks like a little kid. He turns to look at me, a smile wide on his face. It's heartening to see him so excited about something simple.

Looking at him, it's easy to notice his attractiveness and muscular body, but the small things like this really show his true personality, and I feel lucky to be here experiencing it.

"What? You don't like giant roller skates?" he

questions, parking the car.

"I mean, I've never seen a giant one until now."

"Now you can realize the full extent of your love."

He hops out and runs over to the giant roller skate. It's right off the freeway, in front of what looks like an abandoned building. The large white roller skate looks like it's made of wood and plaster. Oliver turns around, arms wide above him, and smiles at me.

When I get to his side, he says, "Let's take a picture!" He pulls out his phone and gets close to me. I see us reflected in his camera, he inches closer and then angles to see the giant roller skate behind us. "Smile!" he says and presses the button.

He looks at it, "Perfect!" and then adds, "Now, just you. You can send it to Jensen."

I smile uncomfortably, and he chuckles, "C'mon Jenna, work it!"

I laugh and can't help but smile bigger, "Yeah, there we go! Turn to the side, tilt your head, oh yeah, perfect, work it, mmhm," he's cheering.

My cheeks turn red and I start to laugh. I whip my hair as he starts whistling and keeps cheering. My hair is going crazy, my hands are up in the air and I'm laughing uncontrollably. He stops and looks down at his phone, "Beautiful," he says and shows me. In the photo, my hair is perfectly wisping around me, my eyes are lit up and happy. I'm mid-laugh with my arms in the air framing the roller skate. I look happy. I look free.

As we walk back to the car, he hands me his phone, "Here, type in your number so I can send you these photos."

"I'm on a road trip with you and we haven't even exchanged numbers," I chuckle as the realization sets in.

"Crazy, right? I'm just that easy to get along with," he winks.

After I type in my number, I hand his phone back, and he immediately sends me the photo of us and a few others he took for me. "You should send that one to Jensen," he says as I look at the one of just me. "You look great in it."

I turn and face out the window to avoid answering him. I try to focus on the beautiful sky and the landscape passing by instead.

"Jenna?" he asks after a few moments of silence. "Are you okay?"

"Yeah."

"Mhm," he replies, completely unfooled.

"It's just...Jensen and I got in a big fight last night."

"Oh. Sorry to hear that. Is everything okay?"

"He was upset that I was coming here with you."

Oliver glances at me quickly and then faces back to the road.

"It's silly. I know. I told him we are just friends, but he was still pretty upset." I continue.

He stays quiet, listening.

"He kind of blew up at me in public and it was really embarrassing."

"What do you mean he blew up at you?" he looks at me, concerned.

"I mean, he raised his voice at dinner, and people were looking at us and it was awkward."

Oliver's eyebrows pull together and he tightens his grip on the steering wheel.

"He apologized though. A lot. It was just kind of awkward. But we are okay now, I should probably just send him the photo," I say quietly, pulling out my phone.

Oliver makes a noncommittal sound but doesn't say

anything.

I send a text with the photo of me and he replies a few minutes later, echoing what Oliver had already said.

You look great! Looks like fun.

"Are you hungry? Should we stop for lunch soon?" Oliver asks, pulling my attention away from my phone.

"Between the turkey sandwich and all the snacks, I'm not hungry."

"How about a treat then?" He nods to a passing billboard that reads FUDGE in all caps.

The look on my face must have said enough because he takes the next exit and pulls into a small shop right off the road. It's a cute store and what you would imagine for a typical candy shop. The floor is made up of red and white tiles, the walls are painted in vibrant colors and every inch of the place is covered in candy. Oliver's eyes grow wide as he looks around, "This place is amazing," he whispers.

We walk up to the counter where a lady with white hair pulled into a tight bun is patiently waiting, smiling.

"How do ya do? Can I help you?" she greets us.

"That rhymed," Oliver jokes.

She chuckles, "I suppose it did!"

Inside the counter are rows and rows of fudge. Cookies and cream, peanut butter, toffee, mocha, mint, cookie dough, orange chocolate, dark chocolate, white chocolate, every flavor I can possibly think of.

"We definitely want some fudge," Oliver says, leaning closer to the glass.

"Would you like to sample some?" she asks pleasantly.

My stomach grumbles instinctively, and Oliver peeks over his shoulder at me, his eyebrows raised. "Not hungry, huh? Seems like you're ready for some fudge."

I bite my lip to hide my smile and look at the woman as I say, "Can I sample the peanut butter, please?"

"I would like to sample the mint, please," Oliver adds.

She gives us a slight nod and grabs a piece for each of us.

When she hands them to us, Oliver holds his piece out, waiting for me to tap it with his in cheers. "To a wonderful road trip," he grins.

I tip my piece against his and pop it into my mouth. It is GOOD. The kind of fudge that melts in your mouth with the perfect amount of chocolate and peanut butter flavor mix and is so creamy.

"Mmmmmm," Oliver says, closing his eyes.

"Was the mint good?" I ask.

"Delicious! The peanut butter?" he replies.

"Soo good."

"Well, okay then. We'll take one peanut butter and one mint," Oliver says, pulling out his wallet.

I'm still looking at the other flavors, and Oliver leans closer to me, "What else?" he asks as we stare through the glass. I turn slightly to look at him and realize how close we are, close enough to touch.

He leans up abruptly and says, "Never mind. We'll take one of each!"

The woman behind the counter lights up and says, "Wonderful!" as she starts pulling out boxes for us.

Oliver turns towards me and puts his elbow on the counter, leaning into it.

"Too bad you aren't hungry," he says, smirking.

"Not so fast, fudge is different. That's like, a different stomach."

He barks out a loud laugh. "A different stomach? How many stomachs do you have in there?" He looks down at my body, and I feel myself grow extra aware of his eyes on me.

"Here are your boxes, my dears," the woman interrupts, handing us bags full of fudge.

As soon as we get in the car, Oliver exclaims, "Which flavor first?"

We decide to take turns trying each flavor. He agrees he probably went a little overboard but "Hey, what's a road trip without some good treats?" he maintains.

We have five hours left. I'm surprised by how quickly the drive has passed so far. Oliver has been a great road trip companion. We've passed the time by playing the license plate game (27 states so far) and by playing the radio game (seeing who can guess the artist and song title first). Oliver was surprisingly good at the radio game and was more than happy to sing along loudly. A few times, the car has fallen silent, but something about Oliver makes me feel comfortable. I don't feel the need to fill the silence, and he doesn't seem to mind it either.

Now is one of those moments of silence. I'm watching the trees and signs fly past the window. It's a beautiful day, thankfully. I turn to look over at Oliver, he's quietly driving, looking straight ahead until he feels my eyes on him and he glances at me. I look away, pull out another piece of fudge, cream cheese this time, and offer him a bite.

"Mmm, good. I give it an 8," he says, holding out his hand for more.

"Have you had a 10 yet?"

"Mint. Definitely. And the peanut butter. The peanut butter might even be an 11."

"I don't believe in 11s," I reply.

"Huh?" He looks at me, "What do you mean you don't

believe in 11s?"

"The scale is from 1-10. There is no 11."

"That's because it's better than the scale, it's off the scale, it's blowing past the rest!"

"So it's a 10, and the rest are less," I explain.

"No, no. That doesn't show the exact exaggeration of how much better it is. It's so good it can't even be on the scale."

"Eh. I don't get it."

He shakes his head, "You're crazy, Jenna."

I feel a squirm in my stomach when he says my name. Why does it do that? I've heard my name said a million times. Why is the way he says it any different?

"Agree to disagree," I shrug.

"About the scale or you being crazy?" he replies, giving me a lopsided smile.

I dramatically roll my eyes back at him and change the subject.

"Why didn't you ever tell me that you own the bowling alley?"

He looks back at me, eyebrows raised. "You never asked."

"I thought you worked there."

"Technically, I do."

I glare at him, and he chuckles, "Okay, okay, I don't know how to bring that up in everyday conversation. Like hey, guess what? I own this place. Cool, huh? Who told you anyway?"

"Olivia."

"Ahh, yes, I should have guessed."

He glances at me again as I wait for him to tell me more. He shakes his head with a smile and continues talking.

"After the accident, I didn't know what I wanted to do with my life. I never really had a backup plan because I never wanted one. I loved football, I was good at football and I was on the right track to continue that. But when all that disappeared, I felt lost.

I started missing classes and had no interest in any of the stuff I was learning, so I stopped going altogether and moved back home. I knew Johnny, the guy that used to own the bowling alley. He was in over his head and didn't know what to do. So I would go to the alley, and we would commiserate with each other and what was going on in our lives. I helped him out a lot, working for free. Then we realized I could help both of us. I had always loved the bowling alley. I had great memories there from when I was a kid. So we figured out a plan for me to buy the place.

Since he was losing money, he sold it to me for as low as he could go. We made a deal that allowed me to pay him over time. Olivia helped me in the beginning, working for free. Between the two of us, we only had to hire a few other people. I could do most of the stuff myself and I spent all my free time there. I fixed it up and painted it, and slowly renovated it over the years. I used a few things I learned from school but most of it was self-taught from business books and videos and a few close friends that are successful business owners. Eventually, the place was fixed up, and I had a few marketing tricks to help get customers back in the door. The biggest one was getting more bowling leagues back in and hosting competitions."

"That's incredible, Oliver." I don't know what else to say. I'm so impressed that he chose to turn his life around instead of continuing to wallow in his pity. If it was me, I'm pretty sure I would have wallowed. All I can think of to say is, "Where's Johnny now?"

"Retired and happy, living in Florida. But I still talk to him often and let him know how the alley is doing."

"You took kind of a big risk."

"Not really. It was the only thing that made sense."

"Buying a bowling alley?" I ask, lifting one eyebrow.

He laughs and says, "Yup. Buying a bowling alley. That's what I was trying to clear my head about the other day. I have to make some decisions about the alley. A woman reached out to me asking about franchising it in some other states."

"Really? So what would that mean?"

"Well, she would do most of the groundwork, but it would all be under the same name as mine. And I would own a part of them. So I would get a little extra income, which would be nice, but it would require some travel from me to go and check in on the places and make sure they are running well. Because if they aren't, it does reflect a bit on me and my name."

"Do you need the money?"

He turns towards me, both eyebrows raised and the corners of his mouth twitches.

"Sorry, too personal?" I backtrack.

"Usually that's not a typical question that you ask someone you don't know very well."

"I mean, we are traveling alone for eight hours together," I point out.

He shrugs and replies, "Fair enough. No, I don't need the money. To be honest, the bowling alley has been doing really well, so I'm making enough of a profit that I don't need the money. I still have some leftover money from football as well. I used a lot to buy the bowling alley, but I kept some in savings."

"Oh, I didn't realize you got paid for playing football

in college."

"You don't. But I had some sponsorships from different companies that paid pretty well for a few years."

"Years?"

"Yeah, they started when I was in high school, actually."

"Wow. You must have been really good."

Oliver smiles, a slight red creeping into his cheeks.

"The power of social media influence, I guess," he replies.

"So you were like a high school prodigy?" I try to think back to high school and if I ever heard of him. He graduated three years before me, though.

He laughs, "I wouldn't call it that, but sure."

"So, are you going to franchise?" I ask.

"I think so..."

"What's stopping you?"

"Logistics, fear, the typical things."

"What do you have to lose?"

He pauses, deep in thought. Then he replies slowly, "I don't know how much of my time it will take...and I don't want to be gone too much. I like being here for Olivia."

I grin involuntarily. "That's adorable."

"I want to be here for her and my customers and for... lots of people," he replies, glancing at me so fast I think I imagine it.

"What about you? How long are you sticking around?" he asks.

I pause, thinking about the future. I have been avoiding thinking about this meeting with Townie Brownie, trying to keep my nerves under control. I know I'm putting too much emphasis on this one client, but they are the first big company I've pitched myself to. In some way, it feels like if they decide I'm not worth their time, I won't be worth anyone's time.

"I don't know. I've been thinking moving to New York could be cool. I could work closer with Townie Brownie, and there are a lot of companies there that I can work with. But honestly, I can work from anywhere, which is one thing I love. I like being back here, but I don't think I want to stay here forever. After this summer, it will be time for me to go somewhere else."

His mouth turns downward slightly, and if I wasn't staring at him, I might not have noticed.

"Let's see if New York is worth it then," he says after a pause.

I feel Oliver gently pat my leg a few times. "Jenna," he whispers. I open my eyes and look around.

"I thought you might want to be awake for this part," he looks back out the window, and I follow his gaze to see New York City stretching out in front of us. The city has the most amazing feel to it. No matter how many times I've been here, it still gives me that feeling in my soul. The architecture is incredible and seeing the never-ending skyscrapers lining the sky brings such an awareness to the city's vast size. In a way, it makes me feel small and big at the same time. The roads are always full of cars and the sidewalks full of people. The energy is high, and I find myself wondering where everyone is going. Each person we pass has a story, a life, and I find myself so curious about all of it.

"I never get tired of this city," I breathe out quietly.

"Me neither."

"How many times have you been?" I ask.

"Only twice."

I help navigate through the city to Robby's apartment building. It's late evening as we pull to a stop. Oliver grabs my bag and ignores me as I try to help. I roll my eyes playfully as he gives me his usual lopsided smile. As we cross the street, I see Robby come out the door and give me a wave. I launch into a run and give him a big hug.

"Hey, sis," Robby says against the top of my head.

Robby is taller than me by a few inches. He has short blonde hair, a few shades darker than mine.

Oliver comes up by my side, "Hi, I'm Oliver," he says, extending his hand to Robby.

"Nice to meet you, Oliver," Robby shakes his hand and grabs a bag from him. He waves to his doorman and leads us to the elevator as we walk inside.

"This place is great," Oliver says looking around.

Robby lives on the 21st floor. It's a small one-bedroom apartment but meticulously well kept. Robby has always been very organized and particular. Oliver gives a low whistle as we walk into the apartment. Inside it's comprised of a small kitchen on the side, with a bar to sit at. He has enough room for a small table, a couch, and a TV. The bedroom is tight with his bed and a small closet, but the most impressive part is the wall in the living room made of windows. They are almost full glass from floor to ceiling and it has an amazing view of the city. Oliver walks over to the windows and exclaims, "Wow, this view is incredible, Robby!'

"Yeah, it's all worth the money right there. I'll put your bag in my room," Robby says, looking at me.

"Oh, no, I don't want to kick you out of your bed," I interject.

"You're not," he laughs. "I made you a bed on the floor."

I laugh and follow him into the room.

"I can't let my sister sleep out there with a boy," he teases.

"Don't you go treating me like a kid now," I laugh.

"I'm well aware you aren't a kid, but I don't want *that* happening a few feet away from me," he laughs.

I smack his arm and remind him, "Oliver and I are just friends."

"Mhm," Robby nods.

"So, Oliver, did you go to Northeast high?" Robby asks, walking back into the living room.

"No, I went to Powell."

"Hm. I thought you looked familiar," Robby replies.

"I played football for Powell," Oliver suggests.

Robby snaps his fingers and says, "That's it! You were their quarterback!"

Oliver nods and then looks back out the window.

"You were incredible. I remember now. You had tons of news articles about you and all these sponsorships right?"

He nods again, not making eye contact.

"Oliver bought the bowling alley," I intervene, trying to change the subject.

"Really? Why?"

I glare at Robby who looks at me confused, "What?" he asks.

"She's just trying to protect my feelings," Oliver explains, turning from the windows. "I got in a car accident and can't play football anymore."

"Oh. I'm sorry to hear that," Robby replies sheepishly.

"It's fine, don't worry about it."

"So! What should we do for dinner tonight?" I ask quickly.

"I was thinking pizza. My favorite place is just down the street a little," Robby suggests.

"Perfect," Oliver and I say at the same time. We chuckle and look at each other.

The sun is setting lower, creating a beautiful glow in the sky as we sit outside the pizzeria, eating our giant pizza slices. They are the kind of slices that are hard to hold because it's so large. It's dripping with grease and cheese and it's absolutely amazing. Hundreds of people are buzzing past us as we eat and I'm sitting back taking it all in. Oliver and Robby are talking about Robby's job while I enjoy the view and sounds of the city. The glow of the sunset is making the buildings look extra magical. It's my favorite time of day here when the sky is lit up from the sunset but dark enough that the lights in the buildings have started to turn on.

"Are you ready for your meeting?" Robby asks, pulling me from my thoughts.

"Yeah, fake it till you make it, right?" I laugh.

"You'll do great," Oliver says, reaching out and gently touching my arm comfortingly.

I feel Robby's eyes on us and I take another bite of my pizza.

"What are your plans tomorrow?" Robby turns to Oliver.

"I want to get my favorite bagel sandwich for breakfast," Oliver replies, then turns to me and adds, "I thought maybe we could get it before your meeting?"

I nod and swallow, "Sure, that sounds great."

"I have to work tomorrow, but I should be home by 6:00. Think you can entertain yourselves until then?" Robby says.

"Yeah, I think we'll have plenty to do," I reply, gesturing around us.

Robby sets Oliver up on the couch, and we all take turns using the one bathroom. When I finally curl up on the floor in Robby's room I hear my phone ping.

How was the rest of the drive? from Jensen.

It was fun. We saw the world's largest lightbulb and a giant hockey player. I reply, including pictures from each place.

Haha, this is great. Tell Oliver he's a weirdo.

Yeah, I'm exhausted and heading to bed. Talk tomorrow!

Goodnight. Good luck with your meeting!

I put my phone down and hear it vibrate again.

I'll be dreaming of that fudge. It's Oliver.

I chuckle, and Robby says, "What are you doing down there?"

"Nothing, sorry."

Me too. Thanks for the company today.

Any time. Goodnight Jenna.

I smile at my phone and turn it off.

"Thanks for letting us stay," I whisper to Robby.

"You're welcome. Always. You know that. How's it going at mom and dad's?"

"How it typically goes. They think I'll be homeless."

Robby snorts. "Not homeless. Just maybe a stripper."

I laugh loudly, "Robby!"

"Kidding. Really. I'm sure they believe in you more than you think. You know how bad they are at showing it."

"I know. It just motivates me to be successful and prove it to them."

"You'll be great," Robby replies quietly. A few minutes later, his breathing gets heavy and I know he's asleep.

12

The next morning I'm awake bright and early to prepare for my meeting. I sneak a quick shower, put on my make-up and pull up my hair. I spent hours debating with Maddie about what I should wear, and I settled on white pants, a soft blue blouse tucked into the front and tan high heels. I look at myself in the mirror and whisper, "You got this."

As I come out of the bathroom, I look in the living room to see Oliver standing up and pulling a shirt over his head. I pause, seeing the tightness of his muscles. My eyes follow the lines down his chest and stomach as they flex, and he pulls the shirt down. He runs his fingers through his wavy hair and then looks up and sees me. My cheeks flush with heat and I quickly look away and duck into Robby's room.

Robby is still asleep, so I tidy up my bed area trying to buy myself some time. Then I slowly make my way back to the living room. Oliver smiles at me from the couch.

"Morning," he nods, the smile on his lips saying he caught me looking at him.

"Morning," I reply curtly, not making eye contact.

"Ready to go get bagels?" he asks. He's wearing a tight white t-shirt that shows off his biceps with light brown shorts and white sneakers. He smiles up at me and I clear my throat.

"Yeah, let's go."

It's a beautiful morning in the city. There is a briskness to the air from the night but the sun is shining. Cars are already lining the streets, and groups of people are walking past us. The energy is palpable in the air. It's contagious and I feel excited about my meeting today. Oliver is looking at me, an amused look on his face.

"What?" I ask.

"Nothing, you just look…happy."

"I am."

"How are your nerves?"

"Fine, actually. I'm ready."

His mouth spreads into a big grin like he's proud of me, and my heart swells back at him.

The bagel place he wants to go to is on the way to my meeting. We have enough time that we decide to walk and enjoy the morning. We admire the buildings as we pass and the cute bodegas on the corners selling bouquets. I stop and smell a few of them, and Oliver snaps a picture of me with his phone. I send Jensen some photos of the buildings and the city and he sends me back a good luck message. But I'm feeling good. For once, I'm not feeling the nerves. I'm not thinking about what happens if they don't like me. I'm taking the pressure off and focusing on this one client and this one meeting. If they don't like me, that's fine. It doesn't have to mean that no one else will. I just have to believe in myself.

Oliver points ahead to a cute bakery. "This is it."

"How did you find this place?" I ask as he opens the door for me.

"The first time I ever visited New York was with some of my teammates in college. One of them grew up here and he brought us all here for the bacon, egg, and cheese. Now I make sure to come back any chance I get."

"Two bacon, egg, and cheese," he says to the woman at the counter. He glances at me, "Do you want anything else?"

"No, thanks."

He nods and hands his card over the counter.

"You don't have to pay for me," I say.

"I figure you're letting me stay with you and Robby. It's the least I can do."

"You drove," I point out.

"True. I suppose on the way back, I'll let you drive, and I'll sleep," he says with a smirk.

Oliver is right. This is the best bacon egg and cheese bagel I've had so far. The egg is the perfect consistency with a runny center and the bagel is soft, the bacon thick. I close my eyes on the first bite, and he chuckles, "Told you so," he says, taking a huge bite.

"Want to practice for your meeting?" he asks.

"Actually, I'm feeling pretty good."

He raises his eyebrows and smiles, his eyes twinkling, "Look at you."

I take another bite of the bagel, and he laughs, "You got a little egg," he says, gesturing towards the corner of his mouth.

I hurriedly grab the napkin and brush it away.

"It's here," he says, grabbing the napkin and slowly cleaning the edge of my lip.

I flush with embarrassment. If this were a movie, it would have been romantic and in slow motion. Instead, my face is burning with embarrassment. Oliver notices the look on my face and quickly pulls back, "Sorry, that was weird."

I chuckle and he looks uncomfortable. "You have a boyfriend," he utters.

"What?" I am confused by his thoughts.

He looks up at me, "Your face. I shouldn't be crossing your boundaries. I'm sorry."

"I don't have a boyfriend."

He looks back at me, an eyebrow kinking up. A smile tugs on the edge of his lips. "Jensen?"

"He's not my boyfriend."

"What is he?"

"I don't know yet," I reply honestly.

"Does he know that?"

"I've tried to tell him."

"I'm sure he doesn't want to hear that," he shakes his head, smiling and looking down at his plate.

I don't know what to say so I take another bite of my bagel and look around us. The air is getting warmer by the minute, and the streets are getting busier. Lots of people are coming in and out of the bakery, and I see people on computers starting their workday.

I think about Jensen and our last conversation and what came after it. He was sweet and patient, not pushing me any farther than I wanted to go. It felt good. He's a good kisser and I thoroughly enjoyed it, yet I was okay stopping. I didn't feel that burning desire to keep going, get closer to him, and feel every bit of him. Even now, thinking about it, thinking about him, it's nice, but I don't ache for him as I would hope. He's texted me saying he misses me. It's nice to hear, but I can't say that I feel the same. I'm fine here, without him. I've talked to Maddie about it, and she says to give it time. But should it really have to take time?

"I feel like he's there a lot faster than me. Like, I am trying to convince myself to fall for him," I say slowly.

He looks surprised. Whether by my statement or my random thought, I don't know. He stays quiet, so I continue, "I just want to fall. Completely, head over heels, easily in love with someone, ya know? I want that romantic sweep you off your feet feeling. But I guess that's too much to ask for."

Oliver keeps his gaze on me, and his eyes seem to darken and turn sad. "It's not too much to ask for."

"Have you felt that?"

"Yes."

"Your last girlfriend?"

He nods. "It happened fast too. Like it seems it is for Jensen."

"But it seems she fell out of it just as fast," he adds quietly. "That's the thing. A sweep you off your feet feeling doesn't guarantee a happy ending. It just means the beginning is great. I think any relationship can grow into that head over heels feeling," he says.

"So you aren't a cynic," I reply.

"A cynic?! No way. I'm 100% a true romantic. I'm a grand gesture kinda guy."

"A grand gesture," I repeat.

"Yeah, I mean, I did bring you a turkey sandwich."

"You think a turkey sandwich is romantic?"

He laughs, smiles and nods his head, "To tell you that I remember you from four years ago? Yeah, I think that's pretty romantic. See, a real grand gesture is all about the intention and meaning behind it. I can buy you a whole house, and sure, it would be a grand gesture, but an empty one if there's no real meaning behind it."

I laugh back, "Okay, I guess I can give you that. Your

turkey story isn't a bad meet-cute."

"Technically, I would tell you that I've always thought you were beautiful and always looked forward to the day you would come back. But meet-cutes are supposed to be the beginning of a romantic couple and as we discussed earlier, I'm not crossing those boundaries, seeing as you are romantically involved with Jensen."

He gives me a lighthearted wink, but my head is spinning. Was he just telling me the truth? I look at him, searching his eyes for clarification, but they are bright and light-hearted as he continues enjoying his sandwich. I try to think back about my many times at the bowling alley. I never forgot our interaction after high school graduation but I didn't see him any of the other summers. He smiles again, and my stomach feels uneasy.

"Oliver," I start, but I'm unsure how to continue.

He looks up from his sandwich at me, waiting. "Is that true?" I ask.

"What?"

"What you said about me."

He smirks and says, "Would it matter if it was?" Then he stands up from the table, "We should make sure you're on time."

I check my watch and nod.

The Townie Brownie office is across from Central Park. We don't talk much as I mentally prepare for the meeting and what I'm going to say. The nerves are starting to come back the closer we get to the office. When we reach the building I turn to Oliver and see him smiling at me.

"You're going to do great," he comforts me as he pulls me into a gentle hug.

"Thanks," I reply, the feeling of unease spreading through me.

We pull apart and he tells me he's planning to take a walk in the park if I want to meet up when I'm done. He wishes me good luck as I turn towards the office. I peek over my shoulder at him one last time as I take a deep breath, and head inside.

13

"I knew you'd nail it!" Oliver exclaims after I found him in the park after my meeting. If you could even call it a meeting. It was a very casual get-together for us to plan and create wireframes. The whole team was very relaxed and comfortable. They let me know they were confident in my abilities and ideas but that it's nice to get together in person and do the wireframes together. When I explained how nervous I was that they didn't like me, they laughed and apologized. Jennifer said she must not have been very clear in her emails because they love me. Once we got through all of that, I could breathe freely.

"I mean, I didn't really do anything. It was kind of a misunderstanding and my anxious personality," I laugh in reply to Oliver.

"Still! You came up with the ideas that they love!" he cheers.

We walk past a line of bikes, and Oliver pulls me over to them. "Let's ride around the park!" he suggests.

I don't have time to respond before he's paying for them and we are pedaling down the street. Central Park is beautiful. It's a large park right in the middle of the city with a six-mile pathway. We pass by all the tall buildings and through large green fields within the park. By the time we reach the second mile I'm grateful Oliver got the electric bikes for us. It's beautiful watching the buildings go by and turning to see Oliver, his eyes match mine with awe. The sun is streaking through the trees, and I'm smiling so wide, living completely in this moment. I feel the breeze hitting my face and brushing my hair behind me. I look over to see Oliver smiling back at me, "This is my new favorite thing to do," I call to him.

"I love your love for the little things," he says back to me. He lets go of the handlebars and manages his balance perfectly as he pulls his phone out of his pocket and takes a picture of me. He pulls his bike closer to mine and holds his phone out to take a picture of us together. I'm a little wobbly and he laughs, snapping the photo. I speed ahead of him and turn around to see him still holding out his phone so I stick my tongue out and continue pedaling ahead of him. He catches up to me, his phone back in his pocket. We don't talk for the rest of the bike path but we stay close and point at all the different things as we pass.

We loop around the park twice and finally drop our bikes off, exhausted but exhilarated as we head towards a food cart. Oliver buys a hot dog and I get a baked pretzel as we sit on the grass, enjoying the sunshine. I make a disgusted face as Oliver takes his first bite of the hot dog.

"What?" he asks.

"You trust street meat?"

He laughs, "Of course. It's New York! I gotta get one of the hot dogs from a cart."

I crinkle up my nose and shake my head.

"Have you had one?" he holds it out to me. I give a dramatic sniff of it and take a small bite.

"If we both get food poisoning tonight, I'm blaming this," I tease.

He laughs and says, "Fine by me! It's delicious." He wasn't wrong, it really was good.

My phone rings, and I look down to see it's Jensen. Oliver sees too and looks away. I stand up abruptly and walk away, "Hey," I say, answering.

"How did it go?" he asks.

"Great!" I tell him all about it and I can hear his big smile through the phone as he says, "I knew it! I knew it would all work out!"

"What are you doing now?" he asks.

"Just exploring the city a little. I'm at Central park right now and —

"Guess what! I got the promotion!" Jensen interrupts.

"What?"

"The promotion I've been working for. I got it! I just had to call and tell you!"

"Oh! Wow. Congratulations!" I say.

"When you get back, I'm taking us out to celebrate!"

"Okay, sure. That sounds great."

"Sweet. I gotta go, everyone is taking me out for drinks tonight. See you soon!"

The call goes silent, and I look down at my phone for a second. I feel a little hollow, as if the excitement has been stolen from me a little. I know that feels childish, I try to just be happy for Jensen. I put the phone back in my pocket and look up to see Oliver watching me. "Ready to head back?" he asks, his eyes searching my face.

I check the time, Robby should already be home.

"Sure, but let's take the scenic route?" I suggest, not ready to let the day end. He nods eagerly and hops up.

We wander through the park a little more and across one of the bridges. I pull out my phone this time to take pictures and Oliver poses. He gives me his best GQ pose followed by a model walk as we cross the bridge. I laugh and he grabs my phone telling me it's my turn. I give him an exaggerated walk full of hip-swaying and sashaying. I laugh and Oliver chuckles, but there's something about the way his eyes watch my body that makes me feel hot. When we reach the stairs, we walk down and see the Bethesda fountain. It looks just as pretty as it does in all the movies and I'm imagining the Enchanted cast running around and singing.

Oliver walks to the side of the fountain and puts his palms on the edge, leaning over a bit to look in the water. I can see his arms flex as he leans against his palms. It accentuates his muscles and pulls the sleeve of his shirt up a little, exposing the end of a small tattoo on his inner arm behind his bicep.

He looks over at me and catches me looking. "Is that a tattoo?" I ask, getting closer.

Instinctively he flexes his arm and looks down at it. "Yeah."

He pulls the sleeve higher and I see a small 3, but it's cracked down the middle.

"That was your number?" I ask.

He nods.

"And you wanted the reminder?"

"I think it's good to remember that I was lucky enough to live my dream, even if it was short."

"But it's cracked."

"Yeah. It's cracked, but it's not broken," he smiles.

He pulls his sleeve back down and looks at the fountain. I don't know what to say. His beautiful perspective strikes me. The idea that something can be cracked but not broken and how amazingly grateful he could be for a part of his life that others would view as tragic. I'm in awe that he can come out stronger and better from a dark time instead of breaking from it. It's beautiful.

He turns and we start walking without saying a word. We walk in comfortable silence until we leave the park. I sneak glances at him, but he seems content to walk in silence, looking around at what we pass.

My phone vibrates and I look down to see a text from Robby.

Got invited to a club tonight with some friends. Want to come?

I show it to Oliver and when he nods, I text back asking where to meet.

"I'm a little formal for a club," I say, looking down at my outfit from earlier.

"You look great," he replies.

We continue walking and we pass by a store. I catch a glimpse through the windows and stop. Oliver walks a few steps and then stops and turns,

"Oh no," he says, seeing the look on my face.

"Yes!" I say, pulling him inside. "I'll be fast. Promise!"

The store is fancier than the typical stores I shop at and I hear Oliver let out a quiet whistle as he looks around. I scan through the racks and try to avoid looking at the price tags. It's a little more pricey than normal, but I figure I can splurge since it was a big day for me. I deserve a little celebration. I pick out a leather mini skirt and a tight red lace top. Oliver is on the other side of the store looking at jackets, so I slide into the dressing room. They fit perfectly. As promised, I buy them quickly, and a pair of black boots to go with the outfit. Then I sneak back into the dressing room, change into the outfit and let my hair down.

When I come out of the dressing room, Oliver is standing there, looking in the mirror at the leather jacket he has on. He sees me over his shoulder and freezes.

"Whoa," he says, slowly turning to look at me.

"You like?" I tease, striking a pose.

"Absolutely," he says, his voice coming out a bit shaky.

I bite my lip and have to look away from his eyes.

"Nice jacket," I say, focusing on it. He looks down as if he forgot he was wearing it, "Oh yeah, thought it looked good," he replies.

He looks really good. It's a simple black leather jacket that fits perfectly through his arms and shoulders. "Not everyone can pull off a leather jacket," I remark, looking at him.

"Careful, Jenna," he says, smirking at me.

The club is crazy and takes forever to find Robby. I notice how close Oliver stays to me as we wind through the crowd. He keeps his fingers lightly against my back, so faint I can hardly feel it, but I swear I can feel the heat and electricity coming from him. We finally see Robby waving at us and he quickly introduces us to a few of his friends. When he orders a round of shots, Oliver politely declines and I hesitate until Oliver leans low, next to my ear and says, "You can drink around me."

I feel chills race up my back as I feel his voice in my ear. I look up at him, questions in my eyes, and he nods. So I take the shot and cheer with my brother. We spend the first hour dancing, laughing and drinking.

Oliver sticks close to the group, showing off his moves. Surprisingly, he can dance well. He jokes that it's his athletic training. I dance next to him, but not with him. When a cute boy comes over and starts dancing by me, I grab his hand and lead him out farther on the dance floor, giving Oliver a flirty look as we walk away. Oliver watches us go, and I see a brief look cross his face, but it's gone so fast I could have imagined it.

The guy I'm dancing with is attractive, and he knows it. He has short black hair that is gelled up for more volume. He's wearing an unbuttoned suit, with the shirt underneath undone one too many times. I imagine he works on wall street, he seems to fit that stereotype. He pulls me close, and he smells expensive, like sandalwood. He holds up his hand, spins me a few times, then pulls me in closer, wrapping his arms around me.

"You are hot," he half yells over the music.

I throw him a smile and keep dancing.

"I'm Nick," he yells again.

"Jenna," I yell back.

He looks me up and down and turns me, wrapping me up from behind. I wiggle lower and closer to him to feel him react. He leans down and tries to nibble on my ear. I pull away a little but keep dancing. Nick moves his hands tighter and lower on my body, holding me tightly, then leans in again to my ear. This time before I can move away Oliver is standing in front of me. His eyes look dark, and his mouth pulls into a thin line. Nick doesn't seem to notice right away, but I stop dancing and he looks up.

"What?" Nick yells, looking confused.

Oliver holds out his hand and I put mine in his. His fingers wrap mine tightly and I feel the warmth run up my arm. Nick continues to look confused, glancing between Oliver and me.

"This guy your boyfriend?" Nick hollers.

I shake my head as Oliver pulls me away. I giggle as I peek over my shoulder at Nick, standing in the crowd, looking confused. Oliver stops and spins me pulling us together. I stand up on my tiptoes to reach his ear, "I didn't need saving that time," I say.

He leans down to meet me and goosebumps run through me as I feel him say, "I never said you did."

He smiles at me and starts dancing with me. We lose ourselves in the song, jumping and dancing together, closer than last time, the song shifts and Oliver does too. He moves in a little closer, grabs my hands, and pulls me against him slowly. I feel my body react to each spot that we touch. He moves his hands down to my hips, moving with them. I can feel his hands burning through my clothes and I wrap mine around the back of his neck, wanting any part of my skin to touch his. I use a little pressure to guide his head closer to mine and tilt up to reach him, our foreheads touching. It feels like electricity is coursing through us, pulling us closer together. My heart is racing as my hips move in sync with his.

Robby suddenly appears next to us, holding out more drinks. Oliver immediately pulls back, and I feel the electricity go with him. My hands feel empty, my knees feel weak and shaky. I wave Robby off and tell him no thanks.

"I think I'm ready to go home," I say instead turning to Oliver.

Robby tips up his drink, finishes it, and says, "Alright let's go!"

As we walk towards the door, I feel Oliver behind me. He's closer this time, his hand in the same spot on my lower back. He's still not quite touching me, his hand floating just inches away and it feels like a tease. I feel my body wanting his hand to be there, actually there, against my skin. I peek over my shoulder at him but he doesn't make eye contact. As we come through the door, the warm night air hits us, and I feel Oliver pull away.

"That was fun!" Robby exclaims.

"Yeah," my voice sounds shaky.

Robby falls asleep almost instantly. I can hear his light snores as I'm lying there wide awake. My body is buzzing. I text Maddie and tell her about the night and all she sends back is

Eeeeeeeeeeeeek!!!

I text back a reply, *not helpful*

MAKE A MOVE. HE IS HOT!

I put my phone down and close my eyes but I know it's useless. I can't sleep. My heart is racing and my stomach is tense. I feel like I'm burning up, even though I'm only wearing shorts and a tank top. I slide out from under the blankets, careful not to wake Robby. I sneak through the door and tiptoe into the living room and I peek around the corner to see Oliver lying on the couch, shirtless, one arm tucked under his head. Glowing lights are coming in from the windows, lighting him up in a romantic way. I take another step into the room and he shifts, looking at me.

"Jenna?" he whispers.

"Yeah."

"What are you doing?"

I'm quiet as I walk closer to him. "I don't know," I reply. I slowly sit on the edge of the couch, and he scoots back.

We sit in silence for a minute, listening to the sounds of the city outside.

"I can't sleep," I say finally.

"Me either."

I slide a little farther back on the couch so my hip touches his. He freezes, and I hear him swallow. I feel my hand reach out, almost like I'm not in control of it, it's drawn towards him. I put it gently on his abs and feel him breathe in.

I relax my hand into him, feeling his muscles. I start to draw lines across his skin, following the curves of his muscles. His breathing sounds shallow. He seems to be frozen in place. I turn in a little bit towards him and he moves with me. He reaches down and puts a hand on my leg. My leg warms where his skin meets mine and I feel tingles run through me. His hand gently rubs up against my leg, higher, reaching the hem of my shorts. My body quivers and I scoot closer, causing his fingers to reach a little higher. I feel him suck in. Suddenly, he sits up. I can see his eyes piercing at me, but he doesn't say anything. His hand is still on my leg, but now it's lower than I want. He seems to read my mind as he slides his hand higher again, this time his other hand coming to my waist. He picks me up with ease and slides me over him so I'm straddling his legs. He keeps eye contact with me as he slowly leans forward, pressing his lips to my shoulder. He moves across my shoulder, across my chest, and up to my neck. It feels like my body is shaking and flames are shooting across my skin as he moves. He's slowly kissing up my neck, getting higher, and my body is aching. I let out a sigh, and suddenly he freezes. He pulls his hands back and sits up taller.

"Oliver?" I ask, searching his face.

"I can't. Sorry."

"What?" I'm confused. He's looking anywhere except my face.

"Oliver," I say again.

"Jenna, I can't. We can't."

I pull back, hurt. I stand up, shakily, my cheeks flushing with embarrassment. "Oh. Sorry. I'm sorry," I keep apologizing.

He stands up with me, "You don't need to apologize," he says as I rush back to Robby's room.

"Jenna, wait," he pleads.

"No, it's fine, I'm sorry," and I run back through the door.

I sit on the other side of the door and hear him sigh. The couch creaks as he sits back down. I'm breathing heavily, my hands shaking. I'm hurt and confused. What just happened? I lay back down and know I'm definitely not sleeping now.

14

When the morning comes, I realize I hardly slept. I throw on my flowy dress and the boots I purchased yesterday and plan to sneak out before anyone else wakes up.

I am only one step into the living room when I see Oliver. His hair is extra curly and messy, as if he also didn't sleep. He's already dressed in black pants and a dark gray shirt.

"Hey," he says quietly when he sees me. "We should talk."

"No need. It's no big deal."

"Jenna..."

"I'm actually on my way out. But it's all good. Really. Nothing to talk about."

He opens his mouth to reply, but I quickly brush past him and out the front door, not looking back.

I spend the morning walking through the city, stopping for a coffee and bagel. I keep thinking back over last night and what happened. Was I reading his intentions wrong? He approached me at the club but maybe he was just trying to protect me. I put my head down in my hands. What if he's dating someone? He's never mentioned a girlfriend, though. Maybe he's just not interested in me. My phone vibrates but I ignore it and stand up to keep walking.

I hop on the next subway stop and ride down to The Battery. I finally check my phone and see some messages from Robby.

Hey, where'd you go?

Everything okay?

I text back telling him where I am and that I'm fine, just wanted to get out and explore. When I get to The Battery, I wander to the water's edge and look out at the boats on the Hudson River. I think back on yesterday, the bagels, the bike ride, the club. It was close to a perfect day until last night. I don't even know what I was thinking. Or what I was trying to do. I feel ridiculous and thoroughly embarrassed.

My phone vibrates, and I look down to see a message from Jensen.

Thinking of you. Hope you're having fun and can't wait to see you in a few days. Where is our celebratory dinner?

My stomach sinks a little. I sigh thinking of Jensen. I know it's not fair to string him along, I'm not trying to. I just can't get my feelings to catch up to his. All I really know is that last night I desperately wanted Oliver. But with Jensen, I've never had to wonder if he likes me. It's obvious how much he cares. There's something so nice and comforting about that feeling. It's like what Oliver said, "Any relationship has the potential to grow into a head over heels feeling." Oliver. Ugh, I'm so embarrassed.

I continue to walk along the water a little ways when my phone rings again, it's Robby.

"Hey sis, where are you?" he asks.

"Walking along the water. I'm still at Battery park."

"Yeah, I came to meet you, I'm walking the water too, but- oh wait, I see you!" he exclaims.

I look up and see Robby waving from down the path. Oliver is with him. I slowly hang up and take my time putting my phone away, avoiding eye contact. When I look back up, Oliver rubs the back of his neck and gives me a small smile.

"Hey, figured we would get out and come meet you," Robby says as we reach each other.

"Yeah, thanks."

"What's next on your agenda?" he asks.

"Uh, nothing really. I don't have plans."

"Cool, let's walk over to Brooklyn!" Robby suggests, leading us back the other way.

I walk to the other side of Robby, keeping him between Oliver and me. Robby is talking about some girl he met at the club last night and how they are going out on a date in a few days. I nod along, throwing glances at Oliver, but he faces straight ahead or looks out at the water. Thankfully Robby is full of things to talk about as we walk the bridge. He pulls out his phone, takes some pictures with me, and says we are obligated to send one to Mom and Dad.

"You should send one to Jensen," Oliver says suddenly.

I trip a little over my feet, dumbfounded by his words. Confusion and anger ripple through me. That's what he's choosing to say right now? My stomach falls, Robby looks at me and asks, "Who's Jensen?"

"Just a guy I'm talking to."

"Talking to or dating?" Robby questions.

"Depends who you ask," Oliver mumbles.

Robby laughs and says, "Uh oh, are you breaking hearts, Jenna?"

Oliver and I suddenly look at each other. His face is completely unreadable. I look away and say, "No. He's just moving a bit faster than me. But he's great, really."

"Cool, let's send him a pic then," Robby says, pulling out his phone to snap a group selfie. He pushes all of us together. My shoulder touches Oliver's and the whole right side of my body is suddenly alert. Oliver re-adjusts ever so slightly so that we are no longer touching and he smiles for the picture.

We finish walking the bridge and go to a nice restaurant overlooking the water. Oliver and Robby talk about football and college and the bowling alley. Oliver is kind and answers most of Robby's questions about the accident and how it led to where he is now. I try not to admire his positive attitude too much, but it's hard. We take the subway back to his apartment and decide to relax and rent a movie. I pause when Oliver sits on the couch. I think back to last night and the way his hands felt on my legs and my waist. I remember too perfectly how my body reacted to his touch. I desperately want that again, and I instantly feel stupid for feeling that way. I shake my head as if that could dispel the feelings and sit on the other end of the couch, allowing Robby to plop between us.

We pack up and leave early the next morning. It's a somber morning, none of us starting any conversation. I pretend I'm tired but really I'm still embarrassed and hurt about the other night.

"Thanks so much for staying with me. It's always great to see you," Robby says, pulling me into a hug. "And great to meet you, Oliver," he says, pulling him into a half hug and patting his back.

"Yeah, thank you for letting me hang out," Oliver replies.

"Come visit soon, please?" I suggest to Robby.

"Definitely before the end of summer. Promise."

He waves as we cross the road, and Oliver and I walk

in silence to the car.

It's going to be a long drive, I think to myself.

"Ready?" Oliver asks as he starts the car.

I nod. He opens his mouth to say something else but hesitates and closes it, facing forward.

We don't talk for two hours. The first hour is filled with a heavy silence. In the second hour, he turns on the radio, but we still don't talk. By the time hour three comes up, I think we'll make it the whole drive without speaking.

"Did you know if two pieces of the same metal touch in space, they will bond and be stuck together forever?"

I jump at his voice.

"Sorry, didn't mean to scare you," he chuckles.

"What?" I ask, confused.

"Metal in space. If they are the same type, they will be bonded forever." He looks at me, the corner of his mouth turned up just slightly.

"Why are all your space facts about things being together forever?" I say.

Oliver barks out a laugh. A pure and loud, happy laugh. The kind of laugh that makes me smile in response. Then he sighs and shrugs.

"Can we talk?" he asks.

"Do we have to?"

"I'm not a big fan of avoidance."

"That's all my family knows," I reply.

"So, do you fall in that category?" he questions.

"...actually no, I hate it."

He smiles as if he already knew the answer.

"But in this case, maybe it's for the best," I add.

He shakes his head, "I don't believe it's ever for the

best."

"I'm embarrassed," I say quietly.

He whips his head toward me, and his eyebrows pull together in confusion. "Embarrassed?"

I fiddle with my hands and avoid his eye contact, but I can feel him glancing between me and the road, waiting.

"I basically threw myself at you, and you rejected me."

"Whoa, whoa, whoa. Jenna. No." he says quickly.

"Yeah, Oliver, that's what happened."

"I–" he starts and then stops. His mouth turns down, and he thinks.

He tries again. "I'm so sorry, Jenna. That was not my intention at all. I promise. I would never want to make you feel rejected."

I steal a glance back at him, his blue eyes soft as he looks back at me.

"Then what happened?" I ask.

He sighs and looks out the window. It's quiet for so long that I think we are going back to not speaking until he finally says, "Jensen. Before you say you aren't dating, I get it. In your head, you're still working on those feelings. But he's not. I've seen it and he's fully in it with you. And I don't blame him one bit for falling so fast for you. I know you're a little confused after that fight and that things are kind of complicated. But it's not fair to him, or to you, to try and complicate things even more. You need to think about what you really want. I'm not going to be that guy, because I've been Jensen before. It hurts being the one that cares more, it hurts being the guy replaced. I won't do that. You like Jensen. You've said so yourself. And I don't know if you're scared of letting yourself feel more, or if you just really don't feel enough for him. But sleeping with me isn't going to help you. Or me."

I swallow, trying to give myself time to take in everything he just said. I open my mouth and close it, unsure what to say. The thing is, he's not wrong. I do like Jensen. And I like Oliver. I don't say that. I don't know how to say it. I don't know what to say. I don't want to just sleep with him, I want to be with him. The pull I feel towards Oliver is something I've never felt before. How do I explain that without sounding like a crazy person?

"I'm sorry," I say finally.

He tilts his head in question.

"For putting you in that situation," I explain.

"You don't need to apologize."

"I wasn't just trying to sleep with you…" I say.

"Oh, definitely don't apologize for that. I mean, who could blame you?" he says with a chuckle and a gesture at his body.

I roll my eyes back at him and say, "So now what?"

"You go home to Jensen and figure out how you feel."

"And you?"

"What about me?"

"What are you going to do?"

"What I've always done," he says with a smile.

The rest of the drive passes comfortably again. We sing along with the music, eat more fudge, and take a detour to see a giant pencil and a large pineapple. This is a new feeling for me. I'm so used to ignoring and pretending like nothing was ever wrong. Oliver is the opposite. He openly talks about how he feels and what he's thinking. It's freeing in a way I've never experienced. It allows us to fall back into the same friendship we had before. We don't have to do the awkward back and forth of pretending it never happened. Even though I still catch myself in my thoughts. I find myself thinking about his hands on me. I think about how close he was, and I remember how he smelled. Then just as easily, I remember the rejection and the embarrassment, and I hurriedly stop thinking about it.

Oliver doesn't walk me to the door when we finally stop at my parent's house.

"Thanks for coming with me," I say.

He nods and replies, "Any time."

I wave again as I reach the porch and look down to see a bouquet of flowers on the step. It's an assortment of different colored roses, and it smells heavenly. I lean down to pick them up and breathe them in. I see a card and read it,

I figured you would be tired, but I wanted you to know I'm excited you're back. -Jensen

I smile and look back up to see Oliver watching me. He gives me a small nod again and drives away.

Maddie is at my house first thing the next morning.

"Tell. Me. Everything!" she shouts, running through my bedroom door.

"Hello to you too."

"Yes, hi, hello, now spill!"

I sit up in bed and think about how to even explain.

"Those flowers!" she exclaims, walking to the bouquet of roses on my nightstand.

"From Jensen."

She freezes and leans back up from smelling them.

"Oh, this is going to be good," she grins, plopping down on the bed.

"Mads, I don't know what to say."

"Well, did anything happen?!"

"No."

"...no?"

"I....tried."

"How do you *try*?" she asks, confused.

"You try by making a fool of yourself. I put myself out there and he didn't want me."

Maddie purses her lips together and thinks. "Why would he do that?"

"He's not into me."

"Did he say that?"

"Well, no, not exactly. He said having sex with him isn't going to make things better for him or me. He told me to come home and figure out what I'm doing with Jensen because it isn't fair."

"Okay, that's not bad then! He's just a good guy! He doesn't want to be a cheater!"

"I wasn't trying to be a cheater."

"Of course not!" she says, patting my leg. "But you could see how that might feel for him, right?" she adds.

I sigh dramatically, and she laughs. "So, what are you going to do?" she asks.

"I don't know."

"Do you like Jensen?" she asks.

"Yes."

"Okay, so start there."

"But..." I start, and she smiles.

"You like Oliver too?" she finishes.

"Yeah...I think I do."

She breaks into a grin. "This is going to be really good!"

◆ ◆ ◆

After a few days in New York, I have a lot of work to do so I sit down with my computer and get started. I start with Joan and finish the new social media graphics of her merchandise to run as ads. Then I reply to a few other companies that I have been pitching myself to. Finally, I start doing some research on bowling alley logos and other fun logo ideas to see if I can finalize some options for Oliver. The day passes quickly, and except for a quick lunch break, I stay in my room working all day. I finish five different logo ideas for Oliver. They range from very basic to a little crazy and everything else in between. I include the one I sketched with Jensen. I tweak it a little bit, but I like the overall concept. The one I like the most is a simple outline of the pins with a silhouette of the building behind it.

I yawn and check the time. I'm surprised to see it's past 5:00, and I stand up to take a shower. It has been a long but productive day. After my shower, I wander to the kitchen for dinner and find my parents there.

"Productive day?" my dad asks.

"Very!"

"That's great."

"We just got a pizza, want to join us for dinner and a movie?" my mom asks.

"That sounds great," I reply.

The movie is a romantic comedy that makes my parents snuggle a little extra close. In the movie, she meets the love of her life right when he has to leave the country for work, so she decides to follow him so they can try to date. My mom says it's completely unrealistic for her to leave work just for a boy she hardly knows. It's all a little crazy but in the end, it works out, and it's adorable.

Unfortunately, it does nothing to distract me from my current situation. When Jensen texts me, I invite him over and he's here within 20 minutes.

"You're quick," I joke as I open the door.

He chuckles and pulls me into a big hug. "Guess I'm just excited to see you."

I peek at my parents, who are still snuggling on the couch and talking. They don't look like they'll be going anywhere soon, so I grab Jensen's hand and pull him back outside to the porch. We sit on the front step, and he asks, "Everything okay?"

"Yeah, I just wanted to talk."

He scoots in closer, putting his hands on my leg. He kisses me on my neck and says, "Let's talk," in-between kisses.

I feel myself relax a little, his breath on my neck. Then I stop and push him away. "No," I say. He looks up at me. "I mean, actually talk."

"Okay, okay," he concedes.

"I really hate the way we left things before New York," I start.

"You mean our hot make-out? I didn't think it was that bad," he smirks and nudges me with his shoulder.

"Not that. The argument at dinner."

He tenses and I see his jaw twitch. "Right. I know. I've apologized a hundred times, and I brought you some flowers. What else can I do?" he says.

"Yeah, that's all fine, but it can't happen again. That was embarrassing and made me very uncomfortable."

"I know. I'm sorry. I really am. I just hated the idea of you being with Oliver. You can't blame me for caring too much, can you?"

"I can if that's the way you show it."

He lowers his eyes and slumps a little. "I know. I know. I promise I'll be better."

I put my hand on his back, "Thank you."

He peeks up at me and then wraps me in a hug. "I missed you so much."

I laugh a little, "I really wasn't gone that long," I reply.

"Long enough," he says. He pulls back and then looks at me, "We're good then?"

I offer him a small nod, and he pulls me in close, bringing our lips together. He's kissing me like we've been apart for months. And I'm letting him because it feels so good to feel his desire for me. He wants me. I find myself thinking about Oliver and his rejection. But Jensen is here, fully showing his desire for me. I push the thoughts away and focus on Jensen. His hands are grabbing at me, and his mouth is pulling me in closer and closer. He's desperate for me, and I love it.

Just as I'm completely losing myself in him, I hear a car door close in front of my house. I pull away and look over. It's dark, so I can't see until Oliver is just a few feet away from us.

"Hi, sorry to interrupt," he mumbles, holding up his hand. He's holding a box of fudge and adds, "I was just going to leave this on your porch." He looks uncomfortable and shifts on his feet.

"Oh, thanks! That's really nice of you," I stand up quickly to take the box, and Jensen stands with me.

"Hey Jensen," Oliver says. "How are you?"

Jensen grunts in response, and I throw him a pointed look.

"Fine. Yeah. Thanks for keeping my girl safe," Jensen says. Is he puffing out his chest, or is that just me? Oliver rubs the back of his neck and quickly glances at me. Then he looks back at Jensen and replies, "Happy to."

"I'm sure," Jensen mutters under his breath.

"Anyway, thanks so much, Oliver," I say, cutting between them.

He looks back at me now, a look on his face that I don't recognize. It almost looks pained. He opens his mouth to say something but stops.

"You're welcome. Enjoy," he finally says and quickly walks back to his car.

I open the box and see a bunch of fudge that we never finished. Jensen leans over and grabs a piece, "Looks delicious," he says, taking a bite.

"Should we continue our conversation," Jensen asks with a wink.

"Actually, I'm pretty tired. I think I'll probably just go to bed." My stomach is twisting as I watch Oliver drive away.

"Cool, can I take you out for my celebratory dinner tomorrow?"

"Yeah, that sounds great."

He smiles and grabs another piece of fudge. "For the road," he says. He leans down and gives me a long kiss goodbye.

15

Jensen is supposed to pick me up in an hour for dinner, so I don't know why I'm standing outside the bowling alley wanting to see Oliver. I know I shouldn't be here. He told me to focus on Jensen. He made it plenty clear that he didn't want me. But I feel like I need to apologize for last night. Or maybe I don't need to, I just want to. I walk through the doors, standing tall and go straight to the counter, but Oliver isn't there. Instead, I find Olivia.

"Hi Jenna!" she says. "You look so pretty!"

"Thanks Olivia. Is your brother around?" I ask looking around.

"Uh, not right now."

"Did he leave you here alone?" I ask, surprised.

"Of course not! Leo and Anna are both working, too!" she points to the other side of the alley and I see a young boy in the arcade and a woman at the food counter.

"Okay...well, I was hoping to talk to Oliver," I say disappointed.

She shrugs and avoids my eyes when she replies, "sorry."

"Oh! Actually, I have something for you," I say, grabbing my purse and digging inside.

I printed off the sticker of her in the rocket ship and put it in my purse, waiting for the next time I saw her. I pull it out of my purse and excitedly hand it to her. Her face lights up instantly. "Jenna! This is so awesome!" she squeals.

She runs from behind the counter and gives me a big hug. I'm hugging her back when my eyes shift up, and I see Oliver watching us from the back of the bowling alley. We make eye contact for a second but then he turns and walks back behind the pins.

I make it back to my house just in time for Jensen to pick me up. On the car ride to the restaurant, he's asking me all about New York. He wants to know every little detail. Where we ate, what we saw, how my meeting went. I tell him everything, well, almost everything. I don't tell him about that night with Oliver. He's made it obvious how he would react. But even as I'm thinking about it, I remember the feeling of Oliver's hands sliding up my leg and the feeling of his lips on my neck. My hand is on my neck gently, as if I can still feel his lips lingering there.

"You okay?" Jensen's voice pulls me back.

"Oh, uh yeah, I'm just tired of talking about me. Your turn. What did I miss?"

Jensen launches into the story about his promotion and the meeting and projects that have led to it. He's been talking about a woman named Mary a lot.

"Sorry, who's Mary?" I ask.

"She's my new manager. I'll be reporting to her now."

I nod as he continues telling me about how this new job will require some travel and how excited he is. His first trip is next week and his excitement is so palpable. It helps bring my thoughts back to the car.

"I'm really happy for you," I say.

"Thanks! I knew I would get it!"

Jensen takes us to an Italian restaurant downtown. Italian is my favorite food, and I'm grateful that he listened this time. The mood in this restaurant is perfect with low light, quiet romantic music, and even flowers on the tables.

"This place is gorgeous," I say, looking around.

"One day, I want to go to Italy," he replies.

"Me too!"

"Here's to Italy one day, hopefully together," he smiles, holding out his glass in a toast.

"So tell me more about what you have to do on this trip next week?" I ask.

"Well, we are going to one of the headquarters in Florida, and I'm supposed to be seeing their warehouse operations and meeting with some other managers there. Basically, I'm there to solve any supply chain delays they are having and help it all flow smoother. But, it's in Miami so I'm very excited about the after-work activities!" he explains.

"Miami! That sounds fun!"

His smile is huge as he nods. "A few of us from the office here get to go, so we've been making lots of plans for after work!"

"That sounds great! I am starting on Townie Brownie stuff this week and finalizing Oliver's logo," I say.

He nods, "I'm proud of you for Townie Brownie! I knew you were just overreacting."

His words are a trigger for me. I don't like being told I'm overreacting. "It's scary trying to earn an income all on my own."

"You just need to believe in yourself."

"I do believe in myself."

"Well, then great! You're halfway there."

"Right. Because that's all it takes. It's just that easy," I reply flatly.

A look of annoyance crosses Jensen's face at my response.

"Does Oliver even know if they need a new logo? Or is he just trying to find an excuse to hang out with you?" he questions suddenly.

I bite my tongue to stop myself from saying that he doesn't need an excuse. Instead, I say, "He told me they need a new logo."

"Did his boss say that?"

"He doesn't have a boss."

"Huh?" Jensen looks confused.

"Oliver owns the place," I reply. I feel proud for Oliver. I feel the need to defend him.

Jensen looks surprised for a moment and then composes himself. "I didn't know that."

"Yeah, he bought it after the accident."

He grunts, and unfortunately, it's a noise I'm starting to recognize. Before this dinner can go completely downhill, he pulls out a pen and says, "I think it's time for your next comic strip!"

"You know, one of the things I like most about you is that we can connect in this artistic way. You bring out the art side of me and not just the numbers and excel spreadsheets side," he says as he starts doodling.

I do love watching him draw. He retreats into the drawing, leaving a quiet peace between us. His face is always deeply concentrated but still relaxed in a way that's hard to explain. I love the light way his hand drifts over the napkin and the way the veins in his hands and arms flex as he moves. I lean in a little closer and see him sketching me. He smiles up at me, and I feel myself smile back. These moments with Jensen feel right. I'm not thinking about Oliver or New York. I'm focusing on this moment, this feeling, and the feeling I had last night as he kissed me. There's no doubt in my mind how much he cares. He's constantly making sure I know it. I can overlook the way he shows it, sometimes it's not always the best, but deep down, I know it's because he just cares so much. I feel like maybe I need to try harder to get to his level. I feel like I need to prove how much I care too.

He stops drawing and shows me the napkin. It's us in Italy together, and we look happy. We look perfect. I want that to come true.

◆ ◆ ◆

"I love this song!" I say right as we stop in front of my parent's house.

Jensen smiles and turns it up loud then he jumps out of the car, comes to my side, and pulls me out. He leaves the car door open as he pulls me close to him and starts dancing with me.

"Have I told you how beautiful you look tonight?" he asks, talking softly in my ear.

"A few times," I chuckle. "Thank you."

"I mean, this dress is amazing," he continues, his hand lowering to touch my skin through the slit on my dress.

I feel goosebumps run down my leg as his fingertips graze me.

"Who knew you were such a romantic? Dancing with me like this," I whisper.

"I could dance with you for hours."

My body feels warm in his arms, and my heart beats

faster at his words.

Suddenly, he grabs my hand and sends me out in a spin. When he spins me back he dips me low, bringing his face down to meet mine and kisses me. I wrap my arms around his neck as he pulls me back up. I peek over his shoulder at the house and see all the lights are off.

"Do you want to come inside?" I ask.

His eyes are bright, and he nods, pulling me towards the house.

The second I close the front door, he pushes me against it and kisses me. I can feel his whole body pressing against me. I tug off his shirt, admiring his muscles as it slides over his head. His hand slides up the slit of my dress, pushing farther than he did outside. I kick off my shoes and hop up to wrap my legs around him. He holds me easily between him and the door, running his hand higher up my thigh. I drag my fingers down his back and kiss down his neck and shoulders. His body seems to rumble with anticipation and he swings me around and walks me over to the couch. As I feel my back land on the couch, my mind starts racing. It's so easy to get caught up in this moment and these feelings, but something is holding me back. Physically I want nothing more than to give in to this moment and give in to Jensen, but emotionally I keep hitting a wall. I catch myself thinking of Oliver.

"My parents," I manage to say as he starts kissing down my neck.

"What?" he asks, pulling back from me and looking around.

"I don't know when they'll be back."

"So?" he's confused.

"So maybe let's not do this on the couch."

"Your room then?" he asks, his eyebrows raised.

I shake my head no as I swallow. "Not what I meant," I say.

He leans back, looking disappointed. He exhales loudly and stands up to move away from me.

"Sorry," I say.

"Yeah. I'm going to need a minute to cool down," he says with an edge to his voice. After a pause, he adds, "I'm wishing you didn't live with your parents right now."

I chuckle but it feels hollow. I can't help but ask myself if I'm actually worried my parents will come home or if I just can't stop thinking about Oliver. I peek over at Jensen. I watch as he walks over and pulls his shirt back on. He sighs loudly again and looks around the room.

"Do you want to watch a movie?" I ask.

He looks back at me as if he forgot that I was there. "Uh, yeah, sure."

He sits down next to me, putting his arm around me. I snuggle into him a little deeper as the movie starts. Jensen pushes the limits a little farther and farther as the movie passes. It starts with soft kissing and quickly moves to his hands drifting higher and higher up my leg. I push his hand back down a few times, but his hand happens to find its way right back after a few minutes. After the third time pushing his hand back, I try to reposition my body a little bit away from him but he catches my arm, keeping me close to him. I look down at his hand wrapped around my wrist as he pulls me closer. I can feel pulsing from the tightness of his grip. I swallow shakily, feeling like I'm in the parking lot with Ty again. Fear is slowly creeping inside me again. I yank my arm away from his and Jensen's mouth twitches. Annoyance flashes through his eyes and I hear the door open, grateful to see my parents walking inside.

Jensen suddenly sits up straighter and leans away from me a bit.

"Oh, hello, you two!" my mom says as she sees us.

"This is Jensen," she says to my dad.

My dad puts on his best smile and comes to shake Jensen's hand, "Nice to meet you," he says.

Jensen shakes his hand and replies, "You too."

"How was the date?" my mom asks.

"Wonderful! I took her to the new Italian place downtown," Jensen answers. I look at him and can't believe how easily he falls into this conversation with my mom. It's scary how different he's acting at this moment.

"Oh, how nice! I've been wanting to try that place!" my mom replies.

"It's great. Next time, you should come with us."

My mom's face lights up, "Oh that would be so fun! Yes! Let's do that!"

My dad nods in agreement and after giving me a look, they head upstairs.

"I think I'm ready for bed," I say.

"Oh, really? Alright," he replies with a wink.

I playfully roll my eyes and give him a serious look as I say, "Really though."

Jensen chuckles flatly, "Okay then. I'll go. Will I see you tomorrow?"

"I'll text you."

The next day I text Oliver in the morning.

I would love to discuss some of these logos with you. Are you free today?

It takes him a few minutes to respond and all he says is, *Can't today. Sorry.*

My stomach instantly knots at his words and I think back to his face when he saw me at the bowling alley. I slam my phone down on the counter in frustration. I don't know what to do. I know it's not fair. He told me to figure it out with Jensen, and I did. So why am I still aching for Oliver? Rather than deal with my emotions, I throw myself into work. After an hour, I feel my mom come and look over my shoulder.

"What are you working on today?" she asks.

"The new Townie Brownie website."

"I like it. It's more fun than what it was before."

"Thanks. Their company grew so fast they couldn't keep up with it."

"Interesting. Did you have fun with Jensen last night?"

"Yeah, the food was great."

"He left pretty quickly after us," she muses.

I nod, unsure what she's getting at.

"You're always welcome to have him here," she offers.

"I know."

"Okay, just making sure. I think you two are a cute couple."

"Thanks, Mom."

"Anywho, I'm off to my office!" she says as she grabs her bag and walks away.

I'm sitting with Joan at a diner downtown, going over some new projects for her site. We've been here for over an hour, devouring burgers and fries and have now moved on to milkshakes. Joan is dressed in a fancy pantsuit today, and when I asked about the occasion, she said, "This is a work lunch, isn't it?" She never fails to make me laugh. "How did you know Dave was the one?" I ask Joan suddenly.

"Hm? Dave? Oh, that was easy. I didn't even have to question it," she replies.

"Why does it seem to happen that way for everyone else?"

"Everyone else?"

"Well, you and Maddie. You fell in love quickly and easily, no doubt."

"Oh, dear, are things not going well with the handsome Jensen?"

"They are fine. Mostly. He has a side to him that I'm not sure I like much."

"Hmm. Well, not everyone is perfect. I'm certainly not. Dave is close but not quite there. I think you just have to find a person that puts up with your flaws and whose flaws are not a deal-breaker for you," she says thoughtfully.

"I'm just not sure, I feel that spark. I feel like I'm convincing myself to like him. I'm kind of tired of constantly trying to prove myself. I'm trying to prove to my parents that I can be successful. I'm trying to prove to my clients that I'm good at what I do. I'm trying to prove to Jensen that I like him. It's exhausting."

Joan reaches across the table and puts her hand on mine.

"My sweet Jenna; if those people don't believe in you, then they aren't worth your time. It's a hard lesson to learn, but your life will be much better when you do."

The bell dings as the door opens and I look up to see

Oliver walk in. My cheeks flush as I watch him walk to the counter. Joan follows my gaze and smiles, turning back to me. "Who is that?"

"A friend."

She smirks at me and raises her eyebrows. Oliver grabs a bag from the waitress, turns, and sees me. He pauses, and Joan waves. He smiles politely until Joan continues to wave, gesturing for him to come here.

He runs his hand through his hair as he walks toward us. My stomach squirms the closer he gets, even though he avoids my eyes. "Hello Jenna," he smiles at me quickly, then turns, "And Joan. I'm a big fan."

"This is Oliver," I stammer, my voice sounding shakier than I want.

"Oliver! So nice to meet you! Jenna and I are doing some work here on my website," Joan says.

"Jenna is very good at what she does," he smiles. He's talking to Joan but glances quickly at me as he speaks.

"She really is!" Joan gushes.

"I actually wanted to discuss the logos with you," I interject.

He turns and looks at me now, his blue eyes unreadable.

"Yeah," he runs his hand through his hair again, there's a hesitation and then he asks, "Are you free tonight?"

I look at Joan, "Uh yeah, we don't have much left here."

"Okay, great. Come by the bowling alley around 8?"

"Sure, I'll be there."

"Really great to meet you," Oliver says to Joan before he turns and walks out the door.

I show up at the bowling alley right at 8 o'clock and Oliver is at the counter waiting for me. I feel nervous seeing him. Things were good after we talked in the car and I thought it would all go back to normal, but I feel so uneasy after he blatantly avoided me the other night. It's the first time I've actually felt nervous around Oliver. Usually, he's so good at making me feel comfortable.

"Alright, Jenna. Let's see what you've got for me," he says, leaning across the counter as I lay out different papers with logos sketched on them.

"Okay, I have a bunch of different ideas here. Please be honest and tell me what you like or don't like," I say. My hands shake a little as I put the papers down.

Oliver looks at my hands and then up at my face. I don't know why I'm so nervous. I've pitched logos a lot, but my stomach tightens with nerves as I watch Oliver look at each page. He nods and makes some noises under his breath as he looks at each one. He grabs two of them, the one that was inspired by Jensen's drawing and the one that I like with the minimalist lines and silhouette.

"These two are my favorite," he says, looking over them. "But I like this one more." He holds out the one that I like with the silhouette. "What are your thoughts?" he asks.

"That one is my personal favorite," I reply, pointing at it.

"Me too. I like the minimalistic style a lot. It's simple but effective."

I'm secretly happy that he didn't choose the one that Jensen inspired. Jensen has absolutely nothing to do with this logo. It was all me and my idea, it's just another way to remind myself that I can do this.

"Great! I can take this and design it on the computer

for you. Then we can do some other fun things with it."

"Thank you," he replies, shuffling the papers back into a stack for me.

"So...about last night," I start. He continues to fidget with the papers, not looking at me.

"You were here. You saw me," I say.

"I was, yes."

"But you didn't want to talk to me."

He stops fidgeting with the papers and looks straight at me. His blue eyes stare at me so intensely, that it's hard for me to look back at him. His jaw muscles tense and he says, "I couldn't."

"Why?"

"I just wasn't ready," he continues gazing at me.

I don't know what to say, my heart is pounding in my ears. His gaze is so strong that I want to look away but also can't. He slowly smiles at me and says, "You looked phenomenal though."

My cheeks instantly flush pink. "Thank you."

"I'm assuming you were going on a date?"

I nod, and he frowns.

"I thought so," he says. "Why did you come here then?" he asks bluntly, staring at me.

"I wanted to apologize for the other night at my house with Jensen."

"Why are you apologizing?" his face is unreadable as he leans closer to me.

"For Jensen. He was being rude."

"You shouldn't have to apologize for someone else's behavior," he replies simply.

"Yet, here I am," I mumble, laughing at my own expense.

He purses his lips and stands up straight again. "I

appreciate the apology, although it's unnecessary."

He busies himself behind the counter and I look around the alley. There are lots of people here tonight, and the energy is high. Yet, sitting here with Oliver feels like it's just the two of us.

"Olivia showed me the sticker you made," he says suddenly.

"Oh yeah, that was just a fun little thing," I reply breezily.

"Well, it's really cool. Have you ever thought about selling them?"

"Not really."

"It could be a great thing to add to your business. You can make custom ones or just a bulk supply of other ones. Stickers are kind of a big deal right now."

"Yeah, that's a great idea. I have a bunch of designs actually that I could use."

"I would love some for the bowling alley as well. I can put them on the counter here for people to purchase," he suggests.

"Thanks. That's really nice of you," I reply.

He throws me a smile over his shoulder as he continues to mess with the shoes and supplies behind the counter. I watch him for a few minutes in silence as he walks around tidying up. He checks the computers and reads through some papers. He has an ease in the way he handles all of this. It makes me wonder if it's always come so easily to him or how hard it was initially. It's so impressive for me to look at this bowling alley with the new knowledge that he did it all himself. I imagine him painting the walls and putting together all the new tables and chairs. I think about the late nights he said he had to have and imagine him and Olivia laughing while working. I look over now to see him chatting with a group of customers at their lane. They are laughing at something he says, and his eyes crinkle as he laughs with them. One of the guys pats Oliver on the back and pulls him closer.

A few minutes later, Oliver walks back to the counter, shaking his head a little and still laughing. He looks up and sees me, he looks surprised.

"You're still here." It's more of a statement than a question.

"Is that okay?" I ask.

He shrugs, "Not like I own the place…" he smiles and says, "Oh wait."

I laugh, and he smiles at me. "You have a great laugh," he says, a softness in his eyes as he looks at me. I feel my stomach flutter and open my mouth to say thank you, but he has already turned to work on something else.

"You've done a great job with this place," I say, gesturing around. "Now that I know all that it took, it really is amazing to see it."

"Thank you."

Oliver is still making himself busy, obviously not in the mood to talk to me so I stand up to leave. He immediately stops and looks up. "Do you want to see something?" he asks suddenly.

I nod, and he comes behind the counter, leading me through the arcade. An eagerness is coursing through my body as I follow him, wondering where he's taking us. There's a door leading to a storage room in the back wall of the arcade. When he turns the light on, I see it's full of boxes.

"What's all this?" I ask, looking closer.

"Stuff that Johnny left behind. I haven't had much

time to go through it since I've been focusing on fixing up the place. But now that things have settled down a bit, I started looking through it. A lot of it is old paperwork, random receipts, things like that. I did find a box of old photos though," he replies, walking over to one of the boxes.

He opens it and I see stacks of photos. The one on top is really old. It's black and white and shows a team of middle-aged men holding a trophy and cheering.

"That's Johnny," Oliver says, pointing to the guy in the middle. "He was in a bowling league before he owned the place. He said winning that tournament is what made him decide to purchase it."

"Wow." I lean in closer and try to ignore the heat that instantly flares inside me as my arm brushes against Oliver's. Johnny looks so happy in the picture. He has one hand on the trophy, his face completely lit up in a cheer, and his team is all wearing classic bowling shirts.

"This is really cool," I say, looking up at Oliver.

"Yeah, I'm going to put together a little display case for some of these photos from throughout the years. I started going through them and look what I found." He flips through a few more photos and pulls one out.

It's of Maddie and me when we were 12. I gasp and lean in closer. "No way!" I breathe out.

"Yeah, it took me a minute to recognize you, but that's definitely you," he chuckles.

I laugh with him. "I'll try not to take offense at that!" I reply.

My 12-year-old self is smiling big with braces, pigtails, and a regrettable outfit choice. We have our arms around each other, smiling wide.

"Johnny got really into photos for a while there. He

has photos of a lot of customers from back then."

"This is incredible. I don't even remember it. I mean, we were here so much I'm not surprised."

I pull out my phone, "I have to take a picture of this and send it to her!"

He laughs and hands it to me, "Okay, but I'll need it back," he smirks.

Oliver starts digging through the rest of the photos and I lean closer to him, our elbows brushing. He doesn't pull away this time. The hours quickly pass by as we move from one box to another, sitting on the floor together and laughing at old photos. We find one of Oliver and Johnny when he first bought the place. Oliver looks younger, and sadder. I can see the pain in his eyes, even though he has a smile. He looks tired, worn down.

"This was when everything started to change," he says, looking down at it. "It finally felt like I wasn't drowning. I actually had an idea of what I wanted to do with my life."

"You never told me how your parents reacted to it all."

"My dad isn't and wasn't around. He left when I was 12. It's the typical cliche, really. He cheated on my mom and left. And my mom, well, she's an angel. She supported me 100%. She helped me through physical therapy, and when that wasn't enough, she helped me with all the logistics of buying this place."

"She sounds great," I reply. Then after a pause, it clicks, "Wait, you were 12? Isn't there a 12-year gap between you and Olivia?"

"Yup. The piece of trash left even though he knew she was pregnant." Oliver replies.

"Wow. That's horrible."

He nods, pursing his lips. "I'll never be that guy," he

says aloud. I'm not sure if he's saying it to himself or me. But I answer anyway, "Of course not."

I reach out and put my hand gently on his knee. I feel his leg tense up at my touch. He puts his hand on mine. It's warm and comforting and I look up at him. He's looking at our hands and slowly looks up to meet my gaze. He stares back at me for a moment, sighs, and pulls his hand back. He runs it through his hair as he looks around the room, a small smile growing on his face.

"What?" I ask.

He looks at me again and smiles, "I'm just glad you're here."

My heart skips a beat. "Me too," I say. It comes out more like a whisper.

16

We spent hours going through the rest of the boxes. Some were full of photos and some full of junk. We even found the old trophy from the photo of Johnny and his team. He put those to the side, promising to display them out front. I stayed around to help him lock up and then I headed home. I was too excited to sleep so I got started on the work that Joan needed. I got most of it done and slowly got started on Oliver's logo. By the time I got to sleep, it was 3 in the morning.

When I awoke I started feverishly working on Oliver's logo again. I got a lot of it done last night and I'm eager to finish it and show him. My phone vibrates and I look down to see a photo from Oliver. My heart beats fast as I open it. It's a picture of Olivia, holding up her notebook with my sticker smack in the middle of the cover.

She's obsessed and says her friends are too. They all want one now. Time to get started on your stickers!

My heart soars at his words and the picture and I find myself staring at the photo and smiling.

"Who's that?" my mom asks.

I hadn't even heard her come into my room. She's peering down at my phone.

"Oh, her name is Olivia."

"She's cute. How do you know her?"

"She's my friend's sister. I made that sticker for her," I

show her.

"That's nice. I actually wanted to discuss that with you," she replies.

My body tenses at her words and I prepare myself for whatever she's going to say next.

"Do you remember Tommy? From the cocktail party?" she starts.

I nod, confused by where she's going with this.

"Well, he actually took your little joke seriously about designing his book cover."

I raise my eyebrows as she continues. "I know you've never done anything like that before. And I told him that. But, he would like to chat with you about it."

"I would love to!" I exclaim, excitement bubbling in me.

She nods, "Okay. I'll send him your number and he'll reach out."

"Thanks, Mom."

She nods again and walks out of the room.

I instantly start researching book designs, information on Tommy, and any advice I can find about pricing. The rest of the day is gone before I know it. I'm just getting out of the shower and into my PJs when I hear my phone ding.

Can I see you tonight? It's from Jensen.

I'm exhausted. Let's do another night.

I'm leaving town tomorrow and want to see you before I go. He replies.

Oh yeah! Your first business trip! So fun!

Aren't you going to miss me?

Of course.

Then come out with me tonight!

I don't want to tonight. I'll see you when you get back.

Send me fun pictures from Miami!

I'll try. See you when I get back Thursday?

Deal.

Maddie comes over the next day for a pool day. We spend the morning lying out and talking about her visit with Ben and my trip with Oliver. She's already heard most of the details from me but loves to make me relive it. I tell her about the other night at the bowling alley, and we laugh again at the picture of us as kids. Being with Maddie is easy. It feels like I'm a kid again and I can trust her with any of my thoughts and feelings.

"That was so long ago!" she gushes, looking at the photo again.

"We've been friends for a long time," I reply.

"And we've been going to that bowling alley for so long, it's surprising we never met Oliver before now!"

"He says he was there a lot too. I'm sure we crossed paths."

"Well, we already know you did at least once," she says, nudging me gently.

"I can't believe that was him," I say quietly. "I remember that whole conversation so well. My whole childhood, I was constantly told to not overreact, to not be sensitive, and to not make such a big deal out of things. I felt like I was just always pushing my feelings to the side and never allowing myself to feel deep emotions. And then in one night, he just speaks right to my soul and says people have no right to judge my feelings."

Maddie is looking at me as I talk, her eyes look sad but she's smiling.

"What?" I ask, realizing I was just rambling

"It's just, I feel really bad if I ever added to those

feelings or ever made you feel that way." she starts, then pauses and adds, "But it's really cute to hear you talk about Oliver like that."

"Oh," My face feels hot, and I say, "Well, I'm not really talking about Oliver."

"Except he is the one that said it to you."

"Yeah, anyone could have said it though."

"But no one else did. It was Oliver," she points out.

I stay quiet, thinking. I remember that night perfectly. It's like a sense memory every time I go into the bowling alley. I remember noticing how blue his eyes are, how they crinkle when he smiled at me, and how his words seemed to be exactly what I needed to hear. I remember it all. The words have been something that I've tried to remind myself of over the years. I'm allowed to feel my feelings. I've thought that during fights with my parents. I've thought that during breakups with boys. I've thought those words during so many moments over the last four years. Whenever I've struggled to feel worthy of my feelings, I've tried to remind myself of those words. My feelings are valid. Oliver's words have guided me through so many big things in my life, and it's strange to think that now he's an actual part of my daily life.

I finish up the logo for Oliver over the next few days and send it off to him. He assures me he loves it, and he raves about my talent for a solid five minutes. He's already ordered a new sign for the bowling alley and wants to do a special unveiling for me. Jensen is still out of town. He's texted me a few times though. One of the texts is a picture of him on the beach with some of his coworkers.

He's shirtless and tan, laughing with two other guys and a woman. I send him a flirty text back about missing his body, and he replies that I'm getting him too excited to come back. It's fun to text back and tease him a little. He says I'm driving him crazy and he wants me. It makes me feel a little giddy hearing how badly he wants me. I enjoy feeling wanted, probably more than I should.

Thursday finally comes, and I'm meeting up with Jensen at a bar tonight. I feel excited as I get ready to see him. This is new for me, for us. Maybe all we needed was a little time apart. I put on a bold lipstick and my black leather leggings. I find myself ready early and eager so I decide to go to the bar to wait for him. As I walk past the window, I stop, surprised to see Jensen already inside. He's in a tight white button-up shirt, and he's at a table with the woman from his picture. She's gorgeous. She has thick curly brown hair, large almond-shaped eyes, and she's wearing a tight dress to show off all her curves. They are laughing and drinking together. As I'm watching, she reaches over and unbuttons one of the top buttons of his shirt. My mouth drops open as I watch. I hesitate outside and watch them continue to laugh, her hand lingering a little too long. I push through the door and walk straight to them.

Jensen turns and sees me, a big smile plastered across his face.

"Jenna!" he says, wrapping me in a hug.

"Hi," I reply tersely, looking at the woman.

"I'm Mary," she says, flashing me a perfectly straight, white smile.

Mary. It dawns on me. This is his new manager.

"I was just telling him that he needs to loosen up when he's not working," she giggles, pointing at his shirt.

He now has the top two buttons undone, and he chuckles. "I mean, if you've got the body, you should flaunt it," she says, looking at his chest.

Jensen laughs again, "You're too kind, Mary," he replies.

I look between the two of them for a second and then perch on a seat.

"So how was the trip?" I ask.

"Oh, it was so fun! I mean, we had to work during the day obviously, but we had one beach day and also got to go out every night!" Jensen raves.

I nod, "That sounds fun."

"Yeah, we had adjoining rooms and the boys kept me up allllll night," Mary says laughing.

I look back at her, scrutinizing her face. She has to know how that sounds, right? Was she trying to get under my skin? Instinctively, I feel myself scoot a little closer to Jensen.

"We were playing video games," he clarifies, looking at me.

"Right," I reply tersely.

"So are we staying here? Or should we go somewhere else?" I ask, looking around.

"Yeah, I thought it might be fun for you to meet some of my coworkers."

I look around for the others. "Are the guys here that went with you?"

Jensen looks at his watch, "Pete should be here by now."

"Oh, he's not coming. Didn't he tell you?" Mary interjects.

"No, I guess not." Jensen shrugs.

"Sounds like Pete," Mary laughs, and Jensen joins in.

My stomach squirms uncomfortably at their ease and

comfort with each other.

"I need a drink," I say.

◆ ◆ ◆

"That was fun," Jensen says, holding my hand as we walk back. Two hours of watching Jensen and Mary giggle and joke about Miami isn't exactly what I would call fun. The more Mary drank, the more handsy she got too.

"I'm glad you had a good time on your trip."

"I missed you though," he says, using my hand to pull me in closer to him.

"Yeah?"

"Definitely. And you flirting with me, oh that just made me crazy. I wanted to come home and kiss you right then," he says, sounding eager.

"Well, maybe you should have," I tease back.

He pulls me in close and kisses me, his hands running down to my waist. I try to focus on this moment, but my mind is still at the bar where I just spent over an hour watching Jensen and Mary laugh and tease each other.

"Jensen," I say, pulling back.

"Hmm?"

"Why was Mary there tonight?"

"Huh?" he pulls back all the way and looks at me, confused.

"You didn't tell me she was coming and when I came in, she was fondling your shirt."

He chuckles, "Fondling? She told you she was just joking about my outfit."

"It was kind of weird behavior for your manager."

"Are you jealous?" he asks, the corner of his mouth turning up like he's a little proud.

"I think it's kind of a double standard."

His smile disappears. "A double standard? How?"

"You go on a trip with Mary and out to drinks with Mary and don't think twice about it. But you get mad about Oliver going to New York with me."

"Jenna. That's completely ridiculous! It was a work trip."

"Mine was too!" I shoot back.

"That's not the same."

"Why not?!"

Jensen sighs, "Your job just isn't the same."

I spit out a sarcastic laugh. "Because you think your job is so much better than mine? Mine is a real job too."

"That's not what I meant."

"I am so tired of trying to prove my job to everyone!" I shriek.

He sighs angrily. "Don't take that out on me. You're so sensitive about that. She's my manager. It's not like I had a choice."

"And if you did?"

"That's a stupid question. If you could come instead of her, obviously that would have been ideal. But that's not really an option now, is it? Oliver had no reason to go with you. It's completely different."

"Honestly, I don't even care about your work trip. Not like you did. But drinks tonight? You would die if I ever invited Oliver to come out with us."

"A lot of people go out with coworkers. It's no big deal."

"It's not even about that. It's about the double standard!"

"And I apologized for that," he says, lowering his voice.

"But do you even recognize how hypocritical you are?"

He steps back, hurt by my words. His eyebrows pull together, his anger building. "I am not a hypocrite."

"Prove it. Oliver is going to unveil my logo at the bowling alley tomorrow. Come and be supportive. No rude comments or territorial behavior. Just come and support me."

He grunts, "Fine. That's no problem."

"Great."

We stand looking at each other for a minute.

"I guess I'll see you tomorrow then," I say, breaking the silence.

"Great."

The new sign unveiling is at 7:00 the next night. Maddie comes along, buzzing with excitement about the sign but also a little too eager to see both Jensen and Oliver in the same place. When we pull up to the bowling alley, Oliver is standing outside, holding a ladder and waving at us. The sign is already up on the building but covered with a blanket.

"Fancy," I joke as we walk up.

"I thought it deserved a full presentation," he replies.

Suddenly, arms wrap around my waist and I feel Jensen kiss my neck. I look up at Oliver but he looks away. I think I hear Maddie giggle, but I'm not positive and when I glare at her she keeps a straight face.

"Alright, let's do this then!" Jensen yells.

Oliver looks at him, a flat expression on his face. Then he looks at me and I give him a smile and a nod. He makes a dramatic performance of climbing up the ladder and then pulls off the blanket with a loud, "TA-DA!"

There is a huge white sign, glowing with the logo that I created. My lines, my idea, all laid out in physical form in front of me on a building. It's incredible. I feel so proud to see it displayed. Maddie and I clap and cheer and Oliver whistles. He hops off the ladder to stand by us in the parking lot to admire it.

"It looks perfect, Jenna," he says.

"It's seriously cool!" Maddie agrees.

"Thank you. It's amazing to see it all lit up," I reply in awe, my heart swelling.

"Yeah, babe. It's great." Jensen adds, giving me an extra squeeze around the waist. "Too bad he didn't choose my design though."

I tense up a little at his words. Maddie looks at him, confused, as Jensen continues, "Yeah, I helped her design one of them. It could have been a team effort. I guess she didn't want to share the credit." He chuckles and pokes my side, as if he's expecting me to laugh with him.

I push away from him. "I wouldn't have given you any credit. Even if he had chosen that one." I retort.

"What?" He looks offended.

"You doodled something on a paper. I turned it into an actual design. You don't deserve any credit."

Maddie and Oliver exchange a look and Jensen stares at me, a mix of confusion and anger on his face.

"I didn't just doodle something. I gave you the whole idea."

"Which he didn't even choose."

"So what? I was just saying that if he *had,* I would have deserved the credit."

"I don't like the idea of you thinking you deserve anything. I don't owe you anything."

"Geez Jenna. Why do you do this? Why do you make everything such a big deal? You're always so sensitive."

I feel my whole body tense up at his words. My fists clench and my body shakes. I'm instantly furious.

"Because it is a big deal!" I shout. I see Jensen's eyes widen at me, but I can't stop now. "It's all been a big deal and I'm sick and tired of you telling me it's not! You said it at the bar when you called me your prize, you said it at the seafood place when you were a jerk about the food, you said it after you yelled at me in public and again last night after being with Mary and *all* of those have been a big deal to me! You don't have the right to belittle my feelings. If you make me feel like crap, then IT IS A BIG DEAL."

Jensen stares at me, shocked. I take a deep breath and look at him, "It's over, Jensen."

"What!" he exclaims.

"We're done. I thought you were what I deserved. I thought the spark would come and make up for your flaws. I thought, this is normal, this is how I'm supposed to feel love from others. But it's not normal. It's not right. I deserve more. I got caught up in the affection. I got caught up in the fact that you care so much for me. And I think maybe you do it in your own way, but that's not the kind of love and affection I want. I deserve more."

"Jenna, don't do this. Just calm down and think. This is just a silly fight. We can get through it," he pleads.

"It's not just a silly fight."

"I don't understand..." he starts.

"Jensen. We're done. Don't make a big deal out of it." I say and then I walk past him, leaving him standing in the parking lot stunned.

17

Maddie runs to catch up to me as I storm through the bowling alley doors. My heart is pounding as she's trying to keep up. "Oh my god, oh my god," she's repeating as we finally slow down inside.

"That was incredible!" she exclaims, pulling me into a hug.

I squeeze her back tightly, closing my eyes as I feel the tears well up.

"Are you okay?" she asks.

I nod, unable to form words yet.

"I'm so sorry," she whispers.

"It's okay. I'm fine. I just..." but my voice shakes and I stop talking.

"I know. That was a lot."

I pull back from her and wipe the tears off my cheeks.

"Ugh, I hate this," I say.

"I know."

Oliver walks through the doors now and comes towards us, his face full of concern.

"Are you okay?" he asks gently.

"Yeah, I'm fine. Is he gone?"

"Yeah, he left," Oliver replies.

"I'm so sorry," I whimper quietly.

"Sorry? For what?" Maddie exclaims.

"That was embarrassing."

Oliver and Maddie exchange a look with each other and Maddie rolls her eyes. "Stop. You have nothing to apologize for or be embarrassed about. I've never been more proud. I'm SO glad I was here for that." Oliver nods enthusiastically as Maddie speaks. I chuckle a little and wipe my eyes again.

"You never told me any of that stuff he said or did," Maddie says gently.

I shrug a little, avoiding her eyes.

"Jenna, no guy should ever make you feel like that," she says.

"I know. I mean, I knew it then. It can just be hard to remember, I guess," I say quietly. "I'm embarrassed," I add again.

"He should be the one embarrassed," Oliver replies, his voice sounding angry.

"I think we need to cleanse this night with booze and junk food," Maddie says quickly, heading towards the food counter. I'm behind them a few steps but I hear her quietly ask him, "Did she ever tell you any of that about Jensen?"

He shakes his head, "She told me about a fight before New York, but I didn't know the full extent."

"I hate that he was making her feel that way. And that she believed it was just his way of showing he cared? Ugh."

"Me too."

Maddie peeks over her shoulder and sees me. She throws me a smile and then faces forward and stays quiet. She walks behind the counter and starts to pour us each a drink, Oliver excluded and then grabs a bunch of cookies for us.

"These cookies are incredible," she says with her

mouth full.

Oliver laughs and looks at me, his eyes shining. I down the rest of my drink and pour a refill. I feel Oliver watching me, but I'm not thinking about judgment tonight. All I want is to feel free.

Maddie and I continue drinking and eating until the cookies are gone, and I feel like I'm floating. I don't want to think about Jensen or the future. I just want to make it all disappear with drinks and terrible bowling. We throw the ball backward, through our legs, through each other's legs, and every other wrong way to do it. We laugh and collapse on the floor in the middle of the lane.

"Okay, you two. I think that might be it for the night," Oliver says, coming over to us.

"Ollllllllie, don't be a buzzkill," Maddie giggles.

"I'm not. But it's time to close up and get you two home," he replies gently.

"Booooo, let's go to a bar instead!" Maddie yells.

"YES!" I yell back. I try to stand up and the world spins. "Whoa," I say, almost falling. Oliver grabs me around the waist and gently helps me down to the floor.

"Yeah, it's time to go home. I'll come back for you," he says to me and then helps Maddie up and takes her outside.

I'm lying in the middle of the lane, looking up at the lights. It's quiet and peaceful down here, I think. The emptiness of the alley surrounds me and I suddenly feel lonely. Another breakup for me. I find some comfort in the fact that this one wasn't my fault, but it's still a failure. Another failed relationship. And now I'm alone again. Suddenly Oliver pops into view above me.

"Hey there," he says.

"Hi Olllllie," I slur.

He smiles and grabs my hands to help me up. He puts his arm around me and supports me. It's so comforting to let him hold me. I love the way his body feels against mine.

"You smell goooood. Why do you always smell so good?" I say.

He chuckles and continues to help me to the door.

"I'm ssssorry Oliver," I slur again.

"For what?"

"New York."

"We've talked about this, Jenna. You don't need to apologize. You apologize too much."

"Sorry," I mumble, then say, "Oh!" and start giggling.

Oliver chuckles softly and helps me outside and into the backseat of his car. Somehow he gets Maddie to her parent's house while I'm drifting in and out of sleep.

"Love you long time," she says to me, giving me a sloppy kiss on my cheek.

"Mhm," I reply as Oliver helps her to her front door.

The next thing I know, Oliver and I are standing on the porch of my parent's house.

"You going to be okay?" he asks.

"I'm a grown woman," I say.

He laughs, "Okay grown woman."

I lean in for a hug and feel safe as he wraps his arms around me. "Thanks for tonight," I say into his shoulder.

He rests his cheek softly against the top of my head. "You're welcome, Jenna. I'm proud of you."

I have my hands on his bicep, stroking it with my fingers, "You have pretty arms."

He chuckles and I like the sound of it. "Time for you to go inside," he replies, pulling away.

Oliver stands on the porch until I get inside and close the door. Then I manage to crawl upstairs and collapse on my bed.

When the sun comes through the window, I wake up with a pounding headache. I'm still in the same clothes as last night, and my mouth takes like vomit, although I don't remember throwing up. I roll over to check my phone. I have two new messages. One is from Maddie

I think I'm dead. My head is going to explode.

The other is from Jensen

Please talk to me. We can work this out.

I shut my eyes and rub my temples as my head throbs. I make my way to the shower and stand under the hot water until it turns cold. After taking some Tylenol, I crawl back into bed and sleep away the rest of the day.

"A little old for partying don't you think?" I hear a deep voice, waking me up from my nap.

"Huh?" I mumble, opening my eyes.

Robby is perched on the bed next to me, a smile on his face. I feel instant comfort seeing him here. He's always been a constant in my life and a good reminder that I'm never actually alone.

"What're you doing here?" I murmur, closing my eyes again.

"Well, hello to you too," he laughs. "Mom and dad asked me to come. Mom is getting an award this week for her book."

I grunt in reply. I don't remember her telling me that.

"You didn't know, did you?"

I grunt again in response.

He sighs. "Maybe you should talk to her more about her life."

I sit up a little, fully opening my eyes now, "Why? That just opens her up to talk about mine."

"Fair enough. I'll stay out of it." He points to a glass of water on the nightstand. "Thought you might want that."

"Thanks. When did you get here?"

"A few hours ago. I poked my head in to say hi and you were passed out."

"Ha. Well, I wasn't partying, for your information. I just had a few drinks with Maddie."

"Ah, Maddie."

"I broke up with Jensen," I admit.

He raises his eyebrows. "Oh. I'm sorry Jenna."

I wave him away. "It's fine. He sucks."

He laughs and stands up to leave. "When you're feeling up to it, let's get food," he says as he gently closes my door.

My head feels a little better, so I get up and throw on denim shorts, a baggy t-shirt, and my sunglasses. I feel a little embarrassed thinking about last night. I remember Oliver's eyes on me as I was drinking and bowling and I remember glimpses of him carrying me home and me openly admiring his arms. He doesn't drink because of a horrible experience in his past, and here I am, getting drunk and sloppy in front of him. I sigh feeling embarrassed. I want to apologize to him. This feels like it's becoming a trend.

"Where are you going?" Robby asks as I come down the stairs.

"I need to talk to Oliver."

Robby smiles, a knowing look on his face. "I'll drive," he offers.

We don't talk much on the drive but when we get to the bowling alley, he says, "I'll stay in the car, give you two sometime."

"Thanks," I reply opening the car door.

"But for the record, I like Oliver. He's a good one."

I turn and look back at Robby. I've always trusted him, and somehow, he always knows exactly what I need. "I know," I reply.

It's a Saturday evening, so the bowling alley is packed, and I can't see Oliver anywhere. I wander through the arcade, my stomach in knots as I continue to look for him. Finally, I see the light on in the storage room, and the door cracked open a little. I knock quietly as I peek in and see Oliver looking through a box. His brown hair looks extra curly today, and he's wearing jeans and a tight white short sleeve shirt, his tattoo peeking out from the sleeve.

He smiles when he sees me. "You're alive."

"Ha! Barely. Last night was a lot."

"Yeah."

"That's why I'm here. I wanted to apologize."

He laughs and shakes his head. "You must not remember me saying you apologize too much."

I tilt my head and think. That does sound vaguely familiar now that he mentions it. It's another blurry part of last night.

"Well, still. I'm embarrassed that you had to see me like that. Especially, you know, considering," I say motioning towards him.

"Considering?" he clarifies.

"You don't drink."

He laughs. It's his loud laugh, the one that makes his

eyes crinkle.

"Jenna. I'm not an uncontrollable alcoholic. You don't have to apologize for drinking in front of me."

I look back at him, and he smiles and continues, "It's fine, really. I'm not judging you at all. Unless you decide to drive, that would be a different story. But it's a personal choice that I made based on experiences in my life. You're fine."

I continue to look at him and he looks back at me, his face and eyes sincere. "Okay...I just, I vividly remember you watching me."

"And you think it was because I was judging you."

I nod. He gives me a lopsided smile.

"You don't think it could possibly be because I have a hard time keeping my eyes off of you?"

I feel my face get hot and my stomach flip. I look away from him, fiddling with my hands.

Oliver chuckles lightly and says, "You seriously underestimate yourself, Jenna."

The next week, I'm inspired. I create 50 new sticker designs and list them online, and I pitch myself to 300 companies. I can feel my motivation picking up with each new task I cross off my list and when my first sticker sells, I feel so proud. I get so sucked into my work that it gives me the perfect excuse to ignore the messages from Jensen asking if we can talk. The farther I get away from him, the more I realize how toxic his behavior was.

My mom was honored at the college, winning an award for her latest book. The family dressed up, putting on our best happy faces and supported her. After the event, Tommy and I met up for drinks and discussed his book cover. We bounced ideas off each other and came up with a few rough sketches. Then I rushed home to keep working. I finished three different book cover drafts, pitched myself to more companies, listed more stickers, and barely came out of my room.

When Saturday morning comes, I hear a knock on the door, and my mom peeks her head in. She sees that I'm awake and working, and she comes to sit next to me.

"Jenna, I wanted to check in on you. You've been hiding in your room ever since your breakup with Jensen. Are you doing okay?" she asks.

I look up from my laptop and reply, "I'm fine, Mom. I've just been working."

"It seems like a lot."

"Yeah, it is. It takes a lot to get going."

"Oh, Jenna. I don't want you to have to work so hard."

"Well, I have to make a living," I deadpan.

"Of course. Yes. I just wish you didn't have to work so hard to do it." She sighs. "How is Tommy's book cover coming?"

"It's great. I sent him some drafts yesterday."

"That's wonderful."

"I've never really thought about designing book covers, but it's kind of fun," I admit.

Her lips pull into a tight line. "Should you spread yourself thin like that?"

"I think it's good to have a lot of diverse things people can hire me for."

Her brow furrows at my words, but she replies, "I suppose so. How is Jensen?" she asks.

I look at her, confused. "I haven't talked to him."

"Poor guy. You two were such a cute couple."

"Mom, you didn't really know him."

"I saw you two together though. I can just tell."

I roll my eyes and sigh. "You can't just tell. You couldn't see the fights we had or his controlling behavior. He acted like he was superior to me. It wasn't good and if we had stayed together, it only would have gotten worse."

Her eyes widen in surprise, "I didn't know," she says quietly.

"I know you didn't."

"Why didn't you tell me?" she asks.

I sigh and look back at my laptop. "We haven't talked like that in a long time. Besides, I was easily confused by how much he liked me. I thought maybe that was enough."

My mom's mouth turns down at my words. She looks around the room and then down at her hands. She opens her mouth and then shuts it. I continue typing the email I'm working on.

"I'm sorry, Jenna," she finally says quietly.

I look up at her and her eyes are sad.

"I'm so sorry you feel like you can't talk to me," she says. "I just want what is best for you."

"I know Mom. But we have different opinions on what is best for me."

She nods, not saying anything. She reaches out and puts her hand on my leg. "You can always talk to me. About anything."

"Thanks, Mom."

"I'll try not to be too judgmental," she chuckles. She pats my leg again and quietly walks out of my room.

I promised Maddie I would take a break from work and meet her for dinner, so I pull myself together, get dressed, and meet her at our favorite burger spot.

"You have been very MIA!" she complains as we sit down.

"I know. I've been so motivated with work that I've just been working like crazy!"

"I know, I've seen your posts and I bought one of the stickers," she beams at me.

"You did?"

She nods excitedly.

"I've only sold two so far," I reply.

"Well, one was me," she smiles proudly at me.

"You're the best, Maddie."

She shrugs one shoulder and says, "I know."

"But really. I want to make sure you're good after everything," she adds, her voice softening.

"I'm good."

"I can't believe that guy," Maddie grunts. "Okay, enough about him. Have you heard from Oliver?" Maddie asks.

"Not since Saturday. I went to the bowling alley to thank him and apologize for Friday."

Maddie laughs, "Yeah, good times. He's such a gentleman! Should we go bug him tonight?"

I shake my head, "No, we should leave the poor guy alone." But even as I say it, I feel a pull in my body. I want to see him.

"Come on! Let's go!" she begs. "You know he loves us," she jokes.

I shoot her a flat look and she laughs again, "Okay, well, he at least loves you!" She wiggles her eyebrows at me, and although I chuckle, my heart feels happy at the thought.

Maddie pays for our dinner and pulls me out the door. "We are going to say hi!" she exclaims. I give in, mostly for selfish reasons and follow her to the bowling alley.

When we get there, the open sign is off and the inside is dark. I check my watch. It's only 9:00.

"It's a little early to be closed," Maddie muses as we walk towards the door. "He's probably still here," she adds. A few lights are on inside and Maddie and I lean closer, peeking through the glass. I see Oliver sitting at one of the tables. He's in a nice black button-up and black pants, and he's sitting across the table from a woman. She has beautiful dark red hair and perfect long legs, her short dress showing them off. They are leaning toward each other, looking down at something on the table. The woman laughs and tosses her hair over her shoulder as we watch. I pull back, a pit growing in my stomach.

"Who's that?" Maddie whispers, still watching.

"I don't know."

"Maybe it's a date!" she gasps. I don't reply and she leans back to look at me. My face must have given away my dread because she suddenly backtracks, "I'm sure it's not a date!"

"It looks like a date," I mumble, glancing at the door.

"It could be anything."

"He closed the bowling alley," I say, partially to myself.

Maddie looks around, "Yeah…"

"Let's go," I urge, walking back towards the car.

"Sorry, Jenna."

"It's fine. We're just friends. I keep telling you that," I retort a little too sharply.

"Right. Yeah," she replies quickly.

18

I throw myself back into work. 10 out of the 300 companies I reached out to got back to me. So I schedule meetings with them and get started on some trial projects. If I can book all 10 companies, it will be a great start for me. I use work as a distraction to keep from thinking about Oliver. I haven't heard from him since Friday. I keep replaying him saying he can't keep his eyes off me. Why would he say something like that and go on a date right after? It seems dirty like he knew how that would make me feel. I don't want to play games. Every time I think I should make a move, he proves that I shouldn't. I spend my energy focusing on clients instead and it works. Out of the 10 companies I do a trial for, I book three of them for a 12-month contract.

"That deserves a celebration!" Maddie cheers over the phone after I excitedly called her with the news.

"Dinner?" I ask.

"Something better!"

"What...?" I ask cautiously.

"Midnight swim at the lake!" she exclaims.

I roll my eyes. There is nothing Maddie loves more than a midnight swim at the lake. "Can't we just swim at my house?" I reply.

"Nope. Tonight. The lake. Midnight! Ben is coming too!"

I laugh but agree.

It's the perfect night for a midnight swim. The air is warm and lighting bugs are flying around the woods. The ground crunches under my feet as I make my way to the dock. The mid-summer humidity is hanging heavy in the air, making me eager to jump in the water quickly. As I'm walking to the dock, I see Maddie and Ben are already there. They are snuggling and laughing with their feet in the water, perfectly content and comfortable in their own little world. When Maddie sees me, she cheers and claps loudly, "Jenna! Here she is! The successful businesswoman!"

"Oh geez, Mads," I laugh uncomfortably.

"Maddie told me about your new clients, that's great," Ben offers, smiling at me and looping his arm around Maddie.

"Let's do this!" Maddie exclaims, pulling off her shirt to show off her swimsuit.

Ben watches her as Maddie gives him a little shimmy and jumps in the water. He laughs, pulls off his shirt, and follows right behind her.

As I'm sliding out of my shorts, I hear steps behind me, and I quickly turn to see Oliver stepping onto the dock. He's wearing bright floral swim trunks and a tight tank top that flaunts his muscles. I freeze as he says, "Hey, Jenna."

"What're you doing here?" I blurt, but it's drowned out by Maddie yelling, "Oliver! You made it!"

"Thanks for the invite," he replies with a wave.

His eyes trace from my feet up to my head. The way he looks at me makes my skin feel warm, and suddenly I'm aware I'm only in a swimsuit.

"What are you doing here?" I repeat.

"Maddie invited me. She said we're celebrating your new clients."

"Yeah..."

"I ran into her and Ben earlier, and they were talking about it," he explains, rubbing the back of his neck. He looks uncomfortable, so I quickly say, "You're obviously welcome."

"Yeah?"

"Of course."

He gives me a nod and the corner of his mouth pulls up in a small smile. "It's been a while since I've seen you," he says.

"Yeah, I've been really busy with work."

"Sounds like it's going well."

"It is. I actually started selling some stickers like you said."

"Really?"

I nod, and he smiles, "That's great, Jenna." He looks genuinely happy for me.

"I have some for the bowling alley."

"Perfect, you'll have to bring them by."

I nod. The silence falls heavy between us. We continue to look at each other until I say, "Well, I guess it's time to jump in."

I scream as I launch myself into the water. It's cold as I first hit it, but my body quickly warms up with the outside air. I come out of the water to see Oliver standing on the dock, smiling as he watches me. He pulls off his shirt and my eyes follow down his chest to his abs. He's muscular in a way that makes you want to reach out and touch him. I think back to the night in New York when my fingers were there on his bare skin. I feel an electric chill run through my body. Oliver looks up at me, a look on his face that makes me worried again that somehow, he can read my mind. He flashes me a lopsided smile and then runs and jumps into the water, splashing right next to me.

"Hey!" I laugh, splashing him as he comes out of the water. His curly hair is splattered across his forehead, a perfect curl hanging down in the middle. I have the urge to reach out and brush it away, but I quickly ignore it. He runs his hand through his hair, pulling the curl back. The lake is lit up by the stars and the moon giving off a romantic glow. I slowly relax onto my back, floating on the water. This has always been a feeling of comfort for me; the relaxing feeling of floating on top of the water, free from the weight of the world. The sky is full of lighting bugs glowing above us and Oliver breathes out in awe as he looks up.

"This is nice," Oliver says, floating next to me.

I don't reply, but I feel his hand brush against mine as we float by each other.

"I'm really proud of you," he says quietly. "I think it's amazing that you are doing it all on your own."

"Thanks. You know how hard it can be."

"I do. But I didn't do it alone, I had help."

"I do too. Joan is the one that started it for me," I reply.

"She seems great. I liked meeting her."

"And I have Maddie." I pause. "And you. I really appreciate you hiring me to do your logo."

"I think you're amazing," he replies.

"I'm proud of the logo we created."

"Yeah, that's amazing too."

I smile to myself in the dark. I peek over at him and see that he's smiling too. I allow myself to drift a little closer to him.

"I should bring Olivia here sometime," Oliver breaks the silence. "She would love the lighting bugs and the stars."

"I admire your relationship with her."

"People assume we are close because I'm a father figure when she doesn't have one. But it's not that at all. I don't try to be her dad, I'm just her brother. Her friend. In a lot of ways, she's taught me more than I could ever teach her."

"About space?" I joke.

Oliver laughs my favorite laugh, the lighthearted, joyful one. "Definitely taught me a lot about space!"

I look around and see Maddie and Ben swimming close to each other, farther out in the lake. She wraps her arms around him and he pulls her in close while she laughs. I can honestly say it brings me joy seeing how happy she is with Ben. I'm so glad that she found someone that fits with her so well. I wish I could find that in my life. I make my way back to the dock and wrap myself up in the towel, dangling my toes in the water.

After a few minutes, Oliver joins me. He rubs the towel through his hair and then gives it a shake, sending water droplets on me.

"Hey!" I laugh. He grins back at me as he sits next to me.

"How long have you and Maddie been coming here?" he asks.

I think about it and reply, "Since we were 14 probably. We used to walk the path together all the time, and then one night we snuck out for a midnight swim and we never stopped."

"That's awesome. How are you doing? I haven't seen

you in a while," he pauses. "I thought you needed some time after the breakup," he adds, turning to look at me.

"I'm good."

He raises his eyebrows back at me questioningly, so I add, "Really. Might sound bad, but I feel lighter without Jensen."

"That doesn't sound bad."

A few minutes of quiet pass, and he adds, "I wish I had known how he was treating you."

"It wouldn't have changed anything. I didn't even really see it at the moment."

"It's just- the whole New York thing. It would have been different."

It feels like my heart stops beating at his words.

"What do you mean different?"

"I probably would have handled it differently."

"So...like you wouldn't have stopped?"

I hear him swallow loudly, and he puts his hand on top of mine on the dock.

"I still would have stopped."

I look up at him, and he's gazing back at me.

"I'll never be my dad. Even if the other guy is a horrible excuse for a man," he adds.

I peel my eyes away from him to look back at the water. Maddie and Ben are making out in the water, and I look up at the stars. I imagine how Oliver must feel, and it pains me to think I tried to make him feel like his dad. I would never want to hurt him in that way. I never even viewed it as cheating because my feelings for Jensen weren't there. But I never communicated that to either Oliver or Jensen. I realize that's my fault now. How would Oliver know that I wasn't just like his dad? My heart sinks at the thought.

"What are you thinking?" he asks.

I glance back at him, unsure how to respond, then I quietly reply, "I don't want you to think I'm like your dad."

His eyes open wide, and he quickly replies, "Jenna, no, never. That's not what I was saying. I just meant that I wouldn't have told you to go back to him and figure things out. If I had known how he was treating you, I would have told you to end it. I thought he might be good for you. I thought you wanted him. I didn't know. I wish I could take it back." He shakes his head and adds, "You are nothing like my dad. His whole situation is so far from yours, that thought didn't even cross my mind."

"But you were comparing yourself to him."

He sighs. He runs his hand through his hair and then leans forward on his palms. "I'm always comparing myself to him. In every situation. I just know I want to be different, better than that."

"I think wanting that already makes you different."

He smiles at me, and once again, I'm distracted by how bright his eyes can shine even in the dark.

I lean in a little closer so that our shoulders are touching. "I'm glad you came tonight."

"Me too."

Maddie and Ben are slowly making their way back to us, and we are quiet for a minute as we watch them. They are playfully splashing each other, and then Maddie is jumping on his back and he's spinning in circles.

"Jenna," Oliver says suddenly. I look back at him, and he turns his body to face me, a serious look on his face. He opens his mouth to speak when Maddie interrupts with a loud, "Hey you two!" as she pulls herself up on the dock.

Oliver closes his mouth and turns back to face her. "Hey! Thanks again for the invite," he says to her.

I continue watching him, but he doesn't look back at me or try to finish his thought.

19

I'm suddenly busier than I have ever been. The three companies that signed with me require a lot of my attention. Thankfully I'm already caught up on things with Joan and Townie Brownie. Between meetings with each company and the back and forth of my work, I don't leave my house. My parents have been supportive in the fact that they've left me alone to get things done. Maddie has texted me a few times to check in but mostly understands that I'm on a roll. I'm finally feeling motivated and successful in a way that is new and exciting. Initially, it was a constant worry that I was not good enough. I had the nagging feeling of needing to prove myself. But with each day that passes, I get more confident and comfortable with my work. It finally feels like I'm not completely wasting my time and that there's a future for me.

My phone vibrates, and I glance down, expecting it to be Maddie checking in again. Instead, I'm surprised to see a text from Ben.

Hey Jenna. I'm coming to town in two weeks, and I need your help with something.

Okay...what's up?

I'm going to propose to Maddie.

WHAT! OMG!

:) Obviously, don't tell her...can you help me set up a few

things?

OF COURSE. Just tell me when and where!

I scream and I can't believe it! I'm so overwhelmed with excitement I run downstairs to tell my parents and find them out by the pool, my mom working on her current book.

"Ben is proposing to Maddie!" I blurt out.

My mom looks up from her book, "That's wonderful!"

"I can't believe it! I mean, I can because they are perfect. But it's just crazy," I say, plopping down in the chair next to them.

"They have been together for a while," my dad agrees.

"And he's such a great guy," my mom adds.

"Yeah, they are really great together."

"It's so nice when you find the one," my dad says, putting his hand on my mom's leg and smiling at her. She giggles, and it makes me smile. Sometimes I feel like they get so caught up in their own work and separate lives that they don't have enough time for each other. But I also catch the in-between moments like this. When possible, they work on their individual things while sitting side by side. They still make time for date nights and support each other at work events. I've never actually noticed how wonderful their relationship really is.

"So, did Ben tell you exactly what he's going to do?"

Oliver and I are splitting what he calls his famous fries together. They are normal fries with two different kinds of cheese melted on top, garlic seasoning, green onions, and a drizzle of buffalo sauce. He's leaning against the counter in a casually attractive position that I've really come to appreciate. I came over to the bowling alley after dinner so that I could tell Oliver all about Ben's text.

I was glad that I was right about him being here. There is something comforting in the fact that I know where he'll be. And if this bowling alley wasn't already such a home feeling for me, it definitely has become one lately.

"Mhm. Actually, I was hoping I could get your help," I smile up at him.

He grins back at me and leans closer, "I would love to."

He leans away when Olivia comes around the corner, her nose in a book, but she looks up briefly and gives me a small wave.

"She's having her birthday here tomorrow," Oliver tells me.

"The big 13, huh? Can I help?"

"Actually, yeah. She would love that!"

"Great! I'll be there!" I reply grabbing another fry.

The next night I arrive at the bowling alley early and see the sign that says it's closed for a private event. I step through the door and see the inside completely decorated with balloons and streamers. There is a hint of a space theme with special galaxy balloons, paper stars hanging from the ceiling, and little twinkling lights lining the whole roof. I look around in awe as I walk and then hear Oliver ask, "What do you think?" I spin around to see him hanging up a birthday banner behind the food counter.

"This is incredible, Oliver!"

"Thanks! Let me show you around," he says, hopping down.

He points to the arcade, "All the arcade games are free tonight, including the photo booth, which I think they'll really love." I nod in agreement as he leads me past the arcade and to the lanes. He's walking backward, bouncing in excitement as he shows me around and tells me his ideas.

"All the lanes will be open, but some lanes are special and silly – like this one, you can only bowl backward, and that lane you can only bowl with your non-dominant hand, that kind of thing."

I laugh and continue walking with him.

"Over here, they can create their own ice cream sundaes and I've got all the other food they could possibly want."

"This is awesome. You've done a great job!"

He collapses on the seat and says, "Thanks. I hope she likes it!"

"You even closed down the whole bowling alley. You don't do that very often, do you?" I inquire, hoping that I'm not being too obvious. I told myself I wasn't going to bring it up, but I can't stop myself.

"No," he shakes his head, "Only for things that are really important or if I'm trying to make a good impression."

I nod slowly, avoiding eye contact as my heart sinks, "Right. Makes sense."

"So, where should I put her gift?" I ask, changing the subject. I made Olivia a space shirt, just like she asked me to.

"The present table is over there," he points.

I take my time putting the present down and look around the bowling alley some more. When I hear the door open, I look over to see Olivia walk in. She's dressed in a silver dress with her hair curled. Her face lights up as she walks in, and she shrieks as she runs at Oliver.

"Ollie!"

He laughs and puts his hands up in a ta-da gesture.

"This is perfect!" she says loudly, still turning and looking at everything.

Oliver shrugs in response and humbly says, "I did what I could."

Olivia turns and sees me, "Hi Jenna!"

I smile and wave back at her as Oliver says, "I want to give you my present before everyone else gets here." Olivia holds out her hands excitedly, and Oliver hands her a small, wrapped gift. She rips the paper off quickly. It's a picture frame, and I see her looking at it closely. I step a little closer and see a certificate in the frame.

"You got me my own star?!" Olivia suddenly exclaims.

Oliver's face lights up in reply and Olivia wraps her arms around him in a big hug.

"Thank you so much!" she exclaims, not taking her eyes off it as she walks over to the food counter.

"Well, you just put the rest of the presents to shame," I joke.

"Technically, I didn't actually buy her the star, just named one after her on a website," he laughs. "But I'm glad she likes it," he adds, fondly watching her.

If you've ever thrown a party for twelve 13-year-old girls, you know exactly how hectic it can be. The girls were all having the time of their lives. There is contagious excitement and joy felt throughout the whole alley. Oliver was right about the photo booth being a hit. Each group starts there and then moves to the pizza, corn dogs, nachos, and french fries. Oliver is a hero to these girls. They giggle as he exaggeratingly makes a pizza, dances with a corn dog, and tells them the story of his famous fries. I stand back and watch as he helps pass out food and drinks to everyone. He's so good with them. He's comfortable and loose and fun. More than twice, I hear whispers about how cute he is and how lucky Olivia is. She is thriving at the party. Her face is pink from laughing, and she is genuinely happy being surrounded by all of her friends. I catch her saying thank you to Oliver multiple times and giving him quick hugs and smiles in between activities.

After they eat more than I thought possible, they move on to bowling, and Oliver and I sit down and watch.

"She seems to be having fun," Oliver says out loud.

"Definitely. You did good."

He gives me a grateful smile in return. "I think we've probably got a few minutes, come on," he says, standing up.

I follow him to the arcade. "What should we play first?"

"Skee ball!"

Maddie and I used to love skee ball and whoever won had to buy the other person a candy bar. It was one of those silly but sweet memories that I love thinking about. The skee ball machine is newer and fancier now than it used to be, but the memories and love are still there. After I score two 100s in a row, Oliver stops and looks at me, eyebrows raised. "I think I'm being hustled," he smirks.

"I never said I was bad at it," I shrug, laughing.

I end up winning the first game, he demands a rematch, and he wins the second game. We decide to leave it at a tie and make our way around the other games. Oliver destroys me in basketball but surprisingly, I beat him in Cruis'n Round and Spy Hunter. When we get to the Touchdown game, I stand back and let him take it. Every time, the ball soars perfectly through the circle.

"Should I even try?" I joke.

After one bad throw, Oliver shakes his head at me and chuckles.

"Hey, I don't play football very often," I defend myself.

He steps a bit closer and wraps his hands around mine on the ball. My fingers tingle instantly, and I look up, my breath quickening as I see how close his face is to mine.

"Put your hands like this," he says.

Realizing I am holding my breath, I take a deep breath in and recognize his smell, it has a woodsy undertone.

I pull my arm back and let the ball sail. It hits the edge and falls through the hole. I scream and jump up into the air, he laughs and gives me a high five. Our hands linger together, and he wraps his fingers around mine and starts to guide me towards the photo booth.

"Oh, you want a signed picture now?" I tease.

"One fake touchdown and you're signing autographs?" he replies with a laugh.

"Worked for you, didn't it?"

He barks out a loud laugh. "Ouch. Fair enough!"

We reach the photo booth and he pulls me in with him. It has a small bench inside that causes our shoulders and knees to touch. I feel heat in each place we touch and he looks over at me, giving me his lopsided smile. He runs his hand through his curls in his typical fashion as I press the start button. We stick our tongues out for the first photo, then he gives me bunny ears, and I laugh in the second. In the third one, I make a funny face and Oliver is looking at me, smiling. For the last photo, I lean my head on his shoulder and smile. When the photos print, I see in the last photo that Oliver is looking at me and smiling. Oliver prints off a copy for himself and slides it into his pocket.

As we walk out of the arcade, the front door opens, and Oliver says over his shoulder, "Sorry, we're closed tonight!"

I look over to see a young boy standing in the doorway, holding flowers and a present.

"I don't think he's here to bowl," I whisper, pulling on Oliver's arm.

He turns and looks at the boy, "Oh," his eyes widen.

Olivia comes walking around the corner now. "Kyle?" she asks.

Kyle breaks into a grin, "Hey Olivia."

I pull Oliver away while Olivia walks up and takes the flowers and present from Kyle.

"What do you think they are saying?" Oliver asks, still looking at them.

"I don't know. He looks sweet."

Oliver glances down at me quickly and then back at them.

"She's mentioned a boy briefly but nothing serious," Oliver thinks.

"She's only 13, I'm sure it's nothing serious," I laugh a little.

We head back to the food counter now, but Oliver keeps his eyes on them until Olivia hugs Kyle goodbye and makes her way back to us, smelling her flowers and smiling.

"So, who was that?" Oliver asks with a bit of a teasing tone to his voice.

"Kyle."

Oliver chuckles and says, "Well, yeah. I figured that part out myself."

"He's a friend," she replies.

"He looks like a nice friend," I say, winking at her.

She blushes a little and says, "Yeah, he's really sweet."

We watch as she goes back to her friends and they all gush over her flowers. Oliver is still watching her. I'm unsure how to read the expression on his face.

"Are you mad?" I ask, curious.

"Mad?" he looks at me, his face relaxing now. "No, of course not." He pauses and adds, "Surprised maybe, but not mad."

"Surprised?"

"She just keeps growing up," he says, a sweet look on his face. "It's amazing to watch."

Oliver turns his attention back to me now, and I lean against his shoulder and nod in response.

After the party ends, I stick around to help clean up. Olivia catches a ride home with a friend because Oliver said there was no way she was going to help clean up her own party. I help him take down the decor and clean up the leftover cups and plates.

"This was a great night," I tell Oliver.

He thanks me and continues moving around the alley, popping balloons. As we are cleaning up, I notice one of the lanes is dark but still has pins standing.

"Hey Oliver, that lane is broken," I point out.

He walks over to it and presses the reset button. He waits a few minutes, but nothing happens.

"I'll probably have to go back there to fix it," he says.

"I'll come with you," I offer, looking around the empty bowling alley.

He gives me a funny smile and then a nod to follow him.

He leads me behind the pins and I smile,

remembering when I was here at the beginning of the summer. Oliver finds the broken one and starts fiddling with it.

"Sometimes this gets stuck," he explains, leaning over to turn something.

I look around the back. It's dark, with just a little bit of light coming from behind the pins.

"Is there a light? I can turn it on," I offer.

"It's fine, I just need to tighten this back on."

"That should fix it," he says, standing up. He steps back and turns, putting us face to face.

We are only inches away and suddenly, I realize how warm it is back here. Neither of us move as we stand inches from each other. Oliver is looking down at me, his breathing heavy. I swallow and realize how loud it sounds in the quiet. I bite my lip and see Oliver's mouth open, he's still gazing down at me. Slowly he moves his hand up and his fingertips gently move across my cheek and to my neck. My cheek flushes under his thumb. Suddenly he moves forward, closing the space between us. His lips are soft and gentle against mine. My heart starts racing, completely caught up in the way his lips feel. I step even closer, bringing our bodies together. His other hand wraps around my lower waist, holding me close to him.

When he pulls back, my lips are tingling, and my breath is shaky. He holds me close, still looking down at me. I hold his gaze and he smiles. My stomach flips, then he whispers, "Well, that was amazing."

I laugh a little in response.

He leans close again and I meet him halfway this time. Both of his hands slide down my back and land on my waist. My body reacts to his, tingling in each spot his hands pass. It feels like I can't catch my breath, my heart racing. Time seems to blur past for minutes or hours, I'm not sure, until we finally pull apart and Oliver gives me a big smile.

"This wasn't exactly how I planned this," he chuckles, looking around us.

"You were planning it?" I tease.

He smiles sheepishly back at me and says, "Not back here, I wasn't. Maybe something more romantic." He slowly drags his hand down my arm and puts his hand in mine.

"I think this is pretty romantic," I reply.

He chuckles and shakes his head, "Of course you do. That's why you're so great. Well, that and your determination."

A smile spreads across my face at his words. It feels so good to hear someone recognize how hard I work.

He walks me to my car, his hand never leaving mine. When we stop I turn and look up at him, "so can I cash in that rain check from four years ago?"

Oliver's face breaks into a wide grin. "Yeah, I think you better."

I clear my throat, "Hi, my name is Jenna and I wondered if you'd like to go on a date with me?"

"Yes. I really would," Oliver replies gently, leaning down to give me a soft kiss.

20

When I wake up the next morning, I check my phone first thing and smile when I see a message from Oliver.

Olivia wants me to let you know she loves your present. That was really sweet of you.

Then another message.

And I had a really great time last night.

A smile is stretched across my face, and I bite my lip to try and contain it. I let out an "eek!" and jump out of bed. I can't remember the last time I felt this giddy about a boy. It's only been 12 hours, and I already want to see him again. And I definitely want to kiss him again. I look at the picture of us from the photo booth, and it feels like a lifetime ago. That kiss changed everything. It was an instant switch for me. Of course, I had thought about it the past month, but that kiss surpassed any thought I actually had. The connection was instant. I felt a spark! For the first time, my whole body felt that undeniable spark! And it was amazing. I long to see him again. I've had this desire before, wanting to see him. I've gone out of my way to go to the bowling alley only to see him. Like when I tried to go with Maddie, and he was with that woman. That woman. My heart sinks, remembering it. Why is he kissing me if he's shutting down the bowling alley to be with her? What did he say last night? He only does that for special occasions or to try and impress someone. The excitement is fading now. What about the whole story about his dad? I thought he never wanted to be anything like him. I pull on my favorite green short jumpsuit and slide my feet into sandals. My hair is holding on to its curl from yesterday, so I give it a quick brush and decide to talk to Oliver.

The bowling alley is quiet this morning. No customers are here yet, but the lights are on and the door is unlocked. I look at the arcade as I pass but don't see Oliver. He's not at the food counter or out on any of the lanes. There's an office behind the counter that I've never been in. A light is on, so I tentatively walk to the door. It's open, and I see Oliver behind the desk, looking at a paper. I knock on the door and he looks up, surprised.

"Jenna!" he exclaims, his face lighting up. I can't help but smile right back at him.

He jumps out of the chair and comes around the desk, moving towards me. I'm feeling nervous that he's going to try and kiss me. As desperately as I want to kiss him again, we need to talk first. His face is gentle, and he seems to read my body language, so he pauses and gives me a gentle kiss on my temple.

"Good morning," he says softly. "How are you?"

I'm wary of the conversation we have to have, but I still wrap my arms around him and hold him tightly. He rests his cheek against the top of my head and I find myself thinking how incredible it is that I can be this comfortable with someone so fast. I suppose it's been happening all summer. We've been slowly building a relationship out of our friendship, but the level of comfort I have with him is something I've never felt this easily with a guy.

When he releases me, he gives me a look up and down.

"You look amazing as always."

My stomach squirms at his look and words but I ignore it and say, "I actually need to talk to you."

He chuckles, "Uh oh. Those are the words every guy wants to hear right after he kisses someone."

He grips the edge of his desk and leans back, his forearms flexing in a very distracting way.

I swallow and refocus. "I just don't know where your head is at. I saw you here the other night…with a woman." I say carefully.

His eyes widen, and he tilts his head, looking at me. "You saw me?" he asks.

I nod, forcing myself to keep holding his gaze. "Here. But you had closed the place. And last night, you said you only did that for special occasions or trying to impress someone, and honestly, from what I saw, it seems like that's exactly what you were trying to do."

Oliver laughs now. "Is that why you asked me? Trying to figure out about the other night? Jenna, you can always talk to me or ask me anything. I promise I'll always tell you the truth."

I look away now, partly because of the strength of his gaze and partly because I'm a little embarrassed. He pushes off the desk and steps toward me. "That was Cassidy. She's the one that wants to franchise the alley. I agreed to work with her, and we were looking over the paperwork."

I'm shocked now. That was not what I expecting. "You did? You are franchising?"

He nods, a small smile creeping into the corner of his mouth. "Yeah, it's been a little crazy but also really exciting. You kind of inspired me actually. All this work you've accomplished the last few weeks and getting those new clients, made me want to continue to grow as well. So I reached out and accepted her deal. She just broke ground on one in Tennessee yesterday."

"Wow. Oliver, that's incredible."

"Thank you." he says, then adds, "Listen, I'm sorry you misunderstood what you saw. I can promise you that if I was dating another woman, I would never have kissed you last night."

He steps a little closer and gently puts his hands on my hips, "And I am very grateful that that's not the case here. Because last night was incredible," he says softly.

I peek up through my eyelashes at him just as he's leaning down to kiss me. My body melts into his instantly as I pull him tighter against me.

For the next three days, Oliver and I are inseparable. I bring my laptop to the bowling alley and work at the counter, keeping him company while he works. He has a lot of meetings and things to do with Cassidy for the franchise, so I end up taking over the food counter when he has to answer a call. The first time this happened, he returned from his call, surprised to see me behind the counter. He slid up behind me and wrapped his arms around my waist, nuzzling into my neck.

"Is it weird how incredibly attractive I find you in this apron right now?"

I giggle in response, and softly kisses me on the neck and adds, "Thank you so much for helping me."

And that was how the rest of the days went. I've helped when needed, kept him company at the counter and when we both have work on the computers, we sit side by side and work quietly, glancing at each other and smiling. It reminds me a lot of my parent's relationship, which in turn makes me smile and understand them just a bit more.

I'm on my computer now, finishing up a project for the baby clothing company that I'm working with. Oliver makes his way over to the table I'm at and slides in across from me.

"I'm taking off early tonight so we can have a proper date," he says.

"Oh really?" I ask, looking up. "I don't mind being here."

"Which means the world to me. But, I also want to go out with you."

I smile, "That sounds nice. I'll go home and get ready."

"I'll pick you up at 7:00."

I find myself a little nervous as I get ready. Sure, I've spent the last three days with him, and we definitely have not shied away from kissing and touching, but we haven't gone on an actual date. We seemed to fall straight into the casually easy things, and now thinking about a formal date is giving me some serious butterflies. Finally, I settle on a casual short, white t-shirt dress and the black boots that I bought in New York with him. I put my hair in a loose braid and add a black hat.

Oliver knocks on the door right at 7:00. When I open it, he smiles and looks at my outfit. "You look incredible as always," he says in awe.

"You're very sweet," I reply blushing.

He also looks great. He must have added some product to his hair because somehow, it looks a little extra perfect. As he hugs me, I notice he smells extra good, and I think I hear him give a little sniff too.

"So, where are we going?" I ask as he slides his hand into mine, and we walk to his car.

"There's a fun bar downtown that I've been wanting to take you to. Tonight just so happens to be their contest night."

"Contest night?" I ask, lifting one eyebrow at him.

He laughs, "You'll see."

Turns out the contest he was talking about is a hot wings contest.

"Oh, I don't know how far I'll get in this," I say, laughing as we sit down. "And I'm slightly regretting this white dress."

He barks out a loud laugh. "Are you planning to wipe it all over your dress?"

"Hey, you never know!"

"Don't regret it. You look perfect."

A bell dings and we look up to see a large man with a bushy mustache make his way onto a small wooden box. He is exactly what I would imagine the host of a hot wing night to look like. He pulls the waist of his pants up and over his gut with a bit of a struggle.

"Ladies and gentlemen! Welcome to HOT WING NIGHT!" he says with a deep voice into a microphone; the whole room cheers in response. The man continues with a thick accent, "Let me tell ya the rules. The wings'll start off mild, and they gon' get hotter and hotter each round. You only get so much water, so once it's gone, it's gone! The table that eats the most gets their picture on the wall, a gift certificate, and eternal braggin' rights. So unbutton your pants and make room cause here comes the first round!"

Oliver laughs and looks at me, his face full of excitement. The first round is delicious. It's a mild barbecue flavor, and Oliver and I easily eat them. We do well during the second, third, and fourth rounds. I start feeling a little full and worry about being able to finish the fifth round.

"These are spicy!" I tell Oliver as I feel my nose and forehead start sweating.

He nods in agreement but continues to eat, he doesn't seem fazed.

"How're you doing?" he checks in as we wait for the next round.

"I don't know," I laugh.

I'm a little surprised at how much fun I am having with him. My mouth is on fire and I'm constantly trying to wipe my hands clean, but it's so fun being here and experiencing it with him. Oliver has this personality that makes everything fun. I think back over the last three days, working at the bowling alley. Even that was fun. The stolen glances and the sweet sneaky kisses make my stomach flip just thinking about them.

As they drop off the next plate of wings, I shoot him a nervous look, and he returns it with a smile. We barely make it through the sixth and seventh rounds. I can't survive the eighth round, partly from being full but mostly because of the heat. Oliver finishes off what I can't. There is only one other pair now competing against us. They are two large, middle-aged men, and I look over at Oliver, wondering how he's going to do it on his own.

"I got this, don't worry. They don't have any water left," he nods over to them. He's right.

I take only one bite before my mouth burns up, and I shake my head in defeat. I peek over and see another guy on the other team also give up. Oliver continues eating the wings and I slide my water over to him. The remaining man continues to look at us, his face red and checking his cup for water. Eventually, he raises his hand, and Oliver takes one more bite before we are officially announced as the winners.

"I can't believe you did it!" I exclaim.

He smiles back at me, his face sweaty.

"I need some milk after this," he laughs.

The waitress comes over to take our picture, and right as she's about to take it, I smear my finger through the sauce on the plate and onto Oliver's nose. He gasps, looks at me and smears me across the cheek. I laugh back at him, and we hear the polaroid camera snap. The picture slowly develops and we stand close to each other, watching it. I smile as it comes into focus and darkens. Oliver and I are both smiling at each other, mid-laugh. He has a smear of sauce on his nose and I have a smear across my cheek. We pin it to the famous wall and escape to the nearest grocery store for Oliver to buy milk.

"I'm still pretty impressed," I say as we are sitting in the park. Oliver is drinking from an individual milk carton.

"I have a pretty good tolerance for heat," he shrugs. "Thanks for sticking around for it."

"I mean, is there anything more attractive than a guy chowing down on hot wings?" I laugh.

"Oh geez," he replies, shaking his head. "I hope I didn't ruin your image of me."

"You think the image I have of you is good?" I tease.

He bumps his shoulder into me, "I sure hope so."

"Okay, so you handle heat well. What else do I not know about you?" I ask.

"Well, to keep going with the food trend here, I hate seafood."

My mouth opens as I gasp. "Are you being serious?" I ask, squinting my eyes.

"Yeah? I didn't realize that was earth-shattering news," he laughs.

"I hate seafood too."

"Well then, aren't we a good match?" he winks.

"Jensen loved it."

"I knew he was no good," he jokes.

"But seriously, I guess that was the first red flag. He took me out for seafood even though I told him I didn't like it. Then he kept pressuring me to try it, thinking I would change my mind. Like somehow, my opinion was wrong. I ended up just eating the free bread."

Oliver is staring at me as I speak. The look on his face is hard to understand, but I recognize the twitch in his jaw.

"That's horrible," he replies, his voice lower and darker. He shakes his head and runs his hand through his hair.

I put my hand gently on his leg, "It's okay. I'm okay."

"Thank God for that," he replies, looking back at me sweetly. Then he adds, "I mean, not all guys are classy enough to take you to a hot wing contest for a first date."

I laugh and lean my head against his shoulder. After a few moments of quiet, I ask, "Does it weird you out how easy this is for us?"

"No."

I wait for him to continue, but he doesn't.

"I'm not saying I do. It's just a little different from my past," I elaborate.

"Well, that's probably a good thing since those

relationships didn't last."

He leans away to look at me, studying my face.

"What are you trying to say?" he asks.

"Nothing, really. I'm glad it's different. I guess I'm just trying to understand why. I've had the casual easy with guys, but it's always been too easy and casual that it felt more like a friendship, and I didn't care that much. Then I've had the physical desire with the hot and steamy emotions-"

Oliver winces as I say it but lets me continue, "But with you, somehow, I have both. I feel that easy casualness with you that makes me feel safe and still have the feeling of my body craving your touch and thinking about kissing you every second."

His face lights up as I finish speaking. "I like that last part there."

I laugh and say, "I'm serious."

"So am I. I think it's really important to have both. And I feel the same, in both ways. I never thought I believed in soul mates or "the one", but the way I feel with you is so different than anything I've felt before."

I hold his gaze as he talks. His bright blue eyes seem so soft in how they look at me. I continue looking at him, even after he stops talking.

"What?" he looks nervous, "Did I say too much? Did I scare you?"

"No, no," I assure him, sliding my hand into his. "Not at all."

21

I've been more than happy to spend all my time with Oliver but it hits me today that I haven't been as proactive with work. This morning, I check my store to see if there are any more sticker orders. When I click on the orders tab my mouth drops open in surprise. There are 100 new orders! I gasp and scroll through the list. A few of them are requesting custom designs but I'm happy to see some are requesting the girl in the space shuttle. There is one large order of 40 for custom order with their business logo, and I see a message next to the order *I need some stickers of my business logo to sell :)* attached is the logo, and it's Oliver's bowling alley. My face lights up.

I just got my first big order for stickers! I text Oliver.

Really? :) He replies instantly.

Thank you.

Thank YOU! I want to sell them at the counter.

I remember you talking about that. I was hoping to ask you if I could maybe display others people could buy too if they were interested?

Of course. I love it! I want to show them to Cassidy as well, and we could possibly have them in each building!

Are you serious?

Definitely.

I feel giddy again as I put my phone back down and finish working.

It's finally the day of the big proposal. Ben got into town yesterday, and today, Oliver and I are in charge of all the finishing touches. We have to make sure everything is set up by 10:00 tonight.

"Do you think Maddie has any idea?" Oliver asks.

"I don't think so! We got lunch the other day and she didn't mention anything at all."

He grins, "That's great. You know how I love a romantic gesture."

"You keep saying that, but I've yet to see one," I smile.

"Hey, I brought you the turkey club, remember?"

"Ah, that's right. And that's romantic?" I kink my eyebrow up at him.

"We decided it was! Because of the meaning!"

"Okay, you're right. It's not bad."

"Can you tell me some of your other romantic gestures?" I ask.

He feigns shock, "Spill my secrets to you? Not a chance!"

"Oh, come on! I promise I won't be jealous."

"You would be."

I scoff, "I'm not a jealous person."

"Really? What about when you saw me talking to Cassidy?" he shoots back with a grin.

I laugh, "Okay, fine. That's fair."

"I'll tell you one. But it was not with a girlfriend. It was for my mom. The first Valentine's Day after my dad left, I got all dressed up and formally asked my mom if I could take her out to dinner. I even picked her flowers from the neighbor's yard and knocked on the front door. She cried."

I look at him, and my heart feels so full, that I'm not

sure I can speak. He smiles back at me, “Are you jealous?” he jokes.

“Ha, no! That’s just, really sweet.” I reply, squeezing his hand a little tighter, “Especially for a teenage boy,” I add, leaning into him.

He laughs, the deep kind that reaches his eyes and makes me smile back instinctively.

After we finish shopping, we make our way to the lake and start setting up. Ben planned everything himself, and Oliver and I are in charge of setting it up while they are at dinner. We start by lining the walkway with little candles and rose petals, leading to the dock. Ben asked us to get a bouquet of roses for the dock, and Oliver expanded on his idea and got 4 bouquets, one for each year they’ve been together. The last task we have is to light the paper lanterns and send them out on the water.

Ben texts me right on time, and Oliver and I quickly send the last lanterns out on the water and hide in the nearby trees.

“This is gorgeous,” I whisper as we wait.

“It is! He did good.”

The water is lit up by 100 paper lanterns that illuminate the night sky. It casts a romantic glow throughout the trees as Oliver and I huddle in a little closer as we wait.

“Thanks for your help,” I whisper.

He just nods and wraps his arms around me. The cicadas are echoing loud in the trees and the lightning bugs are buzzing around the lanterns. We stay silent, our bodies rising and falling together with our breathing.

Finally, we hear steps coming down the path, and I hear Maddie gasp.

"Ben! This is amazing!" she exclaims.

I smile up at Oliver and pull out my phone to take pictures.

"Oh! Oh my gosh! Ben!" I hear Maddie squeal as she sees the dock and starts to realize what's happening.

I quickly start snapping pictures when Ben gets down on one knee and pulls out a ring. Maddie screams, and I hear her start to cry.

"Maddie, I've known from the first day that you were the one. It's only become more obvious with each day that passes. You are everything I could possibly want and need in a partner. You make me better in every way, and I'm so incredibly grateful that you are by my side. I wanted to propose here at a place so special to you because I know it helped you become the person I love so much. When we were here swimming together, you were so happy and full of life. I knew in that moment I couldn't wait any longer. Will you please allow me to try and make you that happy every single day for the rest of our lives?"

Oliver tightens his arms around me as Ben is speaking, and I feel him place a soft kiss on the side of my head.

Maddie vigorously shakes her head up and down and then screams, "Yes! Yes! Yes!"

Ben jumps up to kiss her and says something we can't hear.

I put my hands on Oliver's arms and squeeze him tightly.

"That was beautiful," he whispers, still staying close to me.

I nod, my eyes a little watery.

Maddie and Ben haven't separated since he stood up, so I whisper to Oliver, "Should we try and sneak out of here?"

Oliver nods in agreement, but just as we start walking, Ben hollers, "Jenna, Oliver! Come on out!"

Maddie screams when she sees us, "JENNA! Oh my gosh!" She runs full speed at me and jumps in my arms.

"Okay, let me see it!" I say, grabbing her hand.

The ring is gorgeous and big. Exactly the ring I would imagine for Maddie and her big personality. It's a perfect fit. She can't stop smiling and staring at it. Ben is standing a few feet behind her, his smile glowing as he's looking at her.

"It's beautiful," I say.

"Isn't it?!" she responds, gazing at it.

Oliver pats Ben on the back and pulls him into a hug. "Congrats, man."

"Yeah, thanks for all your help!"

"Happy to help."

Maddie and Ben tell us to stay and hang out, but Oliver and I give each other a look and decide they can celebrate on their own.

"Are you sure?" Maddie asks for the hundredth time.

"Yes, I'm sure. You two celebrate," I wiggle my eyebrows at her.

I take Maddie out to breakfast the next day to celebrate with her, and she's still over the moon, telling me every detail about last night.

"I mean, I really had no idea!" she gushes. "And thank you so much for the pictures! And the setup!" she adds.

"It was fun to be a part of it."

She happily sighs and looks at her ring. I smile

at her and continue eating my breakfast. Maddie has always dreamed of a big, magical wedding. She's told me many times the kind of dress she wants, although it's changed styles a few times over the years. It used to be a big Cinderella poofy dress, then she wanted more of a mermaid style, and now she's decided on a tight-fitted, elegant dress. Ben says he's happy to get married anywhere she wants, and briefly, she wanted to elope to a faraway island, but now she's thinking she wants to get married right here where we grew up.

"Ben really is the perfect one for me," she says, unable to stop smiling.

"I'm so happy for you, Maddie, truly!"

"One day, you'll get it. You'll get this exact feeling."

I don't say anything and hurriedly take a drink to try and hide any emotion on my face. But of course, she catches it.

"What?" she asks, peering at me.

"Nothing."

"Oliver? Do you love Oliver?!" she gasps.

"What? No. We haven't even been together that long!"

She looks at me questioningly, not accepting my answer.

I sigh and add, "But, I'm starting to understand what people mean when they say you just know."

Maddie squeals, "I knew it! Jenna! You are falling!"

"It's too fast," I sigh, putting my head in my hands.

"No such thing."

I glare at her, "There is definitely such a thing."

"Okay, fine. Sometimes yes, but I don't think this is one of them!"

"It just feels so different with him," I say quietly, almost as if I'm embarrassed to admit it.

I've felt it more and more each time I'm with him. It's only been two weeks, but my body seems to react to him in a way that I've never felt before. Not just physically but also emotionally. I finally understand when people say that it's possible to miss them even if you just saw them. I want to be with him all the time. It's the strangest feeling to be so caught up in my emotional and physical feelings with him that the rest of the world just falls away. It's scary to care this much. I feel vulnerable opening myself up like this. I don't know if he feels the same way I do, and it's terrifying.

"I know. I can see it when you're together," Maddie replies. "I'm happy for you."

"It just seems a little silly." Maddie looks at me, confused. So I add, "We've only known each other this summer."

She chuckles and shrugs, "Who cares? Time doesn't determine how strong a relationship is. The people in it do."

I bite my lip, thinking about Oliver and the way I feel with him. Is it really possible to be falling this fast?

22

"You're here early," Oliver remarks as he unlocks the bowling alley door. I'm eagerly bouncing outside the door in the early morning air, holding a box in my arms.

"I just got a big sticker shipment in, and I wanted to bring them by," I explain, holding it out.

"Oh! That's great! Let's set them up on the counter over there."

He leads me to the front counter and helps unload each pile. I brought spaceship stickers, the bowling alley logos and a few quotes.

"Anything new with franchising?" I ask.

He sighs, "Cassidy is really good about keeping me in the process for a lot of it, so it's a little bit of work on my part. She wants me to come out and see the place once it's built."

"That will be fun!"

"Yeah, it will be surreal to see this place somewhere else," he laughs, looking around.

"Well, it won't be the exact same. It won't have you."

He moves a notebook to the side to make room for another pile of stickers, and I see a sticker on its back.

"Wait!" I say, grabbing it.

I flip it over and see that has one of the first stickers I sold. I peer up with a questioning look in my eyes.

The corner of his mouth pulls up as he says, "Yeah, I

bought that from you."

"When did you get it?"

He rubs the back of his neck and his cheeks flush, "Right when you first started selling them."

"Of course. You and Maddie were my first customers," I say as it dawns on me.

I smile widely back at him and lean onto my tiptoes to give him a gentle kiss. I should have known from the beginning.

"Thank you for always believing in me," I say.

The front door swings open and breaks our gaze.

"Good morning!" Olivia smiles brightly at us. She always has a spring in her step. Her eyes widen as she sees the stickers on the counter and she quickly skips closer, "Oooo, are these the new stickers?" She starts looking through the piles.

Oliver smiles as he moves to the end of the counter to tidy up some things, and I lean close to Olivia and ask, "So, how is Kyle?"

Olivia's face turns bright red as she smiles. "He's... perfect," she replies dreamily.

"Wow. Perfect. That's some high praise."

She giggles, "He really is."

"Do I get any more details?"

"Welllll," she starts slowly. "He's in my homeroom class and he's always so sweet. He brings me little muffins or breakfast bars every day. He did that before he even asked me out. Then one day with the muffin was a note asking me out."

"Okay, kudos to him. That's pretty cute. Sounds like the kind of guy Oliver would approve of."

"What did Oliver say about him the other night?" Olivia whispers, peeking over at Oliver.

"That you're growing up too fast," I laugh.

Olivia rolls her eyes, "Of course, he did."

"He's not mad," I offer.

"Oh, I know. I don't know if I've ever seen Oliver mad at me," she laughs.

"I think he'll just be happy for you."

She gives me a grateful smile and walks over to Oliver. I don't know if they are talking about Kyle or not, but I decide to give them their privacy. I wander over to the supply closet that was full of boxes. When I flip on the light, I see it's mostly empty now. Oliver has finished clearing out the boxes, leaving only two in the corner. It looks like it's full of the things he plans to keep. I turn off the light and close the door, making my way back through the arcade when Oliver meets me.

"Hey you," he replies, pulling me into the photo booth. I slide easily into his lap and snuggle in close.

"How do you always smell so great?" he asks, his lips against my neck.

I feel chills run down my spine, and I choke out, "I shower?"

A low chuckle sounds in his throat, and I know I'm a goner.

We lose ourselves in the gentle touches of our lips and hands. He winds his hands up and into my hair while mine sneak into the back of his shirt and explores the muscles of his back. The photobooth feels like our own little world where we can be together and alone. Until a knock comes on the side and Olivia says, "Oliver, I need you out here."

Oliver sits up abruptly as I try to smooth down my hair. When Oliver pulls back the curtain, Olivia looks at both of us, her cheeks turning pink and she whispers under her breath, "Gross."

Oliver turns around and winks at me before he follows her to the front counter. I collapse against the back wall of the photo booth. My lips feel swollen from kissing, and I can still feel the heat in my face. I know I've never felt this way before. It's equally exhilarating and terrifying.

"So, what were you and Olivia talking about earlier?" I ask innocently.

Oliver throws me a look and replies, "Like you don't know. She told me all about your conversation."

I laugh in response and take a drink of my smoothie. We took a lunch break from the bowling alley and let some of the other workers handle it. I'm always teasing Oliver that he needs to let them handle things more and that he's allowed to take breaks. But he cares about the bowling alley so much, it's hard for him to trust others with it. Even if he loves and trusts his employees. Once I finally convinced him, we walked to a shop down the road and picked up some smoothies. It's a beautiful summer day as we enjoy the sunshine while walking back holding hands.

"She was telling me about Kyle," he answers.

"Mmhm," I take another sip, my eyebrows raised, waiting for him to elaborate.

He chuckles, "And wants us to formally meet."

"Oh, a formal meeting? How 19th century of you!"

Oliver barks out a laugh but then gets serious. "This is the first guy she's ever shown any interest in. She wants to get my opinion on him."

"And?"

"And I think he'll probably be great. She doesn't need

my opinion. She's smart enough on her own."

"One of the best things about your relationship with her is that you don't look down on her. As you said, she doesn't need a dad, she needs a brother and a friend."

He nods. "I know."

I laugh, "So when is this formal meeting?" I ask.

"Apparently, he's coming to the house for dinner on Friday."

"Oh, very formal!" I tease.

"You're coming too, right?"

"If you want me there, I'll be there."

He pulls me closer to his side and replies, "Yes, please."

"When do I get to meet Oliver?" my mom asks as we sit down to dinner.

Most nights, between work and events, my parents aren't home for dinner. Tonight since we are all home at the same time my mom decided to make dinner and have us eat together. It's a rare occurrence but one that I'm trying to keep an open mind about.

"Soon," I reply.

"We met Jensen right away," she points out.

I nod, scooping a big spoonful into my mouth, hoping the conversation will end there.

"That's true. He was a good guy," my dad replies.

"Paul." My mom says sharply.

"What?" he asks, looking up. Then he grunts, "Oh. Right. Not a good guy."

I swallow hard and take a sip of my water.

"Oliver is pretty busy with work," I say.

"Yes, you said he owns a bowling alley?" she asks.

I nod.

"That's really something. You don't hear that very often."

"Is it that old one? Near downtown?" my dad asks.

"Yeah. He's completely renovated the inside. It's really nice," I reply.

My dad responds with a non-committal "Hmmm."

And my mom says, "Must be since you spend so much time there."

I bristle at her words, ready to snap back, but she looks at me and softens a bit, "We'll have to come by sometime and see it."

I give her a small smile in return, acknowledging her effort.

My dad starts talking about work and a big sale he got today. I munch on my dinner, quietly listening. I let my mind drift to Oliver and going to his mom's house for dinner. I haven't met his mom yet, but after hearing stories from Oliver and Olivia, I feel like I've learned a lot about her. The thing Oliver says most is how strong she is. He says he only saw her break down once after his dad left, and after he saw it, she sat him down and told him that it's okay to be upset and show feelings. That was a big turning point for him, he said. As a young boy, most people weren't telling him that it was okay to show his emotions and feelings so to have his mom tell him it's normal and acceptable really helped him. He told me I can thank her for his comment to me my feelings.

Olivia has told me plenty about their mom too. She raves about her and says they are best friends. It makes me a little envious to hear about their relationship. My mom and I have our moments, but it still feels like I'm always trying so hard to prove myself to her.

"Tommy showed me a copy of the cover you made, Jenna," she says now, bringing me back to the present.

"Oh?"

"I think it looks great. You really did a good job!" she smiles at me.

She seems to be trying extra hard tonight, and it's a nice effort. I promise to make an effort back.

Tommy and I had decided on a final book cover after sending it to his agent and publisher. The publisher said she was impressed with my work and was going to recommend me to a few of her other authors. Oliver was so excited when I told him about it he said he's going to buy a copy for everyone he knows. So far, Oliver's support for me has been incredible. I've never had someone full-heartedly believe in me like he does. It's such a new feeling for me. And when I talk about failing, he listens and supports me in a way that helps me feel like it's just a minor setback, not a personality flaw.

Friday finally comes, and Oliver and I are driving to his mom's house. Even with everything I know about Oliver's mom, I'm incredibly nervous. My legs are bouncing endlessly on the ride, and Oliver notices, gently putting his hand on my knee.

"You look nice," he says kindly.

I'm wearing black pants, heels and a flowy blush-colored blouse.

"It took me a while to decide what to wear," I reply honestly.

He chuckles, "Don't worry about my mom. I promise she'll love you."

It's comforting, but of course, he would think that. I've only met one of my other boyfriend's moms. It's different dating in college, you don't meet each other's families, and when you do, it's very casual. But with Oliver, I'm in so deep I don't know how to act. I haven't even told Oliver yet how much I care. I just really want his mom to like me. That's all I'm trying to focus on tonight.

"What else do I need to know about her?"

"Nothing really. I promise. She's very mellow. I think she'll be more concerned about Kyle than you," he laughs.

I chew on my bottom lip, nervous. He smiles at me softly and rubs my leg with his thumb.

I've never cared about meeting someone's parents. Everything about Oliver feels different. The way I feel around him, how I think about him, and now, meeting his mom. I know how important his mom is to him, just in the way Olivia is. I smile now, thinking about Olivia. She's told me a few times how much she likes me. And I adore her. She's such a cool kid. She's confident in herself in a way I wish I was when I was her age.

The car slows now, and I see a small brick house with a porch that stretches across the front. There are a few white rocking chairs there, and the front garden is full of beautiful flowers. I can imagine Oliver's mom rocking in the chairs while Olivia and Oliver play in the yard.

"Here we are," Oliver smiles at the house.

"So this is where you grew up," I say, looking around.

He nods. "This place made me."

As we walk up the front steps, I see handprints on the front step.

"No way!" I exclaim, dropping down to look closer.

Oliver laughs and crouches next to me. There are three handprints pressed into the cement. They each have initials next to them. The big one says P.K., the smaller one says O.K., and the smallest one says O.L.K.

"Your mom, you and Olivia?" I ask.

He nods, a sweet, contemplative look on his face. Then he chuckles a little and points at the baby's hand, "We had to add Olivia's middle initial in so it didn't match mine. After Olivia was born, my mom redid the cement on the porch and had us all put our handprints in it. She told us it was a perfect marker for our new beginning. All we would ever need would be right here, in this house, with the three of us."

I choke up a little at his words and look back at the handprints. I reach out and gently touch my fingers to Oliver's small handprint. It's crazy to imagine him being this young and the sudden responsibility of being the man of the house.

I stand up and slide my hand into his. He looks back at me with the softness in his gaze that I've come to recognize. We step through the front door, and he calls out, "Mom?"

The house smells amazing, and music is playing as we step inside. The first thing I notice is the kitchen to the left is bright yellow. The cabinets are white with glass doors and open wooden shelves on the other wall. The dishes inside the cabinets are colorful and Oliver explains, "My mom loves color. It fits her bright personality."

I see Oliver's mom standing at the stove. She has dark curly hair, just like Oliver, and she's wearing a red apron and swaying along to the music as she stirs something on the stove. She starts singing along, and I notice she has a great voice. She does a little spin and freezes, "Oliver!" she scolds. "I didn't hear you come in!"

He chuckles and pulls her into a hug, "Hi, Mom." he gestures to me, "This is Jenna."

His mom lights up with a smile, "Jenna!" she pulls me into a hug. She squeezes me tight, and I notice she smells like sweet vanilla. "I have heard so much about you," she says still holding me close.

"Hopefully, good things," I joke.

She pulls back and laughs. She looks over at Oliver as says, "Definitely all good things."

Oliver's cheeks turn a little pink, and he steps over to the stove. "How can I help?" he asks.

"Oh, I'm just finishing up. You can set the table if you'd like," she says, going back to stirring.

"It smells amazing," I say as I help Oliver grab the plates.

"My mom is a great cook," Oliver replies.

"Where's Olivia?" I ask.

Right then, I hear a knock on the front door and footsteps come running down the hall.

"That's Kyle!" Olivia exclaims.

I hear muffled talking from the other room, and Olivia and Kyle enter the kitchen. Poor Kyle looks terrified. I give Olivia a comforting smile and Kyle holds his hand out for a handshake. It shakes a little as he waits, and their mom chuckles.

"Oh, Kyle. It's lovely to meet you. You can relax," she smiles kindly and shakes his hand, bringing her other hand to his to wrap her hands around his. I see him relax a little, and Olivia smiles. Olivia is wearing a dress and has on a little bit of makeup. She looks beautiful.

Kyle's face is getting a little bit of color back to it, and he replies, "Thank you, Ms. Kearns."

"Oh, please, call me Patty," she replies. "You too," she

smiles at me.

"Let's eat!" she calls.

Oliver wasn't lying, Patty is an amazing cook. She made homemade fried chicken, biscuits, and macaroni and cheese. As we all pile in around the table, I look around and picture this must have been how it was growing up for Oliver. They are all smiles as they load their plates with food and laugh about the day. I look over at Olivia and hope that she recognizes how lucky she really is.

"Patty, this is incredible!" I exclaim after taking my first bite.

She smiles, "Thanks, dear. Cooking is a fun hobby of mine."

"What are some of your other hobbies?"

"I like to paint, as well."

"Really?"

"Yeah, she painted that," Oliver says, pointing to a large sunflower painting hanging on the wall.

It's a painting of one lone sunflower in a field. The field is a little darker, but the sunflower is glowing bright, and the sky is a bright blue. I can feel the emotion that she must have had while painting it.

"It's beautiful," I reply.

She smiles back at me in response.

"Jenna is very artistic too," Oliver says.

"I've seen your stickers," Patty replies.

"Yes!" Olivia exclaims.

"She does other designs too. I've started selling them at the alley," Oliver adds.

I chuckle a little sheepishly, "What about you, Kyle?" I ask, turning the attention to him.

"Yes, what are your hobbies?" Patty asks.

Oliver gives me a small smile and a light squeeze on my leg then turns to Kyle as he responds, "I like to play sports, ma'am."

"Patty," she corrects with a grin.

"Patty," he says. "I play lacrosse."

"Lacrosse! How fun!"

"He's really good," Olivia gushes.

Kyle sits up a little taller, looking proud.

"I always liked lacrosse. I tried to convince Oliver to play, but he was sold on football ever since he was a kid," Patty says.

Oliver smiles and shakes his head. "Here we go," he whispers to me.

Patty laughs and says, "Oliver has been good at football for as long as he's been alive. When he was only two he could throw a perfect spiral."

Oliver shakes his hand and chuckles more. "She exaggerates."

"I do not. I'm sure I have a video of it somewhere!"

"And, of course, Olivia is the brains of the family," Patty says, grinning at Olivia.

Olivia beams back. "At least when it comes to space!" she says.

Kyle laughs and looks at her lovingly. They look really cute together. That first love is such a pure and special feeling. You can see it all over both of their faces.

The rest of dinner passes with great conversation and I eat until I feel like I could burst. Right when I don't think I could eat any more, Patty brings out chocolate chip cookies, and I realize this must be where Oliver gets the cookies from. They are the same perfect consistency of soft, chewy center and crisp edges. After dinner, Olivia shyly asks if she can walk Kyle home. I step into the kitchen to try and clean up, but Oliver insists that Patty and I sit down and let him handle it so Patty and I make our way to the back porch to watch the lightning bugs. We sit in silence for a few minutes, and I'm surprised by how comfortable it is. Oliver was right. His mom is easy. She's kind and fun and instantly makes me feel comfortable.

"Thank you again for dinner," I say, breaking the silence.

"Oh, you're welcome anytime."

"Oliver tells me a lot of amazing stories about you," I tell her.

She smiles and looks at me, "He tells me a lot of amazing stories about you too."

I feel myself grinning back, biting my lip to try and contain it.

"He's very happy," she adds.

"Me too."

"His last breakup was very hard on him."

I nod, but I'm not sure if she sees me in the dark.

"I'm not sure if he's told you about it," she continues.

"A little, yeah. I know it was after the accident. He said it was a hard time for him."

"Very. Losing his dream and his girlfriend all at once. It was very hard."

I don't know what to say, so I stay quiet.

"That's what is so amazing about Oliver, though. He can take a situation like that and come out stronger, better, and somehow happier. He's always dedicated to becoming better and seeing the positive in everything. He's been that way ever since he was a kid. He finds the good in every situation and focuses his energy on that.

He might bend and crack, but he'll never allow it to break him."

I nod in agreement while she talks, and I think about his tattoo again.

"That's a great personality trait," I finally say.

"Mhm," she agrees, "He's told me how strong you are as well. You have your own design company? That's very impressive. Going out on your own can be hard. It takes a lot of dedication and hard work."

I nod as she speaks, and she adds, "But Oliver says you're doing amazing."

I smile at her words, "He's kind. It's picking up a little. It's exciting."

"I'm sure your parents are very proud of you."

I swallow and pause, allowing his mom to look at me, her eyebrows raising in surprise. "Aren't they?"

"Um, I mean yes, I think deep down they probably are. They just don't say things like that to me."

Patty frowns. "That's a shame. A kid should never have to wonder if their parents are proud of them. I'm always telling Oliver that it's a good thing to share your feelings with others. Communication is so very important."

"That's one of the things I like most about Oliver. You've taught him well," I reply.

She beams back at me in response. "Thank you. That means a lot!"

The back door opens, and Oliver comes out. "Oh, better stop talking about him." Patty teases.

Oliver gives a flat laugh and a playful glare at his mom as he sits next to me.

"So what do we think about Olivia having a boyfriend?" he asks his mom.

Patty gets a dreamy, small smile on her face. "He seems sweet. Like a good first boyfriend for her."

"I don't think my parents would let me date when I was that young," I say.

"You never had a boyfriend growing up?" Oliver asks, raising his eyebrows at me.

"Well, I had boys that I liked but never really a boyfriend. Never one that I would bring to a dinner like this," I reply.

Oliver nods. "My mom has always had an open-door policy. She wants to meet the people we care about." I smile at his words, feeling honored to be someone he cares about.

"They are going to like people and spend time with them no matter what I say. The least I can do is be here for my kids and to meet the ones they choose at the moment," Patty explains.

"Wise beyond her years," Oliver smiles.

"Oh, I've got the years," Patty jokes back.

"Your mom is great."

We are sitting on Oliver's back porch now, snuggled up on the bench seat, his mom back inside. "She really is," he replies. "I'm glad you like her. She liked you."

"You think so?"

"Oh, I know so. I can see it." Hearing him say that makes me happy. I really like Patty. She's so welcoming, and I love seeing who raised Oliver.

"My mom asked when she gets to meet you," I admit.

He turns towards me, a slight uplift in the corner of his mouth.

"And? When does she?" he asks.

"Are you free tomorrow?"

"Wow, so soon!" he teases.

I nudge my shoulder into him, and he adds, "I would love to."

"Okay, you can come over and swim. It will be very casual."

The next morning, Oliver shows up right on time, as always. My mom is in the kitchen, trying to play it cool even though she's been buzzing around the house ever since I told her he was coming over. As I open the door, I see Oliver holding a bouquet of flowers. He pulls one out, hands it to me, and whispers, "The rest are for your mom." He grins as he walks inside and kisses me on the cheek. When we come around the corner, my mom turns and looks at us eagerly.

"You must be Oliver!" she exclaims.

He meets her with a smile and hands her the bouquet. She eagerly grabs it and says, "It's so nice to *finally* meet you."

He throws me a lopsided smile as she emphasizes the word.

"It's a pleasure. Your daughter is absolutely incredible," he replies smoothly.

My mom's hand flutters to her chest, and she gushes, "Aww, aren't you a sweetie!" She looks at me and adds, "I like him!"

I chuckle a little at her giddiness in response to him.

"Okay, mom, we are going to go swim now."

"Can't we chat for a minute?" she asks quickly.

Oliver looks at me, one eyebrow pulls up. I sigh in defeat, "Fine, one minute."

My mom's grin is so big that it makes me happy. "Okay. I hear you own the bowling alley?" she asks Oliver as she places the flowers in a vase.

"Yes, ma'am."

"What made you want to do that?"

"Well, I have great memories there from growing up. When my original life plan didn't work out, I decided to improvise."

"Jenna went there a lot growing up, too," my mom says, smiling at me.

Oliver nods, "Yes, it's too bad we didn't meet sooner."

"How did you meet exactly?"

I glance at Oliver and he's smiling at the countertop, then looks back at me. When our eyes meet, my heart skips a beat, and he says, "I actually met her four years ago when she was with her friends at the alley after graduation."

My mom's eyes widen and she looks quickly at me, "Really?!"

He nods, "Yes ma'am. That's when I first met your daughter. It was a very memorable moment."

My cheeks turn pink and I grab Oliver's arm. "Okay, I think that's enough for now."

My mom looks absolutely smitten with Oliver and disappointed as I pull him away, but she nods and watches us go, her hands still clutched at her chest.

"I think you made a good impression," I whisper as we walk away.

When we get outside, he looks around, "This is fancy," he remarks.

I slide out of my shorts to reveal a black swimsuit, and

his eyes turn towards me. "I like that view more though," he teases.

I swat his arm and roll my eyes. But peek over at him while he pulls off his shirt, exposing his smooth skin and muscles underneath.

"You like the view too?" he smirks.

My cheeks flush and I step closer, nodding my head. I slide up onto my tiptoes to give him a gentle kiss on the lips and then pull away and jump into the water.

We spend the whole day in the pool, splashing, swimming and kissing. When we finally pull ourselves out of the water, we relax on the chairs next to each other. I don't fail to notice how similar this day is to the one I had with Jensen, and yet, the feelings and comfort I have today is so very different. I could get used to this, I think to myself. Maybe it wouldn't be too bad to stay here with him. He's lying on his back, his tattoo and bicep flexing as his arm rests under his head and I can't stop myself from lightly tracing his tattoo with my fingers.

"How's franchising going with Cassidy?"

"Great, actually. They've expedited the building, it's almost done. And she bought another bowling alley that was going out of business and is going to make it one of mine," he replies.

"Wow, so you'll have three soon! That's really amazing, Oliver."

He grins in response and says, "It's crazy where your life can end up. Both of us are really going after what we want. It's pretty great." I smile at his words. Once again, he's showing his support in my dream and I'm so grateful.

"Your mom seems nice," Oliver glances at the house.

"She is. I think she's been trying harder. Lately, it seems like she's been asking more questions and getting more interested in what I want. Maybe she's finally accepting that I'm an adult. She should take a lesson from your mom and know that I'm going to do it anyway."

Oliver chuckles kindly. "My mom learned that the hard way."

"With you?"

"No, no. With her. Growing up, she disobeyed her parents a lot. They had strict rules and she would sneak out to meet up with her friends and boys. It put a strain on her relationship with her parents. In the end, she said she never wanted that strain with us."

"And what about you?"

"What about me?"

"Did you listen to her rules?"

"Of course," he feigns being offended, "Why do you think I wouldn't be an obedient little boy?"

Much to Oliver's disappointment, I have to kick him out because I have work to do and a meeting with Joan later. She's really enjoyed having in-person meetings even though I think it's mostly an excuse to get together. It's made me start to think about the future and where I want to go once this summer ends. I've been thinking about New York. There are so many companies there I can work with, I can be close to Robby and I already know it would be fun to work closer with Townie Brownie. Maddie has tried to convince me to come with her, knowing that I can work from anywhere. It's a very tempting offer because she feels like home. But I think it's better to get out of my comfort zone, and that's why New York might be the best choice. Although, after my afternoon with Oliver, I find myself dreaming of staying here with him.

"So, how are things with Oliver?" Joan asks as we finish up our meeting. I've started making strict rules with her that we can't discuss personal things until the business conversations are out of the way.

"Great! He's really great."

"He is," she agrees. "You know, we saw him at the bowling alley the other day," she adds.

"You did? He didn't tell me about that!"

"Mhm. Dave and I went out a few nights ago and he was there. He's done a really great job with the place. We haven't been there in a while, but after hearing these Oliver stories, I figured we better go check it out. And, I got myself one of these," she smiles, holding up one of my stickers. "It looked familiar."

"Oh, Joan! That's so nice!"

She shoos me with her hand, "I wasn't doing it to be nice. It was purely selfish."

"In a few weeks, Oliver and I are going to Tennessee for the opening of the alley there," I say.

"Really? That will be *special*," she says, a sparkle in her eye.

I kink my eyebrow up at her, "Special?"

"You two, alone, out of town…"

I roll my eyes, "Subtle."

"It's very intimate," she winks.

"Yeah, I'm sure we'll get it on at the bowling alley," I snicker.

She shrugs, "Dave and I have had sex in worse places."

My mouth falls open and I laugh loudly. I shouldn't be surprised by what she says anymore, but she still makes me laugh.

"It's not about the location, it's about the person," I hear Dave shout from the other room.

"He's always listening," Joan whispers with a smirk.

The next two weeks pass by in a blur of work, sunshine, pool days with Maddie and date nights with Oliver. Oliver and I meet up every day, sometimes for lunch, sometimes I work at the alley with him, and sometimes we go out to eat and have formal dates. Tonight is one of the nights that we have a date at the bowling alley. He says I'm low maintenance but honestly, I enjoy being here. The food is good, the atmosphere is fun, and most of the time, we sneak into the photo booth to make out. The idea of being caught just makes it even hotter. Tonight, we are back in the VIP section planning our trip tomorrow.

"Can you believe this will be our second road trip together even though we've only known each other a few months?" I ask.

"Guess I'm just that lucky," he smiles. "But technically, we've known each other for four years."

I roll my eyes, "Those years don't count."

"They do to me."

My stomach flips at his words and I'm not sure how to respond.

"I'm really glad you're coming with me," he adds, breaking our gaze.

"Me too. I can't wait to see what they've done with the place!"

"I hope I don't hate it," he laughs.

Oliver stands up to take his turn bowling and his

phone lights up. I glance down as Oliver's phone vibrates, and I see his background is a picture of us from our road trip to New York together. I pick it up and smile at the picture of us biking together in Central Park. The text is from Olivia.

Fiiiiiiiiine. At least send pics for me.

Oliver makes his way back and sees me looking down at it.

"It's Olivia," I say, quickly looking away, embarrassed.

He smiles at me softly. "It's okay, Jenna. I'm not offended if you look at my phone." He takes it from me and chuckles, "Olivia is mad at me because she wanted to come tomorrow."

Realization dawns on me that he chose me over her, and I instantly feel guilty. "Oh no! Oliver, you should take her!" I insist.

"No way. I want you there."

"But I feel so bad! She's the one that helped you with this place," I reply.

"And she can go see the other ones any time. Opening night, I want you there by my side."

My heart warms at his words and I smile back at him. "If you're sure," then I add, "And as long as she doesn't hate me."

He gives one loud laugh and replies, "Trust me, she blames me, not you."

23

Oliver picks me up early the next day. We have a five hour drive to Tennessee, and Cassidy's big opening party is tonight.

"Should we get some fudge?" Oliver jokes as we start driving.

"I don't think I can handle that this early," I joke.

"How about some coffee instead?" he asks, handing me a cup.

"You're perfect. Thank you!"

It's comfortable to road trip with Oliver again. It has me reminiscing on the drive to New York with him. I find myself thinking about how I felt about him then, compared to how I do now. Both times I noticed how sexy his forearms were while driving, but this time I can also think about tracing the veins in his arms with my fingers the night before. During our previous trip, we sang along to the songs, but this time, his hand is on my leg, tapping along to the beat. And of course, just like last time, we have to stop and take a picture in front of a giant reflective bird statue, but this time, we take a picture of ourselves kissing in front of it. I happily post it online, and Maddie instantly comments: OKAY YOU TWO!

We wind our way through the mountains and when we come out the other side, we arrive in the small Tennessee town where the alley opening is.

"Let's go to the hotel and get ready," Oliver suggests.

My stomach flips when I realize we've never discussed the room situation at the hotel. Does he assume we are sharing a room? Did he get two rooms? Am I supposed to pay for my room? I look over at him nervously, but he's looking out the road, drumming along to the music. We reach the hotel and carry our stuff inside to check-in.

"Room number 113," she says, handing over a key. She is smiling a little too friendly at Oliver and glances at me with a cold look. Oliver smiles kindly and turns to me. I gulp as he looks down at me, and an understanding finally seems to dawn on him.

"One room is okay, right?" he asks. "I shouldn't have presumed. I'm definitely not expecting anything. We can get you your own room if you want," he quickly adds.

I grab the key from his hand and smile, "One room is fine." I can't help but throw a smile at the hotel clerk.

The room is big and has one large fluffy, white bed, one small loveseat, a large TV, and a beautiful bathroom with a jacuzzi tub.

"Wow," I say. "This is nice."

"Business expense," he winks at me.

"I'm going to clean up and get ready for tonight," I say.

He nods and plops down on the bed, his hands behind his head. "Take your time!'

The bathroom has a rain shower for that more luxurious feel. It feels wonderful and I try not to think about the fact that I'm naked with only a door and a wall separating me from Oliver. I've never once felt pressure or disappointment from Oliver. He's happy to simply cuddle on the couch with me. But I do find myself aching for him in a way I've never felt before.

After I hop out of the shower, I call to Oliver, "Do you need to take a shower?"

"Is that an invite?" he laughs.

My cheeks flush red, and I quickly say, "No!"

He laughs, "I'm joking, Jenna. Take your time, I showered before I picked you up, so I'll just put on my suit before we go."

Cassidy planned a Vegas-themed night for the opening party and everyone is expected to dress up. I brought a red dress with a low back and a high slit up the side. When it catches the light, it has a black shimmer to it. I curl and pin my hair back, put on my makeup and step out of the bathroom.

Oliver's mouth drops open as he sees me, and he sits up straight on the bed. "Wow." He pauses. "Jenna. You look..."

I blush and smile back at him.

"I'm speechless. You are breathtaking," he breathes out, standing up.

He gently brushes his hand against my cheek and kisses my forehead. "I don't want to mess up your makeup," he whispers. Then he adds, "But I desperately want to kiss you."

My heart skips a beat at his words, and I tilt my head up to bring my lips to his. It's amazing that even after being with him for the last two months, my body can still react like this when we kiss. My stomach fills with butterflies. My knees feel weak and my head gets foggy. The way his lips feel slow and urgent at the same time makes my heart race. He traces his fingertips gently down my back's bare skin and I feel instant chills run through my body.

"This dress is perfect. You're perfect," he whispers

against my ear as he kisses down my neck.

I feel my body react to each touch, and just as I'm about to lose myself, I say, "Ollie, we shouldn't be late."

He hesitates and sighs, "You're right."

He pulls his face back but keeps it close enough that I can feel his breath, "Rain check?"

I smile at him and nod shakily. He looks back longingly at me as he grabs his suit bag and goes into the bathroom.

I feel giddy, waiting for him to come back. His reaction was better than I thought. It seems like everything is better than I thought when it comes to Oliver. I perch on the edge of the bed, fidgeting and eager for the rest of the night.

When Oliver comes back out, he's in a well-fitted black suit with a white shirt underneath and a light blue tie that brings out the color of his eyes.

"Ooookay," I say slowly, looking him up and down.

The corner of his mouth turns up, and he does a slow spin. "You like it?"

I nod and swallow the lump in my throat. It's going to be hard to keep my hands to myself tonight.

Oliver holds open the bowling alley door for me and as I step through, I gasp. It looks exactly like the one back home, except this one is currently decorated with Vegas decor. Oliver's eyes widen as he looks around.

"Wow," he breathes out.

Cassidy rushes to our side, "Hi, hi, hi! I've been waiting for you! What do you think?" she asks, her arms wide towards the room.

"It looks just like mine," Oliver says.

Cassidy claps happily and looks at me.

"It really is incredible," I add.

"Oh good!" she replies. "I wanted to make this one the exact same! You've done such a wonderful job, I just wanted to keep that going! Let me show you around!"

She gives us a tour of the alley, and while it looks the same, there are a few extra arcade games, and there are two fewer lanes, so it's a little bit smaller. After she gives us a full tour, she urges us to get some food and try our hand at blackjack. Oliver orders a fancy Vegas cocktail for me and a mocktail for himself. We make our way to the blackjack table, and after Oliver wins two rounds, I sneak over to the craps table. I roll a 7, an 11, a 7, and a 7. The crowd around me gets bigger the more I win. I actually can't believe it. I've never been very lucky and suddenly I find myself winning.

Cassidy has been floating around the room and introducing Oliver to people. I can see his kindness from across the room as I sit back and watch him interact with everyone. He is so personable with each group. He's funny and lighthearted, and I love the way he can read a person and seem to know exactly the right thing to say. He glances at me from across the room a few times, and my stomach flutters every time we make eye contact. There's something about being able to connect with him, even across the crowded room that makes me feel so special. It feels like we are in our own little bubble, even when surrounded by everyone else.

My winning streak is giving me a natural buzz when I feel arms snake around my waist, and Oliver wraps around me.

"What do we have here?" he asks sexily into my neck, his voice deep and thick.

"Apparently, I'm lucky," I smile, relaxing into him.

"I don't doubt that. Let's see it."

I bite my lip and enjoy the look on his face as he looks at my lips. Then I turn and roll an 11 and the crowd cheers. The excitement I felt earlier is only increasing as Oliver touches me. I feel intoxicated as I turn into Oliver, planting a hard kiss on his lips. His eyes are blazing in response.

"Should you quit while you're ahead?" he laughs.

"One more! Blow on the dice for extra luck," I reply, wiggling my eyebrows at him.

I hold the dice out, and he blows softly on them. I giggle, feeling an intoxicating high watching his mouth. I roll a 12.

"Oliver!" I scold, softly hitting his arm.

He laughs and puts his face in his hands. "I'm sorry!"

I roll my eyes, "You're not lucky! Let's get you out of here!" The excitement is still pulsing through me as I grab his hand and guide him toward the door. I feel a fire inside and when I look over my shoulder at Oliver, I see his eyes reflecting exactly how I feel. He pulls hard enough on my hand to spin me around and back to him. He lowers his lips to my ear and whispers, "For the record, I'm very lucky."

It's time to go.

We say a quick goodbye to Cassidy and race back to the hotel. We don't speak in the car but the energy buzzing between us is so strong that I'm sure even the driver can feel it. We both know what's coming, it's palpable in the air as the electricity flies between us.

The second we walk through our door, Oliver spins towards me and pushes me against the wall, bringing our bodies together. I've never felt this heat and desire before.

I need him closer in every way. He kisses down my neck as his hands get lower and lower down my back. I'm instantly clawing at his shirt, desperate to see and touch his skin. My heart is racing, my body aching as I push him forward. We stumble onto the bed and give in to each other until the morning comes.

24

The first thing I notice when I open my eyes is Oliver next to me. He's sleeping on his stomach, his arm stretched up and under his pillow. His hair is extra messy and I remember my hands in his curls last night. I smile and notice the warmth throughout my body. I'm perfectly relaxed and comfortable lying next to him. I knew it would be better than any other time, but I never fully grasped just how different it could be.

"Hey you," Oliver mumbles. His voice has a sexy rasp to it this morning.

I turn and smile at him, "Hi."

"Last night was..." he smiles, trailing off.

"Yeah. It was great," I finish for him.

He pulls his arm over me and pulls me in closer to him. "Can we stay here all day?" he asks.

"At least until 10," I chuckle, snuggling in closer.

Oliver keeps in constant physical contact with me as we leave the room. His hand is on my lower back as we walk, he holds my hand as we walk to the car, and then his hand instantly lands on my thigh as he starts driving.

I smile over at him and he looks back at me, "What?" he asks innocently.

"Nothing," I chuckle. He continues to look at me questioningly.

"You're very touchy this morning," I reply, looking

down at his hand on my leg.

He laughs and squeezes my thigh, "Can you blame me?" he replies, his eyes twinkling as he looks back at me.

Honestly, I can't blame him. I find my thoughts wandering back to last night. His hands on me, his lips exploring, my body feels hot just thinking about it. I haven't been with many guys, but this was already on a different level than in the past. The way he held me so gently was intimate in a way I hadn't ever experienced. And yet there was an importance and earnestness in each of his actions. How is it possible that he can make it feel slow and yet urgent at the same time?

Oliver looks over at me and I feel exposed, my cheeks turning pink.

"What are you thinking about?" he teases as if he knows.

"Last night," I admit.

He laughs, his eyes crinkling. "Good, me too."

"You know, I've never seen your place," I say suddenly.

"Wow, you really are thinking about last night," he smirks.

I roll my eyes teasingly and say, "But I'm actually serious. You don't have a girl hidden away there, do you?"

"Nope. No girls," he laughs. "How about I make you dinner tomorrow and you can make sure I'm telling the truth?"

"Deal. But be careful, I'm a great detective."

The next morning, I promise Maddie that we can meet up for breakfast because, of course, she wants to hear all the details. For once, she's actually on time. She's practically bouncing up and down in her seat as I step through the cafe door.

"Jenna!" she jumps up.

"Okay, okay," I chuckle, sitting down by her.

"Spill! Now! I already ordered two coffees and bagel sandwiches for us."

"Spill what?" I tease.

She glares at me and I laugh. "I'm not sure you need that coffee," I say. She gives an exasperated sigh and a pointed look.

"It was great. The opening party was Vegas-themed and apparently, I had a lucky streak! It was really fun. Plus, the alley looks exactly like the one here! It's crazy," I say.

Maddie nods as I talk and when I pause, she raises her eyebrows, eagerly waiting.

"....and?"

"And then we went to bed."

Maddie looks disappointed for a minute and then pauses and slowly looks back at me, "Wait..."

"Together," I add and Maddie breaks out into a huge grin.

"I KNEW IT!" she yells and slaps the table. A few people look over at us and I shake my head in embarrassment.

I hear our names called, so I eagerly use the excuse to hop up and walk to the counter to grab the food. When I sit back down, Maddie explodes, saying, "More details please!"

I take a long dramatic sip as Maddie glares at me. I'm having too much fun with her. Then I smile and say, "It was amazing. Like, actually really amazing."

Maddie squeals and asks, "Who initiated it?"

"I think we both kind of did. We both knew it was coming."

"Alright, that's adorable."

"I think I'm falling pretty hard..." I admit.

"Well, duh," Maddie replies matter of factly.

I look back at her and she adds, "It's obvious."

"It's kind of scary. I've never really cared this much before."

I think back to my previous boyfriends. I liked them, of course, I did. But there is something about Oliver that just draws me to him like a magnet. I've always thought of myself as independent but now I actually have the desire to be with someone else. To be independent but independent together. Is that possible?

"It's a good thing to care," Maddie says.

"As long as he cares just as much."

"Oh, he definitely does."

I nod in response but can't ignore the knot in my stomach that tells me she could be wrong. I could be opening myself up to pain. I could be giving him way more than he's willing to give me. Maddie takes my nod and silence as a sign to move on, so she jumps into her wedding planning and my opinions on flowers and colors. I listen as well as I can, but at the same time I'm still thinking about Oliver and how quickly I'm falling. Falling is the perfect word to describe how I'm feeling. It's fun and freeing but at the same time, I have an uneasiness in my stomach as I think about the ground coming closer.

Being the perfect gentleman, Oliver offered to pick me up for dinner tonight, but I assured him that it wasn't necessary. He lives close to me, almost exactly between me and the bowling alley. I secretly don't mind the car ride alone to try and silence the anxiety that's been piling up all day. Ever since I openly acknowledged my feelings for him, I've been terrified it's one-sided and that he's going to break me. I have to talk to him tonight and tell him how I'm feeling, but I'm so scared of his response. I'm not sure I can handle him saying he doesn't feel the same.

His apartment is in a nice building, and he has to buzz me up. My stomach squirms at his voice through the speaker and I take a breath with each step as I make my way to apartment #213.

I knock on the door and hear Oliver shout, "Come in!"

I slowly peek my head inside and hear Oliver say from the other room, "Sorry, Jenna, come on in."

I look around the living room as I step through the door. It's a pretty simple, clean room with a couch, TV, and coffee table. There is a bookshelf full of books on the back wall, and I make my way over to them. He has just about every genre ranging from business and self-help books to romance and mystery. I see a small picture frame and lean closer to see that it's Oliver, Patty, and Olivia. Olivia is younger, maybe 8, and Oliver is giving her a piggyback ride. She's leaning forward, her hair flying around her and her mouth open in a wide, happy laugh. Patty is standing close to Oliver, looking over at them and smiling.

"Hi," Oliver says, walking into the room.

I spin around and smile. He looks casually good in his jeans, gray shirt, and a backward baseball hat. His curls stick out from under his hat, and I want to reach out and put my fingers through them again.

"Hi," I smile back.

He makes his way to me in a few quick steps and pulls me in for a kiss. My body reacts instantly and all I want to do is pull him closer and fall on the couch with him. But I refrain and pull his attention away to say, "That picture is adorable."

He peeks over my shoulder at it and smiles, "Thanks. Already playing detective then?"

"I am a little impressed with your book collection," I reply.

He gives a playful shrug and leads me to the kitchen.

Oliver has all of the ingredients laid out and ready to make pizzas. Together we roll out the dough and practice throwing it in the air. We make a delicious red sauce and a white sauce. We add all the cheese and different toppings. It feels just like a movie when Oliver jokingly throws flour at me, and I instantly launch some back at him with a laugh. We continue throwing flour back and forth until Oliver lunges at me and we fall to the floor, covered in flour and out of breath from laughing. I tilt my face up to meet his and as our lips touch, our bodies melt together. My heart feels so full and I can't stop smiling. Can life really be this good? Can I actually be this happy? It feels like a dream, a movie; this can't possibly be my reality, right?

The timer goes off, pulling us back into reality. I'm completely covered in flour and the floor is even worse after we rolled around together on it. I laugh as Oliver brushes a hand down his chest, trying to get clean before pulling his shirt back on. Then he turns to me and gently starts brushing me clean. His fingers graze across my chest and he freezes. My breathing is shallow as I look up at him and he smiles at me.

"You're so beautiful," he whispers. I swallow shakily

and pull away to slide my shirt back on.

Oliver assures me he'll clean up the mess after dinner so we sit down, the kitchen and our bodies still covered in flour.

"How is it?" Oliver asks as I take my first bite.

"Delicious!"

The dough is sweet and soft with a crispy edge. The flavors of the sauce and toppings mix perfectly. Somehow, he has the ability to take food that I've eaten hundreds of times like pizza, nachos, and cookies and make it taste more delicious than ever. Is it a special talent that he has? Or is it just him? Does he just make everything in my life so much better?

"This is my mom's recipe. We used to make this every Sunday night together. She said it was the best way to get ready for the week," he says.

"Wise woman. Pizza makes everything better."

Oliver nods in agreement as a quietness falls between us. I'm working up the courage to tell him how I feel. I have to tell him how much I care.

"So, Cassidy called me and had a proposition for me," Oliver says, putting his pizza down on his plate.

"Oh?" My stomach squirms uncomfortably waiting for his response.

"She has a partner that loved the alley in Tennessee. He would like to partner with her to create a line down the whole southeast," he continues.

"Wow! Oliver! That's crazy!"

"Yeah, it's great. I'm excited and I honestly never expected anything like this. But ever since the call, I can't stop thinking about it and I just keep getting more and more excited."

His face lights up as he talks. It makes me happy to see

him this excited about something.

"She wants me to go with them through the process," he adds, turning his gaze towards me.

I feel my stomach drop quickly at his words, and a lump forms in my throat.

"Oh. So, what does that mean exactly?" I ask.

"I don't know all the details yet. It sounds like there will be a lot of back and forth between here and other alleys. She wants me to kind of travel around with her and be a part of the process and help manage the alleys. Cassidy and her partner want to be more behind the scenes and have me be the face of them."

I nod but stay quiet, thinking and letting him continue. I don't think I'm going to like the way this is going.

"It seems like a lot and I would hate to not be here with my family, but their offer is really good and both Olivia and my mom told me I have to do it, that I shouldn't stay here just for them."

My heart is racing as I'm thinking about how much he'll be gone and with Cassidy. I think back to my experience with Jensen and Mary. I can't do that again. I can't have those insecurities again. It terrifies me. I'm falling for him so fast, faster than I ever thought possible and it felt safe because I thought he was feeling the same. But now it's suddenly feeling very one-sided. He's going to leave, and he's excited about it. My mind suddenly goes back to that night in New York. It feels like I'm being rejected all over again. I can feel my walls going up. I don't know what to say. Now I'm overwhelmed with the feeling that I care more than he does, making me uneasy. The conversation I wanted to have tonight has happened in the entirely wrong way. But I did get my answer. He doesn't care as much. My mind is racing and I take a sip of my drink to give myself a moment. I'm not going to hold him back. I know that's not the kind of person I want to be.

I swallow and put on a smile and say, "That's awesome, Oliver. I'm so happy for you! You should do it."

A look crosses his face quickly but then he flashes me a smile and says, "Yeah, thanks. I think it's going to be great."

A silence falls between us. I don't have anything left to say. I can feel Oliver watching me closely, but I focus on my food. I'm suddenly self-conscious about the dried flour on my face.

"Here I'll clean up," Oliver says, standing up to help clear the table when I finish.

"Want to stay and hang out? Maybe you could even stay the night?" he asks, smiling at me, but even his smile seems a little unsure.

My mind is still racing as I think about what his news means for us. "Actually, I'm pretty tired, I think I'm going to head home."

He pauses and looks at me, his eyes concerned. "Are you sure?"

I nod. "Yeah, I've just been working a lot, so I'm pretty tired."

"Of course."

He kisses me softly as I stand by the door and I give him a weak smile as I walk away.

25

I cry on the drive home. I've never felt this strongly for someone, and I really thought we were on the same page. But he seems fine, excited even, for an opportunity that will keep him away from me. I call Maddie and tell her everything.

"Okay, first, take a deep breath," Maddie says calmly.

I do as she says, breathing in and out, in and out.

"He wasn't breaking up with you," she says.

"I know."

"He didn't say he didn't care about you."

"I know."

"He obviously really cares about you. Anyone around him can see it. And that's why he brought this up in the first place."

I stay quiet, tears still in my eyes.

"I know you're scared," Maddie says softly.

I'm still quiet, so she continues.

"I've never seen you feel like this, Jenna. And I know that comes with fear. No one likes to feel like they care more in the relationship. It's scary to open yourself up to get hurt. You have to have some risk for the reward though. And I really think, in this case, the reward will be greater than the risk. I've seen the way he looks at you."

A few tears slip out, and I say quietly, "I'm scared he doesn't care as much as I do."

It's Maddie's turn to say, "I know."

"I really like him."

"I know."

"What if I don't know him as well as I think?" I ask. I think of Jensen. I thought I knew him but I was wrong in so many ways.

"Oh, Jenna. Of course, you know him. Don't let your fears change that."

I'm still uneasy when I wake up the next day. It feels like our relationship suddenly got turned the wrong way. I was so confident in us. I've never felt so safe with someone before and I fully trusted him with my feelings. Now, I'm scared. I'm worried that I was just a fun summer fling and now he's off to go pursue his real dreams. He's already lost one dream. I can't possibly stand in the way of his next one.

I don't see Oliver today. I spend the day focused on work. I have enough to do to keep myself distracted and soon the day is over. The next day is off to the same start but as I'm finishing an afternoon meeting, I get a text from Oliver.

I know you're working super hard but maybe you could use a break tonight? Dinner?

That sounds like the perfect idea.

When I see Oliver, my fears and uneasiness from the other night seem smaller. I feel safe again. Maddie was right, it's just scary caring so much about someone. I wrap my arms around him and pull him in a little extra tight. He brings his hand to the back of my head, and I squeeze harder, breathing in his woodsy scent.

He breathes out deeply, "You okay Jenna? Or are you trying to squeeze me to death?"

I chuckle and let go. "Sorry. I just needed a hug I guess."

He pulls me back into a hug and whispers in my ear, "I'm not complaining."

During dinner, I tell Oliver all about the projects I'm working on. He tells me that he's sold a lot of my stickers and he will need more for the new alleys too. He tells me about his meeting with Cassidy to set up a schedule for the future and his first trip will be in a few weeks to meet with her partner and make plans for the next three alleys that he wants to do.

"That sounds really great," I tell Oliver.

He rubs the back of his neck and shakes his head a little, "Honestly, this was never even a thought for me. I don't know how it happened. It's all so crazy."

Our conversations stay safe, I'm too scared to dig any deeper. I'm also too worried to talk about him leaving because I don't want to break down. Dinner is delicious. It's a small southern comfort restaurant and reminds me of Oliver's mom's cooking. It feels like so much has happened between us since that dinner.

We step outside and Oliver grabs my hand and pulls me in close. The air is warm and the lights of downtown are twinkling. I'm not ready for the night to end. I don't want to think about the future, I just want to stay in the moment tonight.

"Should we walk a little?" I suggest.

He nods and I rest my head against his arm as we walk.

"Our favorite bowling team was at the alley today," Oliver tells me.

"Oh no! I'm so sad I missed them!"

There's a team made up of 6 older couples in their 70s and 80s that come in and bowl for hours. They are always hilarious to watch and are more than happy to tell us stories from their lives. I'm laughing as Oliver tells me a story about Gerald and how they used to play pranks on each other when they were young. I'm laughing so hard that I close my eyes while walking and then I hear an unexpected voice say, "Jenna?"

My eyes jerk open and I see Jensen standing in front of us.

He looks between Oliver and me a few times and then says, "I knew it."

His face is angry, and I suddenly feel nervous and alert.

"Hi Jensen," I say, struggling to be kind. I try to step around him to continue walking but he blocks my path.

"This explains a whole lot. It was just a game to you. You were just playing me."

"I wasn't playing you–" I start but Jensen interrupts me and turns towards Oliver.

"All this time you were playing the nice guy but actually stealing my girl," he says, pointing at Oliver.

"Nothing happened while you were together," Oliver replies quickly.

"HA," Jensen retorts loudly.

"You wouldn't put out with me because you were getting it from this guy," he says loudly to me, gesturing at Oliver and looking him up and down in disgust.

Oliver takes an angry step forward.

"Jensen! Nothing happened until after we broke up. Until *after* you treated me like garbage," I now shoot back at him, my face flaming with anger.

"I loved you, Jenna!" Jensen bellows pointing his finger angrily at me and stepping closer. "YOU are the one that treated me like garbage!"

I scoff at him. "You didn't love me. I think you need to back off and stop telling yourself lies," I reply calmly.

Jensen's face turns red in anger, and he yells, "Don't talk to me about lies! Not while you stand there with him! He's the liar! He acts like he's some saint walking the earth when he's the idiot that drove drunk."

I feel Oliver clench up beside me and I gasp. There's no way Oliver was the drunk driver from his accident, right? I can feel the doubt pouring through me.

"You have no idea what you're talking about," I reply shakily.

"The hell I don't!" he yells back. "Your boyfriend has a drinking problem!"

My heart stops at his words. My mind is racing. I'm suddenly thinking back to all of our conversations about drinking and the accident. It can't be true.

But Jensen continues, "And you're too dumb to even notice it. No surprise there. Just another stupid little girl."

My body fills with anger as Jensen takes another step closer to me, but before I can even react, I see Oliver's arm pull back and hear his fist collide with Jensen's face. Jensen stumbles backward and then launches himself at Oliver, tackling him to the ground.

"Oliver!" I scream, but Jensen is punching Oliver on the ground. The sound is sickening. My heart is racing as I grab Jensen and try to pull him off, but he easily pushes me backward and I fall to the ground. I hear Oliver scream my name in response, and he suddenly flips Jensen to the ground and hits him repeatedly.

"Oliver, stop!" I yell, jumping back up.

Jensen's face is cracked open and bleeding but Oliver continues to hit him.

"You have no idea what you're talking about!" Oliver is yelling at Jensen in between the punches.

"Oliver! Stop!" I shriek again, desperate.

Oliver looks up at me, his eyes full of fire. I feel myself shaking and tears are streaming down my face. Oliver's face softens as he looks at me. He shakily lets go of Jensen and stands up. I see the instant regret on Oliver's face. He looks down at his hands and then back up at me.

Oliver steps closer to me and I take a step back.

"Jenna," he says softly.

I look at Jensen on the ground, bleeding and then back up at Oliver.

"Who are you?" I ask.

"What?" he stammers, confused.

"I don't feel like I know you at all." My voice shakes as I say it, and then I turn and run the opposite way. I hear Oliver call my name a few times but I don't turn around.

26

I find myself at Maddie's house, panting. I must have run the whole way here. She opens the door and gasps, "Jenna! What happened?! You're bleeding!"

Confused, I look down at my hands. She gently touches my face and I realize I must have gotten some blood on it.

"It's not mine. It's Jensen's, or Oliver's, I don't even know," I reply as I walk inside. I realize I'm shaking as I sit down on the couch.

"Wait, Jensen? Oliver? What happened?"

"We ran into Jensen after our date. He was saying that I cheated on him with Oliver and that I treated him like trash."

"That's a joke. You absolutely did not." Maddie is shocked and I can see the anger on her face.

"They ended up fighting. Like, full-out brawl."

Maddie gasps and sits next to me. "Is Oliver okay? Where is he?"

"I don't know," it comes out harsher than I intended, but I can feel the anger bubbling inside of me.

Maddie looks at me, a mixture of concern and confusion on her face.

"Oliver wouldn't stop hitting him. I tried to get him to stop and he wouldn't. He looked completely out of control. He was so mad. It was scary." I get angry the more I think about it. "It's ridiculous. I've been in that kind of relationship before. I don't need any more toxic masculinity in my life."

Maddie nods in agreement but stays quiet.

"I don't have the energy for this," I say bitterly.

Maddie's face softens and she pulls me into a hug. "I'm so sorry, Jenna."

I feel tears well up in my eyes. After a few seconds, I say quietly, "I never would have expected that from him."

Maddie stays quiet but continues to hold me. My mind is still racing.

"Jensen said that Oliver was the one that was drinking and driving. That he's the one that caused the accident," I say.

I hear Maddie inhale in surprise and then squeeze me a little tighter.

I stay at Maddie's for another hour. She holds me through the silence. I don't have anything else to say even though my mind and thoughts won't be quiet. I'm bouncing between confused and angry but I'm also scared. I still feel shaky. I decide to walk home despite Maddie offering a ride three times. I crave the fresh air and the chance to think. As I make my way up the sidewalk, I see Oliver sitting on the porch stairs, his head in his hands. His head whips up when he hears me.

"Jenna," he whispers, standing up. His face has dried blood on it, as do his hands. His shirt looks stretched out from where Jensen grabbed him.

I stop walking, and he doesn't step forward.

"I'm so sorry," he says quietly.

I look at him but don't say anything. I want to step forward and comfort him. He looks so sad and hurt, both physically and emotionally. But I stop myself. As much as I find myself caring for him, I can't put myself in this situation again. I physically feel myself shutting off.

"I didn't mean to scare you," he says gently, running his hand through his hair and avoiding eye contact.

First things first, I need to know the truth. "What he said about you, and the accident...?" I ask trailing off.

Oliver sighs before he replies, and then he looks up and says, "It's not true. I wasn't drunk."

"Why would he say that then?"

"Because I *was* at a party that night. And I did have a drink. But I wasn't drunk, not even close. I was fully capable of driving. They tested my blood alcohol limit at the accident and I was well within the limits. But rumors spread quickly. Everyone wanted to see the golden boy fall."

I feel my body relax in relief at his words. He didn't lie to me and he wasn't driving drunk. It's a huge relief. That isn't the only problem though. I can still remember the sound of him hitting Jensen and the look on his face as he continued to hit him long after the fight was over. And can't help but think about the conversation of him leaving. I have so much fear about what that could mean for us. And now after tonight, maybe I really don't know him as well as I thought. I know what has to happen next.

"It was really hard for me. That time in my life. And Jensen tonight, bringing it up. It's just a huge trigger for me. And I hated that he was saying it in front of you. I would never want you to think that I would be capable of something like that," Oliver explains, a look of pain on his face.

I stay quiet as I try to think about how to respond. Finally, I say, "I understand the pain those rumors must have caused you. What happened to you really truly is horrible. But I don't think that's an excuse for how you acted tonight."

Oliver looks down, a pained and disappointed look on his face.

"I know Jenna." he sighs and puts his head in his hands. "I know."

"The truth is, I was already kind of feeling off with us," I say quickly before I lose my confidence.

Oliver quickly lifts his head and looks at me, his eyebrows pulled together.

"You were?" he asks softly.

I nod and continue while I still can. "I'm not sure we're in the same place. I've been feeling like I don't know you as well as I think, and tonight kind of proves that."

I watch as Oliver's face changes. His lips tense up as he comprehends what I'm saying.

"I think we should probably take a break. Some time apart. See if we actually want the same things," I finish.

Oliver nods curtly. "That's what you want. A break," he repeats, not as a question, but almost like he's telling himself, to make sure it's real. I can tell from his body language that he's putting his own walls up to protect himself.

"We moved too quickly. At least I did. I think I just let myself get a little in over my head," I add.

"I don't think we moved too quickly," Oliver says quietly, softly, taking the smallest movement towards me.

"I know. That's kind of the problem. I let my emotions go crazy."

Oliver looks at me, confused and cocks his head slightly.

The anger is gone now, and I'm left with an emptiness. The more I talk, the less I feel. I welcome the numbness. It's easier to close myself off, so I add, "We're just in different places in this relationship. I hope we can stay friends."

"Is this a break or a breakup?" Oliver asks, his eyes searching mine.

I swallow the lump in my throat and blink back the tears I can feel coming.

"Aren't they the same thing?" I ask. Before he can answer I step past him and into the house.

27

Three weeks later

I haven't spoken to Oliver since the night outside my house. I've opened my messages to text him multiple times over the last two weeks but then I stop. I desperately wish he cared as much as me but the silence seems to prove I was right about his feelings. I avoid the bowling alley and throw myself into work. It's almost the end of summer and Maddie is getting ready to go to school. I made plans with Robby to move to New York for a few months to see if I like it. I hope that I like it enough to end up staying long-term. I booked another client so I officially have nine full-time clients. It feels good to finally feel like I have some job security. I've been able to relax a bit and realize that I am worthy and maybe I shouldn't be trying so hard to prove it. Olivia has posted a few times showing her and Oliver in a few different places. He must be working on franchising. Even though it hurts, I'm still proud to see everything he's creating.

I miss him. And I miss Olivia. I cried for two days after we broke up. But then I reminded myself it was for the best. He was going to leave anyway and I was going to get hurt. I would have continued falling for him and we would never have been on the same emotional level. I fell way too fast. I should have known better.

I hear a knock on the door and my mom pokes her

head inside. “I have a surprise for you,” she says, smiling.

I nod my head and she opens the door fully, her hands behind her back. When she steps inside, she pulls her hands out and holds up a book. My design is on the front cover and my mouth drops open.

“It’s done? I thought we still had a few weeks!” I exclaim.

“He got a rush order!”

I jump up and grab the book from her, softly dragging my hand over the cover.

“Wow,” I say as I breathe out. It’s always an honor to see my work in person. To be able to physically feel it is almost as if I can feel the thought and work that went into it.

“It’s amazing,” my mom says, standing by me. “You did an excellent job.”

A grin spreads across my face for the first time in three weeks. “Thanks, Mom. That really means a lot.” She smiles back at me and I can tell she’s being genuine.

“He’s having a small celebration party tomorrow night. Of course, you’re invited,” she tells me.

I nod, unable to take my eyes off the cover. I wish I could tell Oliver. I wish I could show him. Instead, I take a picture and send it to Maddie, who texts back instantly in excitement. I can always count on her.

“This is seriously cool,” Maddie says as we step into the room.

Tommy’s party is in a small room above a bar downtown. In the middle of the room is a stack of his books displaying my cover. At the front of the room, there's a big poster with the image of the book cover, and it makes my heart soar looking at it. I feel so proud of what we accomplished together.

"You made this!" Maddie exclaims as I hold a book in my hands.

I laugh. "Technically, Tommy made it."

She shrugs, "You made the first thing people see." I never thought about it like that and it gives me a buzz to think about.

My mom sees us come in the door and rushes to my side, "I need to introduce you to some people." she says, steering me to the right.

"This is my daughter, Jenna. She designed the cover!" she gushes to the first group.

I feel my heart well up as she talks about me. I can hear the pride in her voice as she introduces me around the room. It's new and it's nice. It's such a severe difference from the last time we were in a situation like this together. Hearing my mom's words seems to open a floodgate inside me. I was so desperate this summer, trying to prove myself to her. When in the end, I only needed to do it for myself. Once I focused on that and stopped trying to prove myself, I found my success a lot more fulfilling. After my mom introduces me to everyone she knows, I pull on Maddie's arm and lead her to the bar.

"So are you excited for school?" I ask Maddie as we sit down.

"Definitely! Plus I'll get to be with Ben way more."

I nod solemnly, and Maddie gives me a comforting knowing look.

"Are you excited for New York?" she asks, moving the conversation away from my thoughts of Oliver.

I smile, "Yeah, I am. It's going to be fun to be with

Robby again."

"I bet. I can't wait to come visit you!"

"Like you'll have time," I tease.

She shakes her head, "I know. Life is crazy. Ben and I officially set a date!"

"You did?"

"Next summer!"

"That's perfect."

She nods in excitement and then pauses and looks at me seriously, "Have you talked to Oliver?"

I shake my head and take another drink.

"I saw that he's in Florida right now for work," she says.

"Yeah. Looks like he's been gone a lot," I reply.

The silence falls between us and she wraps her arm around me comfortingly.

I decide to sneak out of the party early, and despite Maddie trying to come with me, I tell her I just want to be alone. I already know exactly where I'm going. I reach the bowling alley and see my logo lit up above the door. I know Oliver is in Florida, so I'm not worried about seeing him as I walk through the doors. I smell the familiar popcorn smell and my heart breaks a little. This place felt like a second home to me when I was growing up. Then it turned into a completely different place that somehow felt even more special. Everywhere I look has a memory associated with it. It's all flooding back as I walk.

I think of the many kisses exchanged in the photo booth, the food eaten at the bar, the games bowled at each lane, and the slow dances behind the counter. The tears are openly flowing down my cheeks now. I see something new on the wall by the counter and when I get closer, my heart stops. It's a glass case with Johnny's trophy and a bunch of photos. The photo of Johnny's team and the photo of Johnny and Oliver, a photo of Olivia and Patty, and then I see the photo of me with Maddie as kids. The tears fall harder now as I look at it and then I see a photo of Oliver and me together, laughing behind the counter. I'm crying so hard that I can't see through the tears anymore as I turn and run out the doors.

I only have one week left before I leave for New York. I'm ready to go, hoping that some space away will help me forget about Oliver. It's been four weeks since I've talked to him, even though I still think about him every day. He sent me a text a few days ago saying he missed me. I cried when I read it and almost responded before Maddie asked if it would help or just hurt more. I've been focusing all my energy on New York and the future I want to build with my company. It feels easier to focus on that than to think about Oliver.

Maddie wants to go dancing together one last time before she has to go back to school, so tonight will be our last big celebration together. I curl my hair, put on smokey eye shadow, red lipstick, leather leggings, black boots, and the top I bought in New York.

"Wow," my mom says as I come down the stairs.

"Too much?" I chuckle.

"You'll be breaking some hearts tonight," my mom muses. Her tone is more playful than judgmental, and I'm grateful for the turn in our relationship.

My phone rings before I can reply and I see it's Maddie.

"Hey, you on your way?" I ask, picking up.

Maddie's voice is shaky on the other end. "Jenna, you need to go to the hospital."

"What's going on? Are you okay?" I ask, feeling my stomach drop.

"It's Olivia. She was in an accident."

My heart stops and I feel the color draining from my face. The oxygen seems to have left the room as I'm struggling to pull in a breath.

"Is she okay?" I manage to stutter out.

"I don't know. She's in the hospital. I was at the bowling alley with Ben when Oliver found out."

My hands are shaking and I can't think clearly. I'm frozen on the last step of the stairs as the room seems to swirl around me. My thoughts are fuzzy as my mom steps toward me, putting her arms around me. Feeling her touch helps the room steady.

"What's going on?" she asks quietly.

I open my mouth but all I can say is, "I need to go to the hospital."

"I'll drive," my mom responds instantly, grabbing her keys and guiding me out the door. I hear Maddie say to call her later but my brain is still foggy as I hang up the phone.

The car ride is silent. I feel my nerves coursing through my body as we get closer and closer to the hospital. My mom drops me at the front while she goes to park the car and I shakily run to the front desk. They direct me to room #413, and as I'm rushing through the bright white halls, I can't help but feel so out of place and uncomfortable in my outfit. Only minutes ago, I was ready to dance the night away and now it feels like an absolutely ridiculous thing to do.

When I nearly reach the room, I can see the door slightly open. I hesitate, thinking about Oliver, and I slowly peek inside. The room is empty except for Olivia who is lying in a bed, machines beeping around her. I quietly step into the room and make my way over to the side of her bed. Her head is wrapped in a bloody bandage, and her leg is in a cast. She has some lacerations across her face but she seems to be sleeping. Despite her injuries, she somehow looks peaceful. My gut pangs to see how young and fragile she looks lying there. I glance around the room, surprised that no one else is here.

"He went to get food," I hear Olivia say quietly, her voice sounding jagged.

I spin around quickly and see her look up at me.

"What?"

"Oliver. He went with my mom to get food." Her voice sounds weak as she speaks.

I shake my head at her words, "I'm here for you. How are you? What happened?"

"I was riding my longboard and hit a car."

"You hit a car?" I gasp.

"A truck pulled out of their driveway and I hit the side of it. By the time I saw it, it was too late."

"Olivia," I breathe out, sitting down on the bed next to her, gently putting my hand in hers. "How bad is it?" I ask, looking over her body.

"From what they've told me, a broken leg, a gash on my head, and some bruised ribs. But I'll be fine and out of here in a few days."

My eyes are pricking with tears and I squeeze her hand tighter. She closes her eyes but I stay by her side, my hand in hers. She looks so small and frail in the bed. I just want to wrap her up in a hug but I'm too scared to touch her.

"I miss you," Olivia says so quietly, and without opening her eyes, I think I may have imagined it.

Then her eyes flutter open and she smiles a soft, sad

smile.

"I miss you too."

"Ollie misses you," she adds.

My stomach flips at her words and my heart pauses. I try to blink away the tears but I know it's useless. "Does he?"

"So much. He doesn't understand what happened. He said something about you wanting different things?"

"Don't worry about us. Just worry about getting better," I re-direct, quickly wiping away my tears.

She coughs a little and I hand her some water. "Can't you at least tell me what happened?" she asks. Her face is so sweet and eager, even while broken in bed, I can't help but give in.

"It's kind of embarrassing," I start slowly. "I liked him a lot more than he liked me. It seemed so obvious at the end that I didn't know him as well as I thought. I thought he was all in with me, but I guess I was just blinded by how I felt about him. In the past, I was always the one that cared less, it was safe. Once I figured out that wasn't the case here, I just decided it was better to go our separate ways before it got even harder to lose him."

Olivia looked at me, confused. Her eyebrows pulled together, and her mouth turned down.

"You think he doesn't care as much as you?" she asks, confused.

I nod and add, "I know it sounds silly."

"It does," she replies quickly.

My mouth falls open a little, surprised by her bluntness. Then she adds, "Oliver has been in love with you for the last four years."

My heart stops, and my stomach drops. "What?"

"Ever since you came in after high school graduation,

Oliver has talked about you. He said his favorite days of the year were when you and your friends would come back to the bowling alley in the summer. He would make any excuse to take your food orders, get your shoes, and help you any time you came in. We all knew who Jenna was. He regretted not saying yes to you back then but it was after the accident and his girlfriend just dumped him. But this summer you said you were staying here and I think Oliver just about died from excitement. Then he patiently waited while you dated that jerk."

My mind is racing as she speaks. Suddenly, I remember how he knew my name, my drink order, knew that I hated tomatoes on my nachos, and even knew the bowling ball color that I liked to use in the blacklight. I didn't know I had left such an impression on him all those years ago. He's been paying attention this whole time. Olivia continues talking before I can say anything.

"And he told me he freaked out at Jensen. But can you blame him? Sure, he brought up Oliver's past and that's a hard time to relive, but Oliver has hated Jensen all summer. First, Oliver had to wait while you dated him, even though he cared about you. Then he finds out that Jensen wasn't treating you right. Of course, he's going to take the chance to punch the guy. I would have too."

I'm speechless. I have no idea what to say. My mind is all over the place, and my head feels like I might pass out. I stand up, unsure how to process everything she just said. I open my mouth to reply but shut it just as quickly because I still don't know what to say. I shake my head as if to clear my thoughts, and then I hear a noise and look up to see Oliver and Patty in the doorway.

Oliver's curly brown hair is messy; I know it's because he's been running his hands through it. His eyes look sad as he looks at me, and then at Olivia.

"She had to know eventually," Olivia says, defending herself.

I stand up and walk toward Oliver. I watch his eyes trace over my body and then hold my eye contact. I have so many emotions just looking at him again. My body instinctively reacts to being in the same room with him, it's like our bodies are magnets and I have to hold myself back from him. My mouth feels dry, but he stays quiet.

"Can we talk?" I manage to choke out.

He nods once and follows me into the hall. We are quiet as the door closes and I hear Patty say, "Kyle is on the way. I called his mom."

The silence in the hall feels heavy between us. I'm not sure how to start, but the way he's looking at me makes my skin feel hot.

"You look amazing," he says, the corner of his mouth turning up.

My cheeks flush and I blurt out, "Was she telling the truth?"

He rubs the back of his neck as he pauses but then puts his hand down and meets my gaze. "Yes."

"Why didn't you tell me before?"

"I don't know. I didn't think it mattered."

"You didn't think it mattered?" I repeat with a dry laugh.

"I mean, I just always figured you weren't as interested in me. Then when I found out you weren't, I didn't think there was any point in telling you."

"You think I'm not into you?"

He looks confused now. "You said we were in different places."

"Because I thought you didn't care about me."

Oliver's mouth drops open in shock. Then he shakes his head and laughs, "I'm in love with you, Jenna. Every day, I've regretted not saying yes to you four years ago. I know it wasn't real but it's felt real to me ever since. I haven't been able to stop thinking about you. This summer I told myself that I couldn't let you go again. I've felt broken these last few weeks."

My heart stops at his words and it feels like my body goes numb. I stare at him, unable to say anything and he chuckles, the sound that I've come to love so much. He takes a step closer, close enough that I breathe in his familiar scent, and my heart instantly starts racing again. He tilts his head closer to me, his blue eyes holding my gaze.

"But your dream of franchising the bowling alleys. I thought that meant you didn't care about being with me," I whisper. It sounds silly now as I say it.

"I want to have passive income. I need to make money without having to be there. I want to follow you wherever your dreams take you. You're my dream now."

My body completely melts at his words. I feel that safety and security in his words. I believe him. I know him. I step up and pull his face down to meet mine. It feels so good to feel him in my arms again. To feel his lips on mine, to taste him. It feels like home.

I pull back just long enough to say, "I love you too," and then I collapse back into him, letting our worlds melt together.

EPILOGUE

One year later

Maddie looks absolutely gorgeous in her dress. Her hair has a soft wave to it, pinned back with beautiful pearl pins. She chose a tight dress with a long train and a slight flare at the bottom. Pearls make elegant designs throughout it.

"You are stunning," I say as she does a little twirl for me.

She beams in response. "Thank you for everything. I couldn't have done this without you. Love you long time," she replies. The past year had been full of ups and downs throughout her wedding planning process. I took my position as maid of honor very seriously, and I was with her every step of the way.

"Love you long time," I smile back at her.

I step outside, waiting in my position to walk down the aisle. Maddie was kind and didn't pick an ugly dress for me. Instead, it's a gorgeous emerald color that fits perfectly. As I wait for the music to start, I hear steps coming toward me.

"Hello beautiful," I hear, and I turn to see Oliver walking toward me. He looks amazing in his tight black suit and my stomach still fills with butterflies when I see him, even after all this time.

"Back at you," I say with a wink.

"That dress is gorgeous. Matches your new jewelry quite well," he winks. I look down at the diamond ring on my finger and grin. It does match perfectly.

"You ready?" he asks, nodding towards the aisle.

"I'm ready," I nod. "Are you?"

He smiles back at me and his eyes twinkle as he replies, "Definitely."

I peek out into the crowd and see my parents in the back; they give me a small wave. Olivia and Kyle are sitting in the third row next to Robby. They are chatting animatedly and Oliver says, "She's probably telling him about the next space launch."

I giggle and turn back to face him.

After the hospital, I moved to New York just like I had planned. Oliver continued helping with franchising, but instead of North Carolina being his home base, he came to New York with me. After a few months of traveling, Oliver had enough that he could cut back and now would only have to travel once or twice a year. I continued to work with my nine clients and have since added on another five. I also designed another book cover from one of Tommy's referrals.

Oliver has been by my side every step of the way. During one of the days I was struggling, I looked at him sadly and said, "I don't want to let you down. You are following me and my dream. I just want to prove that it's worth it."

He gently lifted my chin and looked at me softly. Then he said the new words that I would remember and remind myself of throughout the years. "Jenna, I love you. Unconditionally and always. You're done trying to prove yourself. You never have to prove yourself to me."

Made in United States
North Haven, CT
11 January 2023

30924545R00157